# Forever's Just Pretend

## a Hector Lassiter novel

### CRAIG McDONALD

BETIMES BOOKS

First published in the English language worldwide in 2014 by Betimes
Books

www.betimesbooks.com

Copyright © 2014, Craig McDonald

Craig McDonald has asserted his right under the Universal Copyright
Convention to be identified as the author of this work

ISBN 978-0-9926552-9-7

*Forever's Just Pretend* is a work of fiction. Names, characters, places, and
incidents are either the product of the author's imagination or are used
fictitiously. Any resemblance to actual persons, living or dead, events, or
locales is entirely coincidental.

Cover design by JT Lindroos

# ALSO BY CRAIG MCDONALD

# PRAISE FOR *FOREVER'S JUST PRETEND*

"I really hope Brinke Devlin comes back. I loved her the first time she came on the page and I loved her at the end, too. She's a fascinating character. Those of us who are male writers can really appreciate how difficult it is to write such a strong and believable female character." —James Sallis, author of *Drive,* regarding the character of Brinke Devlin in *One True Sentence*

"Experiencing the work of Craig McDonald is akin to experiencing a painting by Picasso, a dance by Baryshnikov, music by Tchaikovsky. No two people will experience it exactly the same, but everyone who does experience it will walk away richer." —Jen Forbus, *Jen's Book Thoughts*

"The competition for the future of crime fiction is fierce, as it should be, but don't take your eyes off Craig McDonald. He's wily, talented and—rarest of the rare—a true original. I am always eager to see what he's going to do next." —Laura Lippman

"James Ellroy + Kerouac + Coen brothers + Tarantino = Craig McDonald" —*Amazon.fr*

"The best new crime writer in the country." —*Wisconsin State Journal*

# INTRODUCTION

If any label best describes the Hector Lassiter series, it's probably "Historical Thrillers." These books combine myth and history. The Lassiter novels spin around secret histories and unexplored or underexplored aspects of real events. They're set in real places, and use not just history to drive their plots, but also incorporate real people.

As a career journalist, I'm often frustrated by the impossibility to nail down people or events definitively. Read five biographies of the same man, say, of Ernest Hemingway, and you'll close each book feeling like you've read about five different people. So, I've concluded, defining fact as it relates to history is as elusive a goal as stroking smoke or tapping a bullet in flight.

History, it's been said, is a lie agreed to. But maybe in fiction we can find if not fact, something bordering on truth. With that possibility in mind, I explore what I can make of accepted history through the eyes of one man. The "hero" of this series, your guide through these books, is Hector Mason

Lassiter, a shades-of-grey guy who is a charmer, a rogue, a bit of a rake, and, himself, a crime novelist.

Some others in the novels say he bears a passing resemblance to the actor William Holden. Hector smokes and drinks and eats red meat. He favors sports jackets, open collar shirts, and Chevrolets. He lives his life on a large canvas. He's wily, but often impulsive; he's honorable, but mercurial.

He often doesn't understand his own drives. That is to say, he's a man. He's a man's man and a lady's man. He's a romantic, but mostly very unlucky in love. Yet his life's largely shaped by the women passing through it.

Hec was born in Galveston, Texas on January 1, 1900. In other words, he came in with the 20$^{th}$ Century, and it's my objective his arc of novels span that century — essentially, through each successive novel, giving us a kind of under-history or secret-history of the 20$^{th}$ Century.

Tall and wise beyond his years, as a boy Hector lied about his age, enlisted in the military, and accompanied Black Jack Pershing in his hunt down into Mexico to chase the Mexican Revolutionary Pancho Villa who attacked and murdered many American civilians in the town of Columbus, New Mexico. Villa's was the first and only successful assault on the United States homeland prior to the events of September 11, 2001.

Much of that part of Hector's life figures into *Head Games*, the first published Hector Lassiter novel and a finalist for the Edgar and Anthony awards, along with a few similar honors. That novel is set mostly in 1957. Its sequel, *Toros & Torsos*, opens in 1935. Subsequent books about Hector similarly hopscotched back-and-forth through the decades upon original publication.

The Betimes Books release of the Hector Lassiter series will try for something different, presenting the books in roughly chronological order—at least in terms of where each story starts as the novel opens. The series now opens with *One True Sentence*, the fourth novel in original publication sequence, but the first novel chronologically.

Set in 1924 Paris, that novel is now followed by its intended sequel, *Forever's Just Pretend*, enjoying its first-ever publication and completing a larger story revealing how Hector became the guy we come to know across the rest of the series: "The man who lives what he writes and writes what he lives"; friend to Hemingway, Orson Welles and other 20th-Century luminaries.

The rest of the repackaged series unfolds in similar fashion, a mix of the old and new titles.

The Lassiter novels were written back-to-back, and the series mostly shaped and in place before the second novel was officially published. It's very unusual in that sense—a series of discrete novels that are tightly linked and which taken together stand as a single, larger story.

Welcome to the world of Hector Lassiter.

**Craig McDonald**

*This novel is for James Sallis*

*"Dream as if you'll live forever;*
*Live as if you'll die tomorrow."*

# CHRISTMAS
## 1924

*"Christmas is a holiday that persecutes the lonely,*
*the frayed and the rejected."*
—Jimmy Cannon

# PARIS
## Hector & Victoria

It was warm and crowded in the café. The liquor was flowing and everyone was laughing and wishing one another a Happy Christmas. Back slaps, cheek kisses and toasts all around.

Victoria sat in a corner of Le Select next to a sprawling, slightly overweight cat, watching Hector at the bar chatting with his fellow writer, Hemingway. The two authors had already spent most of Christmas Eve together. Victoria envisioned a good deal of the day and perhaps even the holiday evening would be spent with the Hemingways, as well.

Oh, Vicky liked the Hemingways just fine. They were fellow Americans, and Midwesterners, at that. Hadley and Hem recalled the people Victoria had grown up with back home. But they also had a young son, "Bumby" or Jack. The Hemingway child was a kind of knife twist for Victoria just now.

Quite soon, she would be going back there, back to the States, and going with Hector who had at last decided to return home after several years roaming Europe, an unintended odyssey that began with his ill-fated service in the last war.

Hector had met Victoria under bizarre circumstances earlier in the year, right around Valentine's Day, she guessed. Hector had actually saved her life, rescuing her from a killer. She had heard another woman close to him—his lover before Victoria, a woman named Brinke Devlin—had fallen prey to the murderer.

Although Hector had eventually taken Vicky into his life, then into his bed—although he was paying her way back to the States—he'd always made it clear he wasn't looking for a permanent entanglement with her. Hector had warned Victoria from the start that the New Year would find him returning to America, and then moving on from New York alone, headed for parts unknown.

Yet it should be different now, she thought.

Hadn't they been mostly happy together these past few months?

Seemingly, Hector respected Victoria's remaining secrets, and she respected his—including the sense that some other woman evidently waited for him back there in America. She never confronted Hector about that. She never put the question to him directly.

But sometimes the pale-skinned, raven-haired Victoria caught Hem or Hadley looking at her with this curious mix of affection and concern, almost as if she reminded them too vividly of someone else, someone Victoria could only believe must have been close to Hector. Maybe it was the dead woman? Perhaps it was this Brinke?

It should be different, she thought again, watching the handsome young author.

It was Christmas, and they were lovers, and Hector had at last secured publication of his first novel. They should be returning to their homeland as a triumphant married couple, Victoria thought. Returning to celebrate Hector's new novel and their departure from this old European city that had stripped so much from them.

But it wouldn't be like that.

Tonight Hector would be in her arms of course.

This Christmas night he would be hers, but not in the ways that truly counted or mattered most to Victoria. And of course it wouldn't endure.

This night in the City of Lights, engulfed in laughter and music, Victoria already viewed Hector Lassiter as the one who got away.

# KEY WEST
### Brinke, Miguel & Mike

Christmas? It didn't feel that way at all to Brinke Devlin. Oh, someone had tipsily strung some colored lights around the bar, and a drunken Creole was playing plinking Christmas tunes on a ukulele, but for a Midwesterner like Brinke, an Ohio girl who had grown up with snow on the ground most Decembers, it felt like a false holiday.

Yet she couldn't bear to spend this night of all nights alone, holed up somewhere in silence and solitude, wondering what Hector Lassiter might be doing this Christmas night back in their city, so far back there in the City of Lights: Hector, handsome, charming and solo lobo.

So Brinke had brought her notebook to this "blind pig" and found a corner table. She was bent over the table now, all concentration and writing by candlelight, about halfway through the first draft of a new novel.

Her efforts to compose worthy prose in this bar were so far a mixed success. The noise and the music was a welcome distraction from her thoughts. Brinke was making some progress in her writing.

Yet as an unattached, fetching woman in a bar full of drunks, Brinke was also a target of opportunity.

So far, she was successfully rebuffing occasional approaches, rejecting all offers of free drinks calculated to lead to something more.

Brinke was mostly so far successful in ignoring the lustful, baleful gazes she felt upon her, including those from the tallish, rather strapping Cuban man at the bar. She'd heard the bartender call the man "Miguel," or something like that. This Miguel was the one she sensed might be the most difficult to cool off at this point. He seemed full of passionate intensity.

Fortunately, he was also nearly legless drunk.

So for her part, Brinke figured she could wait out *Miguel:* let him get so plastered he wouldn't be a threat of any kind, so there'd be no danger of him following her out of the bar.

Focused on Miguel, Brinke never really registered the rather fat, balding man sitting in a corner opposite hers. Mike Rogers, publisher and editor of one of the island's two local newspapers, was sitting at a table with his own notebook and pen.

But Mike wasn't writing a book, or even penning a news article tonight for his rag.

Mike was instead putting away the rum and colas and drawing pictures of Brinke nude in his notebook.

Focusing again on her prose, Brinke drifted in and out of the bar in a sense, trying instead to stay immersed in the country of her story. She was determined to use her creativity to distract herself from thoughts of Hector at ends in their former city. From thoughts that at least two months remained before she might possibly see Hector again.

*Hector Lassiter.* Just thinking of the name made Brinke smile.

# CAYO HUESO
## (BONE KEY — THE *LAST* KEY)

Valentine's Day, 1925

*"He lives the poetry that he cannot write. The others write the poetry that they dare not realize."*
—Oscar Wilde

# 1

The man sat sweating in the shade, awaiting the sunset and watching the child.

The room the man had rented for the past three days had a patio that faced the narrow, stingy beach. Each day he'd sat sweating in the shade of that patio, wearing shorts and a damp T-shirt, brooding and watching the other hotel guests laughing and loafing by the shoreline.

Most of them were older, retired men on holiday with their wives. Probably refugees from the Midwest based on what he could hear of their accents. "Snowbirds," the Floridians called them.

There were a couple pairs of newlyweds, and, now, another, still younger couple who wore no rings. Probably those last two had sneaked off from some other part of the Sunshine State for a first night of lovemaking. That girl would probably wind up pregnant.

Or, given what the man was going to do to the hotel once the sun went down, maybe not.

There were two or three families; some with young children.

One of those families had a single child. She was a cute, pudgy little blond girl whose coloring echoed her mother's eyes and hair. The girl was clearly a first child, doted on and fretted over.

The man had noticed the girl and her parents the first day he'd checked in. He'd made a point to find their room number.

If it wouldn't put him at risk, perhaps later in the evening he'd go ahead and knock on their door, try to give them a fighting chance. Call it salve for his conscience.

Now the little blond girl was waving at a distant ship with a tiny shovel. The man's stomach churned. Yes, maybe he would do that, try and give them that chance for flight.

The hotel was old, hell, just this side of dilapidated. The man figured none of his fellow renters could be well off.

The hotel, more of a motor court when you came down to it, was the kind of place you booked sight-unseen because it fit a price-range. Or perhaps because it was the kind of place you just ended up in, road-ragged and beat to the wide, exasperated after exhausting all better possibilities. The last rooms on the last Key.

The man looked up at the paint peeling from the wooden overhang above his room's patio, then at the crisp scrub grown up close to the hotel's perimeter. It was the dry season and it hadn't rained in more than a week. The place was a tinderbox for certain. With the sea wind whipping across the shoreline, combing that dry beach grass, the man figured he'd only have to focus on two or three units. The blast-furnace wind would see to the rest.

The man checked his pocket watch. Two more hours until sunset.

Sighing, his stomach sour, he poured himself another glass of lemonade, frowning and then belching from the stomach acid that bittersweet lemon concoction brought up.

Chewing his lip, the man kept watching the little blond girl and her parents now frolicking in the sand and creaming surf.

# 2

Hector Lassiter stood at the corner of Truman Avenue and Windsor Lane, staring up at the twin spires of St. Mary, Star of the Sea Catholic Church. His mouth was dry and his stomach unsettled. He pressed his hand to his belly, surprised by his own nervousness. A woman approached. She was pushing a baby carriage. Hector smiled distractedly at her as he stepped off the sidewalk to make room for mother and baby to pass.

Babies, family... houses?

*Right.*

The last time he had seen Brinke Devlin had been the previous February on a cold night in Paris. February had been blustery in the City of Lights that year, and when it wasn't raining, it was nearly always snowing. This February Florida evening the temperature was still in the high seventies, very humid, and Hector's white cotton shirt clung to his back.

Hector looked up a last time at the twin crosses topping the church, a hopeful man convinced he was without faith. Churches, for Hector, for some reason, were places he wrote in.

He stepped into the shadow of the church's canopied entrance and tugged at the door.

A lone woman sat in a back pew. A single candle flickered in a small alcove.

The woman's hair was blue-black and just brushed her shoulders. In Paris Brinke had worn her hair almost as short as his own, cut in fact by Hector's Parisian barber.

Now she wore a white dress, the straps glowing against her bare, bronzed shoulders. She heard his footfalls on tile and took a deep breath, squaring those proud, brown shoulders. Without turning her head to look back, the voice he remembered, the voice that dogged him so many days and in dreams since last February, said, "Please, God, it better be Hector."

He placed his hands on her shoulders and squeezed. Her hands closed over his. Hector leaned down to kiss the dark down on the back of her neck.

He slid into the pew next to Brinke and cupped her chin. She hugged him to her so tightly it robbed him of breath. They kissed, long and hard. He touched her breasts through her dress. Their tongues were in one another's mouths. She leaned back, stretching out across the pew and pulling at her skirt, urging him on top as she fumbled with his belt buckle.

"We can't here," he said.

Her breath on his neck. "We *can*. There's been nobody by for the hour I've sat here."

Brinke wasn't wearing anything under her dress. She spread her legs and pulled his pants down around his thighs. "Hurry, Hector," she said. "Please."

After, she led him a short distance from the church and down to a small strip of beach. She slipped out of her dress and walked naked into the water. Hector shed his clothes and followed her in.

The sand quickly subsided to rock and shells that hurt underfoot so they swam back closer to the shore and made love again in the water. They climbed back up onto the sand; his knees were still trembling. They stretched out naked in the shade next to the haphazard pile of their clothes, close by an old banyan tree. "We'll be okay here, like this," she said. "I swim here every day."

Hector smiled, squinting against the sun. "Just like this? Nobody else comes here?"

"Not so far. And people wouldn't care. Probably most swim naked."

Hector noticed then her lack of tan lines. Brinke said, "It's seemed like forever. I can hardly believe you're here, Hector."

"I had to come," he said. "There was never any question of that."

That knowing smile of hers he loved. "Of course there was. You're the kind who always has options."

He shook his head. "No. Not when you said that I'd find you here. There was no choosing then."

Across the Key, the man on the patio checked his watch and took a deep breath.

The little blond girl and her parents were packing up for the evening.

That child was balling up everything for him. Kid was wrecking all his dark and bloody plans.

*Still.*

The man drained his lemonade, made a sour face, then rose and stretched. He walked around the end of the hotel to his car to begin his preparations.

# 3

They were sitting on the patio behind the restaurant, looking out across another small, short beach at the setting sun.

Brinke said, "It's beautiful, isn't it, darling? Sunsets here are an event. It's as if everyone stops to watch the sun slip away, regardless of how long they've lived here."

"It's the berries, for sure, just truly gorgeous," Hector said. Orchids hung in baskets from the latticed roof of the patio's enclosure. The salt air was scented with hyacinth. Gulls squawked overhead. From somewhere, Hector heard a Nighthawk call.

He smiled, watching his lover eat. Brinke's insatiable appetite hadn't changed since he'd last seen her. He'd often wondered how this slender, athletic woman could maintain her fetching figure with her linebacker's capacity to put away the grub. Brinke had already made short work of her own swordfish with almonds and sautéed spinach. She was helping herself to spoonfuls of Hector's conch chowder and bites of his Sicilian-style swordfish. The fish had been rolled in breadcrumbs and then grilled with olive oil. The fish was crunchy around the edges and smoky tasting.

"Yummy," Brinke said. "Damn, I should have had this."

"You are now," Hector said, smiling and scooting his dish closer to her side of the table. "God, you still eat like two of me."

She shrugged and said, "How long have you been in Key West, Hector?"

"Came in on the train this morning. Been walkin' around since and getting a feel for the place. It's everything you said a year ago. God, how I love it. How long have you been here?"

"Since before Christmas," Brinke said. "Before that, it was a lot of running and weaving. Making sure everyone but you believed me dead. Making sure that horrid, murderous woman Estelle wasn't on my heels. I wanted to get down to this island knowing we could be safe here. Serenity of certainty, you know? It's the perfect place for us, beautiful, bohemian and off all the tourist maps."

Brinke leaned across the table, crossing her bare, bronzed arms, studying him. "And look at you, you're already tanning. Me? I went straight to sunburn my first day here. You look wonderful. Even handsomer than I remembered."

He reached across and squeezed her hand. "You are the looker. I like your hair longer like this."

"I was going to grow it out even more, but in this climate?" She squeezed his leg under the table. "You know conch's an aphrodisiac?"

"So I've heard," Hector said. He smiled. "But we won't need that kind of help. We haven't so far."

"It has been a year," she said, smiling. "But a week from now? Maybe then…?"

"Nothing will have changed. We have forever now."

Brinke smiled sadly and shook her head. "Forever is just pretend, Hector."

He said, "We'll just have to see about that. Where are you staying?"

Brinke hesitated, then took the plunge. "My last two novels have been doing gangbusters, really selling like daiquiris in hell, so I took the earnings from those two books and bought us a pretty little love nest." She studied his face again. Evidently encouraged by what she saw there, she was emboldened to press on. "It's on the corner of Green Street and Elizabeth. You can see the ocean from the front window. Real estate is crazy here in Florida right now, Hector, and getting ready to boom even more, they say. It's a great investment." She bit her lip. "Have I scared you buying us a love nest, Hec?"

"You, the nomad, bought a house?" Hector could hardly believe what he was hearing. Brinke was the consummate globetrotter. He bit his lip, watching her. Well, well.

"We promised one another so much in Paris a year ago," Brinke said. The candlelight flickered in her charcoal eyes. "All this time apart has only made me goofier for you. A real Dumb Dora. I mean to keep my vows, darling." She put down her fork and squeezed his hand. "So what about you?" She was holding her breath.

"I'm here," Hector said.

"We made another promise, remember, Hector? A promise about vows. Remember?"

"I proposed. I remember just fine. I asked you for a trip up the middle aisle and meant it."

"And I accepted." She held up her left hand. The candlelight caught the diamond in her ring. "I still have this. I've never taken it off. The only tan line on my body now. But are you still sure? You've always seemed so proud and protective of your solitude. In Paris, you were always declaring yourself solo lobo and pleased and proud to be that way. At least to all appearances."

"Playing the lone wolf was souring, even back then," he said. "You can only make yourself your own mark for so long before it becomes your life or plays out very badly. Let's get that ring a mate."

Brinke smiled and squeezed his hand harder. "When?"

"Just as soon as you can arrange it. That church, St. Mary, Star of the Sea—why not get married there? Do it lickety-split?"

"You mean that, darling?"

"No second thoughts," he said.

Something was flicking further down the shoreline, an orange glow, shuddering and pulsing in the dying light.

The waiter was suddenly looming at Hector's elbow. Hector raised his empty glass and said, "Another of these, whatever the hell it was. Sucker hit the spot."

"A mojito," their young Cuban waiter said. The waiter added, "May I get you anything else?"

"A bowl of gazpacho," Hector said. "I find myself still strangely hungry."

Brinke smirked at Hector, then smiled at their waiter. "Two slices of Key Lime pie, too."

The waiter nodded and moved to take his leave. Brinke caught his arm. She pointed at the glow down the beach. "Any idea what that is?"

The young man nodded. "A fire. The hotel down the beach is burning down."

Brinke bit her lip, nodding. "Another hotel fire?"

The waiter nodded. "It was very old and in poor condition. All made of wood. It was bound to happen sometime. Some rummy probably fell asleep, smoking in bed." He raised his arms. "Whoosh!"

When the waiter was gone, Hector said, "This hotel isn't the first to burn down?"

"No," Brinke said. "There have been several fires lately. Some suspected to be arson. That's the mixed blessing of this island. It's beautiful, remote…" She ran her fingers back through her black, wind-whipped hair. "But lately, this island is rather dangerous, too."

# 4

They stood naked on the beach under the stars, brushing sand off one another's backs and backsides, waiting for the balmy night air to dry their skin from their swim so they could dress again.

"See that," Brinke said, pointing at the sky. "It's the Crux. Key West is the only place in the United States where you can see it."

Looking up, Hector said, "Crux?"

"The Southern Cross," Brinke said, shivering.

He wrapped his arms around her. "Ah. What's that light?"

"It's the lighthouse."

Hector nodded. "And *that* one?"

"The burning hotel, I think," Brinke said. "Terrible. Like I told you, fire is a deadly serious thing here. Nearly all the houses are all-wood construction, and many are built very close to one another. So they roofed the houses with tin so the sparks have a harder time jumping from one burning house to a neighboring roof."

"Is your house built close?" Hector zipped up his pants and shrugged on his shirt.

"Our house, and you'll see soon enough," Brinke said. "At least it's away from this blaze. Two years ago, there was another terrible fire, Hec. It happened around Whitehead Street, in twenty-three. Forty-three houses were destroyed. Forty families left homeless."

"So they're rebuilding?" She turned her back to him and he zipped Brinke's dress.

"Sure, but not rebuilding them for those burnt-out families. The property is worth too much now for that." Brinke rested her head on Hector's shoulder. "Whatever that is burning down over there will be some speculator's boon tomorrow, likely. If it is old, insurance will never cover costs for new construction. The landowner will be given some offer he can't possibly turn down, and in a month, there will be some new hotel or resort space under construction. Wait and see." She kissed his arm. "We should probably head home now, yes?"

Hector nodded. "Surely want to. But my stuff's still at the train station. Just need to make a call and tell 'em where to deliver it." He held Brinke's hand to steady her as she slipped on her shoes.

"We'll call from a hotel, our place doesn't have a phone yet," Brinke said. She kissed him again, then reached into her purse. She pulled out a Navy Colt and handed it to Hector. "You better carry this. You really know guns like this. You should probably give me lessons soon."

Hector hefted the gun, cold suddenly. "What in God's name is this iron for?"

"Protection," Brinke said, frowning. "As I said, nights here get a little rowdy. And there have been some other bad things happening. Women raped. All of them attacked and then beaten to death."

"Christ Almighty," Hector said. "What the hell is going on on this rock?"

Brinke nodded. "The question everyone is asking. We'll talk more about that later. Right now, I just want to get you home and naked again."

It was a small white house, one lot away from the corner. It had a sheltered front porch with a chair swing dangling from its eaves. As Brinke had promised, from the front of the house the view included a patch of ocean. With the windows open, in the quiet of the night, Hector guessed one might just hear the waves slapping coral.

"It has an extra bedroom. That room could be made into a nursery," Brinke said. She shrugged her bare shoulders. "If we want to go that way."

Hector said, "If?"

Brinke shrugged again. She arched an eyebrow. "When?"

Hector tried to read her expression, made a guess, then said, "No, let's stay with if."

Brinke stroked his lower back through his damp shirt. "Right. What do you think?"

The house had a New England air about it, and its tin roof was painted hunter green. The lot was shaded front and back with tall old palm trees. He could smell the tang of the ocean.

"It's perfect," Hector said. "Really jake."

"You can be happy here?"

"With you here with me? It's going to be idyllic. I already love it."

In the distance, Hector heard a scream; what sounded like a police whistle—men yelling. Perhaps a gunshot.

Brinke took his hand. "Probably just bell bottoms or spongers on some drunken tear. Just another Saturday night in Key West, darling. Now come inside with me."

Hector lay sprawled on the damp sheets, struggling to catch his breath as the oscillating fans on either side of the room caressed them.

Brinke's cheek was pressed to his belly, her head rising and falling with his ragged breath. He raked his fingers through her damp black hair. He said, "Why in God's name are you carrying a gun, darling?"

"You snuck around with a gun, last year in Paris. That big old Colt of yours." The old 1873 Peacemaker was in Hector's steamer trunk, in fact, oiled and wrapped in soft cloth and tucked between some shirts. Hector thought of the old, dying fiction writer who'd gifted him that gun so many years ago on the far side of the Mexican border. Poor, wicked Ambrose Bierce— dying alone and far from family who, admittedly, hadn't struck a young Hector as particularly close to the old man's dark heart.

Hector stroked Brinke's hip. "Sure, but I'm me. You didn't carry a gun in Paris. What's goin' on?"

She brushed a thick comma of hair from over his right eye. "I told you, things here are dangerous lately. Some pretty terrible things have been happening around here."

Hector, still stroking her body, said, "You mean all these fires?"

"And murders, Hector. Quite a few of those, too."

"Murders? What the hell?"

"Vicious slayings. Senseless killings, on face. Then there are these fires. Most think the arsons and the murders are linked in some way."

"Brinke, you're not poking into these crimes, are you? Your penchant for playing detective is what cost us what could have been our first wedding anniversary this month."

"It's different this time, Hector. This isn't just some other country I'm passing through, soaking up color for another mystery novel. This is home, now. This is our place, yes?"

Hector combed his fingers through her hair. "Yeah, well, Europe is pretty balled up about now, too, Brinke. Did you hear that bastard Mussolini has turned Italy into a dictatorship?"

"Don't change the subject, Hec. Point is, this is the place we're going to live. This is home now."

"Brinke…"

Her chin was pressing into his belly. She said softly, "The fires apart, it's women being killed. Raped, then murdered, like I told you. Beaten to death with baseball bats. The papers have given the killer a spooky name. They call him the Key West Clubber. It's giving all the women on the island the heebie-jeebies. You can count me among the terrified."

"For God's sake."

"Lurid, I know, but it sells papers, Hec. All these crazy, bloody scream headlines."

"And it could sell books aplenty," Hector said. "Dark novels. Could be fodder for the next Bud Grant crime novel, couldn't it?" Bud Grant was Brinke's new penname, one Hector had coined for her. Brinke had this perplexing impulse, drawing on her life to feed her fiction.

She raked her nails through his chest hair. "No, Hector. I learned my lesson last year. Learned it very well and at a too-stiff price, as we both know. I'm not going to write about anything happening here. But I have… skills. I have them, and so do you. I can see that very clearly, now. It's

27

wrong for us not to use those talents to set things right here in our new home."

"You've now seen the scars on my back from our last bout of playing detective, honey. And all our dead back in Paris? Hell, our best friends in the Quarter think you're among the fallen. Leave it to the local law, darlin'."

Brinke shook her head. "No can do, love. The local law is an elected official in the hip pocket of other elected officials. A rube. Probably a crooked rube."

"Yet all of these elected officials must have wives and sisters and daughters who could fall victim to this so-called Clubber," Hector said. "Way I see it, there's no damn percentage in this top cop doing flat nothin'. Not if he wants to stay in office, sweetheart."

Brinke shook her head. "It's against my instincts. And against my conscience. Against yours too, if you knew the whole story."

"This is sure ghoulish pillow talk for our first night back together, Brinke."

"Then we'll save that chat for breakfast. For now, let's spoon and neck and pet some more." She kissed her way up his chest. She bit his neck. Then Brinke sat up suddenly. "Oh, I need you to inscribe my copy of *Rhapsody in Black*. You wrote a great crime novel, Hector. It's a hell of a debut. And you surprised me with that ending. That never happens anymore."

"Thanks. You're the one who prodded me to write the novel, you know. Wouldn't exist without you. Hence the dedication."

She kissed him. "And I thank you for that. But only you could have written that book, Hector. It's dark and sad and wonderful. Fearless in its way."

"Your first Bud Grant novel, *Triangle.* Now, that was a hell of a book."

She kissed him. "You're so good to say so." Then she put her fingers to her lips to hush him. She slipped naked from the bed and turned off the fans. Brinke was all Sheba—Hector never tired of looking at her.

Brinke settled back on the bed with Hector and said softly, "Just shush and listen for a minute, please? This is my favorite time of night. Only the wind chimes and the ocean. Sometimes the horn from some far-away ship. But it's wickedly hot without the fans, so I don't do it often."

Hector gently kicked off the sheet. "Well, then we'll just sit and listen for a while. Heat's no big thing. A nice change from your drafty garret in the *Quartier Latin.* Let's just listen to those sounds you love."

# 5

Terrible shrieks wrenched Hector from his sleep.

"Holy Jesus, I feel like I'm on a farm." Hector struggled up onto his elbows, bleary-eyed and frowning at the screeching outside.

"Those things are fighting cocks," Brinke said, making a face. "The island is lousy with them. They roam the streets, sometimes attacking even the dogs. There are cock matches held all over the island. Horrible blood sport. Makes bull fighting look almost palatable."

Hector stroked her longer hair. Smiling and shaking his head, he said, "Christ, this sand dab really is like some border town."

Brinke kissed his shoulder then playfully bit it. "Already having second thoughts about living here?"

Hector leaned over and kissed her breast; tasted heady salt. "Nah, it feels right. Definitely my kind of place."

Brinke pressed his face to her breast again. She stroked his unshaven cheek and stood and stretched. She pulled on a light silk robe that didn't reach her knees. It was something Oriental that Brinke had picked up in her travels, Hector figured. He saw himself as quite the maverick, but Brinke was five years older than he was and consequently had covered that much more ground. The woman was the consummate explorer. She looked at him and said, "For weeks I've imagined this morning, waking up and seeing you there in that bed. Our bed."

"With the imagination you've got I can't imagine reality is shouldering up too comfortably to your dreams."

"You're right," Brinke said. "This is so much better."

Hector cupped her chin in his hand and kissed her, soft and slow. He whispered in her ear, "They say you should be careful what you dream, because eventually, your dreams will be dreaming you." He softly nipped at her ear lobe with his teeth.

Brinke hugged him closer. "You pinch that pearl of wisdom from Gertrude Stein? Perhaps Jim Joyce?"

"My grandfather."

"Is he still alive?"

"He is at that," Hector said. "Men that side of my family live a long, long time somehow. He lives on Corpus Christi Bay. Well, mostly. He's on the road a lot, too. Lives large and wide."

Brinke bit her lip, said, "We have an extra room here. See if he'll cross the Gulf. One of us should have family at our wedding and my side's not an option. Think he'd come?"

Hector stretched back out on the bed. He crossed his hands behind his head. "Asked? Sure. He'd likely be flattered. I could send him a wire later today."

"So let's do that very thing, Hec. I'd love to meet him. Now, you loaf, lover man. I'll make us breakfast."

Hector arched a dark eyebrow. "No offense intended, but you cook, honey?"

"Didn't have to in Paris where there was always someone offering to buy me a drink or dinner," Brinke said. "But yes, I can cook. Tomorrow it'll be your turn in the kitchen."

"What makes you think that I can cook?"

"*Rhapsody in Black*. Specifically, chapter eight."

"Could have been researched."

Brinke shook her head. "You're not that kind of writer. You're like me, the write-what-you-know sort. The write-what-you-live breed." Hector wasn't so sure about that, so he just bit his lip.

Hector pulled down a black T-shirt over his khaki pants and slipped on a pair of leather sandals. His dark brown hair was wet from the shower and still showing comb tracks. Brinke whistled lowly. "Wow. Quite a change from my Paris Hector with his sweaters over sweatshirts and his leather jackets."

Brinke was wearing white shorts and a worn white fisherman's shirt with faded blue stripes. The soft fabric draped her breasts. She had a pair of sunglasses resting atop her head. She wore white sandals. "You look like an ad for a cruise," Hector said.

"Too studied?"

"Too beautiful to be real. A living doll. I feel like undressing you again. But I'll soldier on. What do we do, our first full day together on Key West?"

Brinke pulled down her black cheaters, hiding her blacker eyes. "There's a restaurant down by the docks I want to introduce you to. Well, restaurant is pretty much overstating it. More like a shanty shack. But it has the freshest seafood you can imagine. It's pretty rustic décor-wise, but sits on a dock and it's great. We can watch the tarpon roam between the pilings, eat in the breeze."

"Sounds like a diamond in the rough," Hector said. "But let's hit a store on the way. Need to get myself some sunglasses."

They were on foot. Hector said, "Not much point in owning a car is there?"

"There are a surprising number of flivvers on this rock." Brinke took his hand. "But, no, most things are in walking distance if the heat isn't on. If it's too hot to walk, you just hop on the streetcar. But the island kind of shuts down in the afternoons. Like an island-wide siesta."

Hector could smell the docks before they reached them. There was some commotion as a sport boat's catch was hoisted up on onto the big scales. The tuna, dripping and oily gray-blue in the sun, topped three hundred pounds.

Brinke said, "Some monster, huh?"

"Very surely a big boy," Hector said. "Catchin' 'em looks like some kind of exercise."

Brinke led him down an inclined ramp, encrusted with salt spray. They ducked into a tin-roofed shanty. From outside, it looked like the next tropical storm would lay waste to the dump. But it was cooler in the shade and a single, intricately weaving pulley band drove several overhead fans. Those fans and the sea breeze made the open-air clam shack pleasantly cool.

Hector slipped off his sunglasses and hooked one of their arms in the front of his T-shirt. The day's offerings were scrawled on a chalkboard above the bar—many misspellings there.

"Think I crave something new and different," Brinke said. "Maybe something like that leviathan they're weighing out front." After some questions put to the bartender, she instead settled on grilled grouper with raw artichokes and a side of conch fritters. Brinke slid onto a stool at the bar and asked for a daiquiri. A tune played from a distant boat; they could just hear snatches of "Rhapsody in Blue," then of "Dixie."

Hector took the stool next to Brinke's and ordered himself a mojito. He selected tarpon with some dirty rice. Hector sipped his drink and watched the cook go to work with a knife, slitting the fillets into strips running nose to tail. "I'm wondering what else I should order," he said. "I mean as you'll no doubt be eating mine."

"I'd stick my tongue out at you now if it wasn't so childish," Brinke said. "And I'm not that hungry this second."

A woman edged behind the bar. She was fiftyish and overweight. She wore a floral print dress and a white headband that held down the hairnet on her head. The woman said, "Hey there, Dev. You're nearly becomin' a reg'lar."

Brinke said, "Hey, Rose." She waved her arms around them. "You know I love your place. And it's the best seafood in town."

The woman gave Brinke a half-smile and said, "Who is this big lug with you? This your fella, the Texan, you've been gabbing about since Christmas?"

Brinke smiled and slipped her arm through Hector's. "That's right. Hector Lassiter, meet Rose Thorpe."

Rose wiped a hand on her apron and stuck it out. Hector shook it. "Great place," he said.

The older woman said, "God, they do grow 'em tall in Texas. He's the bee's knees, okay."

"Smart, too," Brinke said. "Capable. Boasts what a French cop calls grace under pressure."

Rose nodded and said, "On that note, Dev says you may be able to help figure out who hurt my baby girl, Mr. Lassiter. Help get to the bottom of what happened to my Louise."

Hector raised his eyebrows. "Your Louise?"

Rose nodded. "She was murdered, Mr. Lassiter. A month ago, yesterday. Sheriff Mel hasn't done a thing about it, so far as I can see. Mel is such a goddamn Palooka."

Craig McDonald

Hector shot Brinke a look. Brinke said, "It's true. 'Sheriff Mel' is Melvin Hoyt. He's useful as a pair of tonsils."

Hector smiled sadly at the older woman. "Sorry, darlin', but cops don't much cotton to private folks playing flatfoot. Trust me, Rose, I have painful first-hand knowledge of that." He felt the scars on his back chaffing his damp shirt. "So does Brinke. She has more experience on that front than me, in fact."

Brinke squeezed Hector's knee. "Hear her story, Hector. Please."

The old woman looked at him hopefully, big, sad eyes that implored.

*No graceful way around it, goddamn it.*

Hector shook out a cigarette and struck a match on the underside of the counter. He cupped his hands to protect the flame from the warm wind off the water. He smiled. Letting a little smoke into his voice, he said, "What happened to your daughter, Rose?"

Word 'round Bone Key was the crime wave started with the Great Fire of 1923. The flames licked house to house, driven by the sea wind and falling, spiraling and burning palm fronds that touched off the dried grass. The blaze left a big burned wasteland in the middle of the Key.

In 1924, in late October, came another fire at the lumberyard, then, a week later, the church-furnished home of an island clergyman burned down.

After that arson against the padre, the attacks on women commenced. The first of those came in December of 1924.

The woman was raped and then beaten to death with a club or metal pipe. Possibly a baseball bat. Three more similar attacks quickly followed.

Rose's daughter, Louise, was killed in late January. Louise was a schoolteacher, twenty-six-years old. She was beaten and molested and then clubbed to death less than twenty yards from her schoolroom, apparently attacked on her way to work. A student found Rose's body. That same day, another woman was found dead in her home. She had also been molested and murdered.

And now, with the recent hotel fires, the arsons seemed to be resuming.

Hector ground out his cigarette. "Louise had no boy-friends who were questioned? No students who may have been infatuated with her?"

Rose's eyes were hard. "She had no boyfriend, mister. And she taught elementary school. Her students were too young for infatuations, Mr. Lassiter. In fact, the boy who found my Louise, all naked and bloody, he was seven. Hardly more than a baby. No child did this."

"It was a question that had to be asked. And please, call me Hector." He thought a second and then said, "These fires and rapes—the murders—how'd they come to be linked? They're pretty different beasts as crimes go. Frankly doesn't make sense to me one man would do all of them."

"Sheriff Mel says it's so," Rose said. "He said clues at the crime scenes leave no doubt. The sheriff's said so to the news-papers. 'Course he hasn't said how the clues tell him that, 'xactly. Hasn't said what those clues are."

Hector nodded. "And it was that local newspaper that came up with this spooky moniker, the Key West Clubber?"

"That's right." Rose passed Hector his plate of fish. She said, "Brinke said you two might could figure out who did this, since the police here ain't showin' signs of doin' it. She said you two helped stop some murders back in Paris, France." She handed Brinke her plate.

Hector rose, his plate in hand. "Let me think on all this a few minutes, okay?" He took his food and walked to a tall table, seaside. He glanced over the rail and saw more tarpon sliding, long and silver, just an inch or so from the surface, gliding between the piles, just as Brinke had predicted.

He looked up from the cruising tarpon as Brinke pulled out a stool and sat down across from him at the table. He said, "You're some kind of unbelievable, sister."

Brinke nodded and combed her fingers through her black hair, getting it off her damp forehead. The heat was already taking hold. "So sorry to snooker you like this, darling. But you see now, Hec? And Rose is a friend. One of the first people here to be really nice to me. She helped me find our house. I like her. I really want us to help her."

"Was it all this that prompted you to get that gun you gave me to hold for you last night?"

Brinke forked off a sliver of Hector's fish. "Yes." She hesitated. "Well, it was what you know now that drove that purchase." She bit her lip. "That, and some more, actually."

Hector said, "More?" His voice went hard. "What more is there?"

"A week ago, a man followed me down Duval, Hector. I'd been in a coffee shop, a Cuban place, writing. Stealing speech patterns. You know, snatching bits of overheard dialogue that rang true as sentences. Anyway, this man followed me. Never got a good look at him, but he was shadowing me, dogging my steps, no question about that."

"How can you be sure?"

"I ran half-a-block. He gave chase. I ducked into a hotel. Then I took a taxi back to the house. The next day I went to a pawnshop on Simonton Street and bought my own Colt."

Hector sipped his mojito. "Okay, I'm gettin' my back up now. Hope you're happy."

"I am, but not like you mean. But now you will help me to help Rose?" Brinke took another forkful of Hector's tarpon. "If it isn't quite enough, there's more I could tell you."

Hector scowled. "What? You mean still more involving you? Some direct threat, or what exactly?"

"That's right, a threat. Or I think so. The last couple of nights, I spotted someone sneaking around our house. Or maybe he was sneaking around the neighbors' houses. Either way, whoever it was, they were lurking with intent. Of that much I'm certain."

Hector sighed. "Okay. Obviously you've been nosing around already. What do you know so far, darlin'?"

"*Nada,*" Brinke said. She made a face. "Or given the events of last year, I should say nothing. Nothing that makes sense yet. I'm with you, Hector. Based on past experience, and being an above-average student of crime, I don't see how you have an arsonist and a rapist-killer inhabiting the same body. This is something more than just one lunatic. I'm convinced of that."

Hector sampled a little of his quickly disappearing tarpon. He might have tried a little of Brinke's grouper, but it was already gone somehow though he'd never seen Brinke touch it. He said, "Me either. So what exactly, then?"

"I'm at a loss, so far," she said.

"These women, did they all live alone?"

"I don't think they were married, anyway," Brinke said. "I scrounged around and found some news articles. I checked some obituaries. No mentions of husbands."

"That doesn't preclude shack-ups," Hector said.

She wrinkled her nose. "Shack-ups?"

"Couples living in sin."

"Oh," Brinke said. "Sinners like us, you mean."

"Right." He smiled. "But not for much longer, yes?"

"No. That reminds me, you should wire your grandfather after this."

"Sure. Once we do that though, we're fully committed. You know that, don't you?"

Brinke smiled. "Exactly! I want this, fiercely. I'm furiously in love with you. On that note, you've seen the house is pretty Spartan. Thought we'd shop together for more furniture, and soon. But I get right of refusal. You being from Texas, God only knows what you regard as décor. Maybe steers' skulls and lariats or the like." She feigned a shudder.

Hector smiled. "Place I was born wasn't all that different from here in some ways. Just the other side of the Gulf."

"So where do we start together working on these crimes?"

He rubbed the back of his neck. Hector stared into the water, contemplating the cruising tarpon. "I'm thinking on that, still."

Rose was coming their way, smiling. She wiped her hands on her apron. "How was it?"

"Great," Hector said. "Delicious. Best I almost had. By that I mean Brinke ate most before I got there."

Rose smiled. "Dev's an eater, okay. Still hungry then?"

"No, but very thirsty," he said. "Another of these would hit the spot." Hector lifted the glass and swished around the dregs of his rum drink. "Another daiquiri for Brinke, too."

Rose winked. "Done. You thought about this other? About my Louise?"

"We'll nose around for a tad," Hector said. "But let's keep it our secret, eh, hon'? I'm new on this island and don't want to get on Sheriff Mel's bad side. I suspect that's a mighty treacherous place to be."

# 6

The man threw down the newspaper, his stomach churning.

Four had been killed in the fire. One was a child. No way to know if it was the little blond girl, though he'd taken the trouble to rap his knuckles on their room's door as he made his escape.

So maybe that tow-headed toddler was okay.

Maybe. Jesus Christ, he hoped so.

He'd contracted for three jobs. The next was a private residence on Elizabeth Street and a restaurant at Mallory Dock still remained.

He'd planned to space the arsons out more, but he didn't want to hang around the island and hear more about that hotel fire and maybe the kid. He didn't want to be around for the news coverage of the next two jobs.

So he decided he'd double-up and finish his hellish contract before morning.

The man had other job prospects in Miami, work for some bunch of greasy Guinea hoodlums out of Chicago who were angling for a muggy winter beachhead now that John Ashley was safely dead and his gang in tatters, he guessed.

That was more his line of work than this Key West gig was proving to be.

Killing kids? Killing children was not his thing. Not at all.

# 7

Hector finished the text of the wire to his maternal grandfather, the man who raised him after his parents' deaths, and read it over once. As he was about to hand it across the counter to the clerk, Brinke snatched it away. Turning her back to the clerk, she slipped on some reading glasses and read it. Vain, pretty Brinke: always hiding those spectacles and her weak dark eyes.

Shaking his head, Hector said, "Meet with your approval, darling?"

Brinke took off her glasses and handed the slip of paper back to the clerk. "Oh, the message is just fine, Hector. I was just seeing what your granddad's name is. Beauregard Stryder. Can't be many men with that name." She folded her glasses and slipped them back into her purse.

"That's the drastically shortened version," Hector said. "His whole name runs Beauregard Ballou Strapp Stryder." Hector furrowed his brow. "Hell, there might even be another name or two in there I missed."

"We'll stick with Beau Stryder," Brinke said, putting away her reading glasses. "Sounds quite dashing—that handle, to use one of your terms. Think he'll give me away?"

"I'm frankly more worried about him trying to take you away," Hector said. "He was, and remains, least ways in his own mind, quite the lady's man."

"I can hardly wait." Brinke hugged him. They kissed. "So now we're committed, like you said."

"Utterly."

"So we should look for wedding bands."

Hector furrowed his brow. "Not at the same place where you bought that shooting iron?"

"Lord, no. A proper jewelers." She took his hand and tugged. "C'mon, I'll show you."

Hector had their wedding bands in a small envelope he'd thrust into his pant's pocket. He was fiddling with the envelope in that pocket and jingling change in the other, standing under a canopy and waiting for Brinke. She'd ducked into the general store to buy more ribbons for her typewriter. Between the two of them, and given their respective writing speeds, Hector figured to go through many miles of that stuff in the days to come.

Hector turned and looked into the storefront behind him: a realtor's office, "Last Key Realty." Taped to a large piece of cardboard in the front window were photographs of various homes and properties for sale. There was a second sheet that was laid out more as a kind of plat. Hector eyed that rendering and realized it was comprised of an entire block of property, or perhaps even two or three blocks given the haphazard pattern of the island's streets. The land was being sold in parcels.

The properties all seemed to be centered around White-head Street. Then Hector remembered what Brinke had said about the 1923 fire that had wiped out more than three dozen houses on the Key in that vicinity.

A man ducked his head out the door. He was wearing a sweat-stained white shirt, the sleeves rolled up below matching sleeve garters. His hair was parted in the middle and slicked severely down on either side of his head. The man grinned and said, "I'm Denton Stokes. Looking for property, brother?"

Hector shook his head. "Nope, I don't think so. Just looking at this sheet here. This place is an island, and pretty densely developed. What, God suddenly make some more coral bed for you all to build on? That looks like a mighty big chunk of the Key for sale."

The man wiped his forehead with a ragged handkerchief, the screen door resting against his shoulder.

"Yeah. That's from the big fire a couple of years ago. That took out a passel of places."

"Most people would rebuild," Hector said.

"Thems with enough or any insurance would," the man agreed. "But some of those places that went up in smoke, hell, most of 'em if you ask me, weren't worth spit standin'. Best thing that ever happened, that fire. Certainly good for my line of work."

Hector looked again at the board with the pictures of still-standing houses for sale. He said, "Looks to be so."

The man leaned out a bit further and offered Hector a business card. Hector reached up and took it. "In case you change your mind," the salesman said. "No better time to get yourself some Florida property than now, brother, and this is the place to buy it. Last Key. Like you said, the Lord ain't gonna grant us more dirt. Opportunity stops at the southern-most point."

"That last sounds like a slogan," Hector said.

"It may be now," the realtor said, clearly proud of himself.

# 8

They were standing on the pier watching the bobbers skim the waves. It was overcast and Brinke was blinking back the first rain in many days.

Squinting against the light drizzle, she said, "We're on an island, Hector. We're surrounded by seafood caught and prepared by others. What is this about? Why in God's name did you buy this fishing stuff when there are all these others who make their living doing this? Why are we trying to catch fish?"

Hector recast his line. "I enjoy it for one thing. But I did it mostly because of my granddad maybe coming. Grandpa Beau is an avid fisherman. He made sure I fished, all the time, everywhere we went. It's been a few years since I've done it. And if Pap saw I lived someplace surrounded by water and didn't own any tackle? Hell, he'd ream me. It'd kill him. Just want to make sure my casting is up to snuff. That and what comes after."

Brinke wiped rainwater from her forehead. "With all that tackle and the rods, you could have at least bought a couple of rain slickers. That's the other thing about this place, it doesn't last long, but you get rain here nearly every day. Or so they say. I haven't seen much until now."

"Takes off the heat a bit," Hector said. He nodded at the bobbers. Brinke's was dipping below the waves. "Think you've got a bite."

Brinke looked over the rail, suddenly excited. "Hey, it is going up and down!"

"Wait until the bobber goes under and stays a moment, and then tug back, firmly, but not crazy hard."

Brinke squealed as the bobber went under and she jerked back, a bit too sharply Hector thought, afraid she'd lose the fish.

To his surprise, there was still tension on the line. Brinke said, "Okay, what do I do now?"

"Turn the reel and pull him on in!"

Hector ended up reeling in his own line and setting his pole on the planks to help Brinke. Whatever was on the end of her line was big.

They finally got it up out of the water and Hector reached over the rail and hooked a finger through its gill slit and hefted the fish.

Wide-eye, Brinke said, "What is it?"

"My lunch that you enjoyed, tarpon. But relatively small for tarpon."

"That's small? So we throw it back?"

"Hell no. We take it home. You catch it, you clean it. Then you eat it. The rules."

Brinke looked worried. "But I don't know how to clean it."

"I'll show you how," Hector said.

Brinke sat back in her chair in their under-furnished kitchen. "Well, if the bottom falls out for my new character, Horace Lester, and for your next novel—if the wolves are baying at our door—at least we know we can survive on what you catch and cook. There'll be no heating bills here and we don't need much in the way of clothes. I think we're set for the poor life, if things go all to hell. We'll do just fine."

"That's a cheerful thought," Hector said. "Tarpon was okay?"

"As good or even better than the one at lunch," Brinke said, sipping some white wine. She reached across the table and held up the bottle. "Thank God you thought to smuggle in some of this from the civilized world. That's the one thing about Paris I miss, the readily available legal and proper booze. Outside of Rose's place, and a couple of rough bars downtown, it's all speakeasies and codes and wink-wink to get a drink. And mostly rum. I've missed fine wine."

"Prohibition can't last," Hector said. "It's making too many criminals rich."

"And that's why we'll get to drink again?" Brinke smiled and shook her head. "It's certainly a crazy world, isn't it?"

Hector poured himself some more white wine. "Another quiet, panting night at home, or what, Brinke?"

"Thought we might get out a bit. We could see a movie. The theatre is showing Erich von Stroheim's *Greed*."

Hector made a face. "Isn't that film something like ten hours long?"

"They've severely edited it, according to the local paper."

"What, to a brisk five hours?" Hector shook his head. "How about drinks, dinner and bed instead?"

"Sold! But first I need to do some shopping. You're right about stamina and us. Want to get some fresh fruit and some illegal hooch for the in-between times. While I do that, you can wander the island maybe. But not quite yet." She turned on the radio. "In Shadowland" was playing.

That look—bedroom eyes. He took her hand, pulled her up to him.

Brinke said, "Think bed'll still be sexy when we're legal?"

# 9

The woman was slender, tall. She was black-haired and pretty. A real tomato. The man searched for a word to best describe her and settled on "coltish."

Pulling on a bottle of Coca-Cola, he thought about how he'd drawn himself a winner with this one, okay. One to savor. The last two had been, eh…call 'em plain.

He'd been spying on the woman for several days, ever since he was given her name and address. He'd learned her routines and picked his time and place.

The woman paused at a fruit stand. She touched and weighed various bits of produce. She wore khaki shorts and a sleeveless white shirt that tied at the back of her long, tanned neck—a shirt that bared much of her bronzed back. She was leggy and busty. He looked a long time at her legs, those stems without end.

And Jesus, that chassis?

Yes, he'd really hit the mother lode with this broad.

The houses on either side of the woman's house were empty. The man was responsible for one of those vacancies; a fire had taken care of the other. He smiled, remembering the woman who had lived in the vacant house. The woman he'd killed.

Veronica Duggan. A dirty blond, just shy of plump. Thick ankles and wide-hipped. A real Mrs. Grundy. She'd fought him to her final breath, for all the good it did her, which was none.

He smiled, remembering.

Because there were no immediate neighbors on one side to hear, the man had decided on the raven-haired woman's house as the site of his attack. He'd already confirmed she was unmarried—no man he'd seen around the house the past few nights that he'd troubled himself to watch. Yes, she lived alone.

He'd have privacy in her house and the time to savor her before he put out her lights. He'd already hidden the baseball bat in a shrub by her front door. He could hardly risk walking around the island toting a Louisville Slugger. Not since the newspapers had hung that bogeyman moniker on him and the others. The islanders were crazy with fear for a visit from the Clubber because of those scream headlines. Goddamn muckrakers.

The pretty, dark-haired woman was paying for her produce; a fetching smile for the Cuban clerk. The woman pulled sunglasses down out of her wind-tangled hair.

The man watched her, smiling. Watching that long brown back, shapely backside and those endless legs.

They'd be his soon. All his.

The man followed the woman, pausing just long enough to scoop up a peach and a newspaper, then tossing the fruit monger a couple of coins. Something there about commerce on the cover. A pull quote from President Coolidge: "The business of America is business."

Right-o. Some other item about new FBI chief J. Edgar Hoover.

Folding the paper under his arm, the man bit into the fuzzy, succulent peach.

Delicious.

He looked at the fruit where he had bitten into it: pink, glistening. Reminded him of a woman.

# 10

Hector realized, standing at their locked front door, he hadn't yet been given a key to their new home.

Not that a doorkey would have helped him now: the screen door was fastened from the inside with a catch-and-eye hook. Hector called out to Brinke once, twice. No answer. Not to his knock, either.

The seam between the screen door and frame was a crude one, a fair amount of gap there. Frowning, Hector pulled out his notebook and edged its cardboard cover into the crack in the door and eased it up, popping the hook. Too damn easy. Right there, Hector promised himself a cool, early next morning re-hanging the door to prevent anyone else getting in the way he had just done. Brinke was cautious enough in some ways, yes. But in others?

Hector slid into the shade of the living room. The room was cool from a cross breeze through the open windows, front and back. He heard the palm trees creaking in the wind.

Discarded clothes lay on the floor: a white blouse, some sandals. Scraps of clothing were dropped along the path to the bedroom. Shorts and bloodstained panties, crumpled on the floor, set Hector's heart beating faster and left him wondering if Brinke had undressed herself. His suitcases were still sitting in the middle of the room, mostly unpacked. Hector frowned and slipped his hand under a stack of shirts and pants and shook loose his '73 Peacemaker. He hefted the long-barreled Colt revolver and then edged into the darkened bedroom. The shades were drawn and the fans going. Hector's eyes were still adjusted to the harsh Florida sunlight, so the interior room was all but black to him. He stood there a moment, waiting for his eyes to adapt to the dark.

Hector saw that Brinke was sprawled faced down on the bed, nude.

Softly, he said, "Brinke? Are you okay?"

No answer.

Frightened now, he walked softly to the bed and pressed two fingers to her throat; felt a pulse. Her head turned. Groggy, Brinke said, "Hector?"

"What's wrong sweetheart? I was very worried."

Brinke rubbed her eyes and looked at his Colt. "I guess you were, worried, I mean. You can put that gun away, Hector. It's not like that."

"You okay?"

"I—well, it's that time of the month. Never had it hit me so hard, before. A migraine, cramps. Sorry about the mess, but I just had to get cool and to bed. Sorry for scaring you, darling. But I was so sick, so hot. And I hurt."

Hector saw now that Brinke had spread a towel under herself to protect the chenille coverlet. She clutched at her lower abdomen and groaned. "Oh, God, this is awful."

"Cramps again?"

She shook her head and said, "The worst. And this is so embarrassing. Having you see that…this."

He waved a dismissive hand. "Don't be silly, darling." He uncocked his Colt and placed the revolver on the nightstand. He stroked her hip, curving around her pelvic bone to massage her belly. He began unbuttoning his shirt. "Those cramps, I expect I can help with those." He unfastened his belt.

"Not now," she said. "Not with me like this. You can't want to."

"Hell I can't," he said, kissing her forehead and kicking off his pants.

Her eyes shone in the light through a crack in the blinds. Brinke said, "Sorry again for the mess."

He smiled and said, "Quiet now. It's nothing."

She kissed his shoulder. "You're right, though. It did help with the cramps. Headache's gone, too. So I guess in addition to all your other fine qualities, you're medicinal, too."

"Sure I am." Hector brushed the black bangs back from her forehead.

"This thing may be the death of me," she said, stroking him there, then frowning at the sticky blood on her hand.

"Given your passionate nature, it's more likely to be the death of me," Hector said.

"You regretting my passionate nature, Hec?"

"Heaven forbid." He slipped his arm under her head. He softly massaged her belly with his other hand. "Any good restaurants on this island? By that I mean joints with linen table cloths and waiters in jackets or ties?"

"A couple," she said, sounding sleepy as she continued to stroke him there. She still felt her blood on him, tacky between her fingers. She said, "Already feeling homesick for Paris, Hec?"

"Nah. Or not like you mean. The City of Lights is worse than you remember. It's tourist hell now, and I mean all the way up. A legion of new, would-be expatriates arriving every day, crowding out the bistros and cafés. Just thought it would be nice to put on some glad rags. Puttin' on the Ritz, you know? Like we used to when we crossed the river and stepped out on the Right Bank."

"Let's do that," she said, stretching her neck to kiss his cheek. "Been months since I dressed to the nines. And it'll give you an excuse to finally shave again. You're going native."

"Don't like the scruffy look?"

"Not on you. Yeah, shave and then let's paint the town."

"Only if you're still feeling better."

"I'm great now," Brinke said. "Completely copacetic." She closed her hand, warm and firm around him, said, "And if I relapse, I'll just take another dose of Hector."

Car doors slammed outside; commotion. Some dogs barked off a ways. Hector heard men talking, gruff and officious sounding. After a few minutes, someone rapped hard on the front door, belligerent knocks that telegraphed trouble. Brinke and Hector exchanged looks. He said, "I'll get it." He rose and cleaned up with a towel before pulling on his pants. Shrugging on his shirt, he called through the open window, "Just a goddamn minute, right?"

Hector closed the bedroom door on Brinke and began buttoning his shirt as he crossed the living room to meet their caller.

A man in a uniform was framed in the screen door. Hector squinted his eyes against the glare through the screen and realized it was a police uniform. Some island Bull was silhouetted there at the door. The Bull had stains under his arms and his forehead was shiny with sweat. The sun glinted off his badge. Squinting, Hector said, "Officer. Is there some problem?"

The cop said, "Is indeed. Name?"

"I've got one, yeah. Hector Lassiter. Your name, officer?"

"You live here, fella?"

Hector was taking a swift dislike to the cop. He said back to the Bull, "All things in their time. You have a name fella?"

The cop—standing an even six-feet, and going maybe two-ten, Hector guessed—said again, "You live here, mister?" There was another cop behind him, now. That policeman smiled politely at Hector, shielding his eyes from the sun with a maimed hand—the second cop's middle finger was missing.

"Yeah, live right here," Hector said. "What's up, Oh Unnamed Flatfoot?"

"You live here alone, mister?"

Brinke wrapped her arm around Hector's waist. She was wearing her saucy little Oriental robe. She said, "He does not." She flashed her left hand and Hector saw that Brinke had slipped on the wedding band for cover. "This is our place, officer."

The lead cop nodded, eyeing Brinke. "How long have you been together?"

Brinke slipped her arm through Hector's. "We met last February."

The cop made a face. "I meant today, Ma'am."

Brinke shrugged and smiled sheepishly. She beamed up at Hector; he thought she was laying it on a bit too thick. "We're newlyweds," she said. She smiled at the sheriff, all sex. "You know what I mean. Why do you ask?"

The cop said, "There's been a murder. Two doors down. A woman was killed." The cop paused, looking Brinke over again. "She looked more than a little like you, Mrs. Lassiter."

Hector edged closer to the door, read the cop's nametag. "So you're the storied Sheriff Mel Hoyt."

The cop scowled. "What of it?"

Hector said, "Nothing of it."

The Sheriff pressed, "You've heard of me?"

"Plenty," Hector said.

"What's that mean?"

Hector shook out a cigarette. He fiddled with a box of matches, struck one. "Like I said, not much."

"What's that fuckin' mean?"

Brinke looked tense, warning Hector with her eyes to back down.

Hector rolled his eyes. "Nothing. It means nothing."

"Don't you fucking adopt some attitude with me," Hoyt said. "Don't you do that."

"You're the one with attitude, constable," Hector said. "No identification, even when asked twice for it. I'm the one who was napping peacefully until you banged on the door and began running your belligerent mouth. All that coarse language in front of a lady. Tell me, who over your head can I complain to about your sour demeanor? You seem to have forgotten you're a public servant."

The sheriff sighed and looked over his shoulder at his flunky with the missing finger. "Fuck this. These two are a goddamn waste of time."

The second cop lingered long enough to say to Hector, "Thanks for your time, sir. Very sorry for the intrusion." The cop looked a little contrite for his superior's surliness.

Hector watched them leave, opening and closing his fists. Brinke rubbed his back, said, "You need to get a handle on your temper around that one. He is a low, mean bastard, that's a given. But you can't antagonize that man. Right or wrong, he's the law on this island. There's no court of higher appeals."

"He's a dirty piece of work. You're too right about that. Comes off him in waves."

"So you do see what I've been saying about Sheriff Mel?"

Hector nodded. "I see it, sure. Did you know this woman he says was killed, this alleged twin of yours?"

"No," Brinke said, biting her lip. "I didn't. But I don't know anybody around here, not like that. I'm not exactly the friendly neighbor type, you know that, Hec. And this island's a live-and-let-live kind of place. They don't run Welcome Wagons on Bone Key, as far as I can tell."

Hector closed and locked the storm door, then wrapped his hands around Brinke's waist. She draped her arms around his neck. He said, "You told me earlier someone's been lurking around here. Spying, or the like."

"They have indeed." A quaver in her husky voice. Hector felt something tighten inside.

"Christ. This dead woman a house down? Knowing that someone's been casing this area? You've really painted me in a corner, haven't you, honey? Got me right where you want me and forced to poke my nose into this thing with you, haven't you? Dammit all."

Brinke squeezed his hand. "You're only finally seeing what I've been saying all along is inevitable. What's necessary. Those skills we have, we have to use them. It's honestly that simple."

Hector said, "You are at least right about that cop. He's worse than useless."

Brinke slipped off her robe and let it slide to the floor. Hector closed the front door with his toe so she wouldn't be visible from the street. "Right," she said. "He may even be culpable." She began unbuttoning Hector's shirt.

"Maybe," he said. "Either way, he's a thug with a badge." Hector watched Brinke fumble with his shirt buttons. He shook his head, half-smiling. "More cramps, darling?" He studied her eyes.

Brinke nodded. "Not as bad as before, nothing like that. But I can feel them coming. Figured we could nip 'em in the bud." She smiled and kissed his chin. "I trust that's okay."

# 11

The man snagged a stool at the end of the rough-hewn bar. Pelicans skimmed the surface of the warming Gulf waters, distracting him. A light cough and the woman behind the bar was suddenly standing in front of him. He winked at her and said, "What's good, toots?"

The woman said, "What's to your taste, mister?"

"Gin and tonic. Fried oysters if you can make 'em."

"We can surely do both."

The man watched the woman mix his drink. He watched the cook begin preparing his food. The man said to the woman, "What's your name, gorgeous?"

The middle-aged woman rolled her eyes and gave that the smile it deserved. She said, "Rose. What's yours?"

"What time you close this shack down, dollface?"

Rose gave him a look like he couldn't possibly be interested in her. She made sure her rings were prominently on display. "We close at eleven. Except Friday and Saturday nights. We go past midnight, then. We hate to run a clock on people who are happy and paying."

This job was a de facto thing for the man. One made necessary because the previous man had lost his stomach for the assignment after burning down a hotel and killing a child. Unprofessional on that bum's part, the new man thought, watching Rose. But the new man had another job prospect of his own, a possible insurance-scam torching just north a couple of Keys. That job interview was at nine. The money sounded very good. So sparking this dump was going to have to be a rush job. He just couldn't wait for the place to clear out for the night.

Oh, well. Too goddamn bad for this Rose woman.

Brinke said, "Presentable?"

"You're never less than that," Hector said.

She wore a floral print dress that showed a lot of leg. Brinke also wore a pearl necklace and white high heels. She had her hands behind her head. "Could use some help with this," she said, turning. He saw then that the dress was backless and tied behind her neck. She had gathered the ends of the dress' collar in her hands for Hector to secure them.

"You look ravishing," Hector said as he took the dress's straps in hand. Impulsively, Hector let go of the straps. The front of Brinke's dress dropped around her waist. He cupped her breasts, running his thumbs' tips across her stiffening nipples. She sighed and tipped her head back against his shoulder and he kissed her throat. "We'll miss our reservation," she said huskily. "Take a check on this fine thing?"

"A check, sure," he said, pulling her dress's front back up over her chest and tying it behind her neck as she held her hair up so he could see. "Something to look forward to."

Brinke said, "Don't you dare tie some killer Boy Scout knot you can't get out fast, later."

Hector smiled. "Not a chance. Trust me, this one will come loose, pronto."

They rode the trolley through the darkened streets. Hector was wearing khaki slacks, a white shirt and a blue blazer, figuring Brinke might need it later when the temperature dropped. She sat close beside him in the trolley seat, stroking his thigh. "This takes me back," she said.

He leaned over and kissed her forehead. "Back? To Paris, you mean?"

"Yes. I miss it. Not so much the city, you understand, but the people. Sylvia, Hash…Gertrude. Hell, I even miss Alice. A little. Even goddamn Ford. You miss them, Hec?"

He brushed a comma of hair from above his right eye. His forehead was already damp from the humidity. "You forget that a few weeks ago, I was still there. Old Ford is still the same breathless, anecdote-spewing bore. Poor Sylvia still talks about you. Mourns you. Her heart is broken at what she thinks happened to you. Gertrude was also wrecked, in her way. Hem wore a black arm band for weeks."

Brinke nodded, looking guilty. "I wish I could do something about all that." Her eyes went hard. "But Estelle Quartermain is still out there somewhere, gunning for me. That cop friend of yours in Paris still regards me as some kind of criminal." She shrugged. "In other ways, being presumed dead by the world is quite freeing. Certainly has been artistically."

They got off at Whitehead Street in a block that had been spared the 1923 fire. They walked by a big old empty Spanish Colonial mansion with an adjacent coach house. A second floor porch wrapped around the perimeter of the mansion. The porch was supported by wrought iron columns. Brinke said, "A few novels down the road, maybe we could afford to buy and restore that place. It has potential, don't you think? It was built by Asa Tift in 1851."

"I like it a lot," Hector said. "It's wonderful. But a bit big for just two. And you've really steeped yourself in local history, haven't you?"

"You know it," Brinke said. "This island fascinates me. She reached out and took his hand. "For instance, this place we're eating tonight? It's next to the place where they launch passenger pigeons. They call it the dove cote."

"Interesting."

They were seated under a small palm festooned with Japanese lanterns. Hector ordered another bowl of gazpacho, vermouth shrimp, French-fried devil eggs and eggplant chips. Brinke selected swordfish with broccoli rabe. It looked succulent. Brinke took a bite, arched an eyebrow, then surprised Hector by offering him a couple of forkfuls. As he was leaning in for his second bite, Brinke said, "Didn't realize this dish was so lousy with garlic. This way, having had some yourself, you can't complain later about me. We'll neutralize one another."

"Always the ulterior motive with you," he said. "Never drawing an uncalculated breath."

Brinke said, "Yours looks really good." Hector smiled and turned his plate so Brinke could transfer some of his entrée to her plate. She took a few bites and rolled her eyes. "God, this is amazing." After a time, she said, "So, Hector Lassiter, author—what's your next novel?"

"You first," Hector said. He figured Brinke was probably using Key West as the setting for her next Bud Grant crime novel featuring "Horace Lester" and didn't want to presume to big-foot on her new tropical territory. Hell, she'd found their new island, after all.

"I'm calling the next one *Havana Jump*," Brinke said. "I've been making some runs over to Cuba here and there. In this one, Horace falls for a British diplomat's daughter who may be less, or more, than she claims. Your turn, Hec."

"*The Big Siesta*, is the title I've settled on," Hector said. "A Miami private investigator ventures into the Keys on a missing person's case, looking for a rich man's too-young wife. He doesn't make it back to Miami. It's a death trip, at bottom."

"Sounds dark, and still I'm looking forward to it," Brinke said, putting down her fork to squeeze his hand. "After this, I thought we'd hit the Bamboo Den. It's a lounge-cum-speakeasy. Sort of a collision of Cuban and Hawaiian décor. Great little band plays there weekends. Something like Calypso-Jazz."

"Sounds perfect," he said. "We'll get a couple of nightcaps and then get you out of that damned pretty party dress." Brinke frowned and let go of her hand and pressed it to her belly.

Hector combed a wave of hair behind Brinke's ear. "Pain's back?"

"Just a flutter," Brinke said. "Nothing a couple of drinks can't fix. And you, of course. You keeping up with my needs okay? I feel like I'm just using your body like this, greedily."

"Doesn't faze me. It ain't torture, after all. And at least your current condition means we get to be reckless again."

"We do have that," Brinke said softly. She looked up at the Southern Cross. "Any word from Beau?"

"None as yet," Hector said, following her gaze to the Crux. "But that's not to fret. It's not his way to jump to with a return wire. He'll turn up in a morning or two. Or he won't."

Brinke leaned across the table, propping her chin on her palm. "Tell me some more about Beau. What's this man like? How long since you last saw him?"

"Guess the last time was 'round about 1920," Hector said. "But he's looked the same for, well, hell, for years. Tall.

Southern-gentleman sort, like some Kentucky colonel, or such. Given to wearing white linen suits. You know, like Mark Twain. He's just a little younger than that house you were admiring. He was born in 1853."

"Civil War vet?"

Hector slapped at a mosquito on his neck. "Uh, no. God knows both sides were conscripting teenage boys right and left, some to be Bugle Boys or drummers. Though those boys ended up as dead as anyone else in the fog of that bloody war. But, no. Beau, well, he kind of dodged all that bloody mess. Never been such a fighter, my Paw-Paw. He went abroad with his mother, who, to hear him tell it, was quite the woman. She was a kind of extremist Bohemian. A freethinker and such. Another kind of pacifist, I guess you could call her."

"So what's Beau's trade? I mean, I figure at his age, he must be retired. But how'd he make his living? He another author? The one who passed those creative traits down to you?"

Hector shook his head. "Beau's no writer. Maybe a raconteur, but he's no author."

Brinke stroked the back of Hector's hand. "What then? Oil man? Texas Ranger?"

"God, no, on both counts." Hector hesitated and said, "And he's not exactly retired."

"What's left in terms of options then?"

Hector lifted his hand, traced the line of Brinke's jaw. "Think I best let him try to characterize it for you, darlin'."

Brinke sighed and pressed his hand to her cheek. "Now I'm even more intrigued. You're right, this old man, he might just win my heart. Particularly if he has your looks."

"Count on it. You liking him, I mean. If Beau wants you to love him, you will."

# 12

The clerk was having a bad morning. For starters, his first cup of coffee was burned by his wife, tasted of charred grounds. And then she'd turned him down for an early morning tussle, the cow...

And now this damned customer was working his last nerve, poor mouthing and playing the sob sister. The woman pleaded, "The promotion said children under ten are for free, mister. Please."

"That offer expired yesterday," the clerk said.

The woman raised her hands. "It didn't say anything about an expiration date in the newspaper, mister. I have the ad here somewhere," she said. "I know it." She began to dig through her big, shabby purse.

The little boy at her side looked worried. He said, "Momma, we won't have to go back home, will we?" He tugged on his mother's threadbare dress. "Will we?"

The old man in line behind the woman and her son saw then the boy's black eye. He moved to get a better look, and saw the mother's corresponding black eye and the bruises on her wrist. Those last looked like fingerprint marks from a big, strong hand. Black and olive bruises dappled her skin. The old man drew quick conclusions; his blood roiled. That temper—he'd always had a hot streak of his own. It ran in the bloodlines. Thank God, comparatively young, he'd mostly learned how to channel his own anger, to focus it.

The clerk said, "I'm sorry, lady, but the boy has to have a ticket. A paid-for ticket. Now pony up or push on. I've got other customers to tend."

"But I don't have any more money, sir," the woman said. "I used the last of our money—'cept what we'll need for a meal on the boat. I spent it on this ticket for me."

"The rules are the rules," the clerk said. "I don't have time for no more poor-mouthing. Step aside with you now. Go ahead on. Other customers are waiting, like I told you."

The old man in line behind the woman smiled and shrugged. He said, "I'm just fine. See to the lady's needs, please." The woman looked at the elderly man in line behind her. The old man was tall and courtly. His thick white hair was brushed back from a high forehead and just reached the collar of his shirt. He had the palest blue eyes and a thick, white moustache. His skin was deeply tanned.

The clerk said, "Ease off, Pops. This is not your concern." The clerk turned on the woman again, wagged a finger. "Look, step aside, lady, or I'll call a cop on you. I ain't kiddin'."

"I just want a refund then," the woman said impulsively. "I can't use this ticket if my boy can't come along. Just give me my money back. Please, we're in a terrible hurry."

"Just give the ticket to him, then," the clerk said, nodding at the boy with the black eye.

"He's just a child," the woman said. "He can't go alone! Please, mister, if you knew what we're running from, you—"

"Not my damn problem." The clerk pointed over his shoulder at a sign: NO REFUNDS. He said again, "I will call the law on you, Ma'am, you don't step aside. I mean now, sister."

The woman looked panic-stricken. The boy was on the verge of tears. The old man took the woman's arm, leaning in close. "How much do you need, sweetheart?"

"Ten dollars," the woman said. "But I couldn't accept your—"

"I'm not offering my own money," the old man said softly, smiling. "You just step behind me, sweetheart. You keep hold of your ticket, and bide your time. But you listen real close to this to come. You'll learn something doing that to help you down the road if you need more money and fast. Strikes me you might at that in the uncertain days ahead."

The woman, still flustered, stepped behind the old man.

The clerk smiled an oily smile. "And you, sir? What do you need?"

"Passage for one."

The ticket salesman said, "Where bound?"

"Where that very ship is headed, to Miami," the old man said.

The clerk nodded, still a bit surly from the woman before. He said, "Ten dollars, sir."

The old man smiled, forked over a twenty-dollar bill. The clerk took it; handed across a ticket and a ten-dollar bill in change. The old man moved to leave, then snapped his fingers and pointed behind the sales desk. "You know, I could use some change." The old man placed a twenty dollar bill on the counter. "Can you break this for me?"

The clerk nodded, then counted out three fives and five ones.

The old man scooped them up, then slapped the counter and said, "Hell, don't know what I was thinking. I really don't want a bigger roll then I'm toting, and you can probably use the singletons for change more than me. I'll give you these ones back for a ten." He dropped a stack of ones on the counter.

The clerk shrugged and slid across a ten-dollar bill at the old man who scooped it up.

The clerk picked up the stack of ones and started counting. "Sir, there are only nine one dollar bills here."

The old man frowned. "Oh, must have miscounted." He put down another dollar bill and said, "Here's one more dollar for ten. So we don't get confused, you've got ten there on the counter. Here's another two fives. How about you just give me my original twenty back and we'll call it even?"

The clerk smiled. "Sure." He passed the old man a twenty dollar bill.

The old man accepted the twenty. Behind his back, the old man held a ten-dollar bill between his fingers, waving it at the woman behind him. He felt the bill tugged from his fingers. Heard a whispered, "God bless you, sir."

The old man smiled at the clerk, struck a match on the counter and lit a cigar. He blew a smoke ring at the man and said, "Pleasure doin' business with you, old pal."

The old man waited just long enough to confirm the woman's ticket purchase for her child was consummated.

When the transaction was closed, the old man smiled and stepped out onto the dock and into the ragged line to board the ship. He figured he'd be safely in dock on the other side before the clerk realized the shortage in his bill tray.

# 13

The Cuban woman said, "Not that I don't want the sale, sir, but this coffee is awfully strong. And you've already had three cups."

Hector smiled. "What are you saying? You telling me you have to train to drink this excellent java of yours?" He waved a hand and grinned. "Hell, I live on this stuff, hon." That was true enough. For Hector, black coffee was like fuel.

The older woman, black-eyed, black-haired, smiled and said, "You'll be days awake, gringo. Trust me, you have to work up to this."

"Day is young and we'll all sleep plenty when we're dead, honey," Hector said, holding up his mug for a refill. "More of that Joe, please. Pour in a little milk if it'll salve your conscience about my tender gringo innards."

The woman nodded and handed Hector a small loaf of bread. "Here, hombre, on the house. Chew on a little and preserve what's left of your stomach lining."

"You're a jewel, *señorita*," Hector said, tearing off a piece of the soft hot Cuban bread.

His hostess, more a *señora* likely, smiled and made *loco* circular finger motions at her own head. Hector smiled, reopened his notebook and uncapped his pen to resume work on his novel.

An hour later, a man came in. He pulled the Cuban woman aside, whispering urgently. Hector watched them, capping his pen. He closed his notebook as the woman began to sob.

The man was leaving. Narrowing his eyes, Hector grabbed the man's arm as he passed by. "Hey, brother. What's the trouble, pal?"

"Very bad news," the man said, taking Hector's hand from his arm. "Her friend died last night."

"Unexpected?"

"Should say so. Her business burned down. Terrible, no?"

Hector sighed. "Christ, yes. What was her friend's trade?"

"She ran a restaurant. They say the grease fryer sparked it. Set the floor on fire. Burned down the whole place. Rose didn't get out. Goddamn it." The man crossed himself.

Hector shook his head. "Rose's place? That shanty restaurant over at Mallory Dock?"

"That's right. You knew Rose?"

Hector slammed a fist down on the table, making his empty coffee mug jump. "Just."

Brinke was at her writing table, pecking away at the keys. She saw Hector and smiled. He held up his hands. "Sorry, darling," he said. "Didn't mean to interrupt."

Brinke stretched and stood. "No apologies. I'm not composing. Just transcribing."

"Feeling any better, sweetheart?"

"Much. Think the worst is maybe past." Hector hugged Brinke to him and kissed her forehead through careless black bangs.

She said, "What's wrong? What's happened? You look shaken."

So much for his poker face, Hector figured. "I've got some bad news, Brinke. Terrible news, I fear, darlin'."

Brinke tipped her head up. "Oh God, what's the matter?"

"Rose is dead, honey. I'm so sorry. It looks like murder."

Brinke was stricken. She fell back into her chair. "Dear God! How?"

"Some one burned down her place. They say Rose died in the fire."

Brinke hung her head. "Goddamn it! You're sure, Hector?"

"I went down and poked around the scene myself. There's nothing left, darlin'. Fire burned a hole right through the deck. And it's in the newspapers. About Rose's death, I mean. No doubts."

Brinke rose and squeezed him tightly to her. "Oh, damn it, Hec. My God!"

"I'm sorry, sweetheart," he said. She beat on his back with her fist. After a time, Brinke looked up at Hector with angry black eyes. "No more soul-searching, then. No more fence-sitting from you. We need to find out who's doing this. We need to stop it. We're the only ones who can around here."

Hector's fingers combed through her black hair. "Yeah, figure that's sorrily so. Time we did all that."

Brinke said, "Those papers you read say when they're going to bury Rose?"

"Thursday at ten in the morning at the Key West Cemetery," Hector said.

"I've walked that cemetery," Brinke said. "The graves are above ground, like in New Orleans. You know, because of the water table here. Lizards sun themselves on the head stones. That bothers me, somehow. I would hate to be buried there."

Hector nodded, biting his lip. "So noted." This funny chill. "Don't plant me there, either, hear?" He got out a cigarette.

Brinke said, "Butt me, too, would you?" Hector shook loose a second cigarette for Brinke. "It's been a while," she said. "I've nearly given up the habit. But this one time?"

"I've been cutting back, too," Hector said. "'Specially with this tropical climate. Somehow this place doesn't encourage smoking in me. Well, maybe cigars would feel right. Cubans, of course."

"Not in this house," Brinke said. "I hate the smell of those things. Well, Hec, we should get down to cases, and I mean this very minute. We need to start asking some of the right questions. We need to try and get a handle on this bloody mess. I'm just so sorry we're starting too late to save Rose."

# 14

The reporter used his napkin to wipe the sweat from his forehead. The woman sipped her sweating mojito and stroked her black hair behind her ears. He couldn't believe his luck to be sitting here with the very woman he'd been lusting after Christmas night.

The reporter said, "So, Miss Tessa Templeton, what about the rings there on your hand?"

"Those are my mother's rings," Brinke lied. She waved her left hand, considering her left ring finger. "Call the bangles discouragers. They leave a lady the option of choice."

The reporter grinned. He had very crooked teeth. "A façade then?"

"More of a tactic," Brinke said. "Come-ons by boors don't send me." Brinke had borrowed one of Hector's T-shirts, a v-neck that was too big for her and whose plunging neckline exposed the tops of her breasts. She leaned across the tiny table, crossing her arms under her breasts and pushing up her décolletage. "The rings see to it that the also-rans stay never-tries." She smiled, full on. "Do you know what I mean?"

The reporter, Mike Rogers, smoothed his thinning hair and smiled, rubbing down his damp palm on his pant's leg under the table where Brinke couldn't see. She was the most attractive woman who ever accepted one of Mike's drink invitations. He had butterflies just looking at her. He was afraid of saying something stupid, something that might send her on her way. "I get it," he said. "I do. And you probably get a lot of also-rans, looking beautiful as you do. No end of them, I expect. You must get come-ons all the time." He smiled and winked. "Tell me I'm not right."

Brinke shrugged and changed the subject. "Wow, boy, some story you're onto, huh, Mikey? The Key West Clubber. You come up with that nickname for him yourself? It's sure some spooky thing."

"Sure. I mean, he beats the women to death. It made sense to me as a name." He smiled, showing those crooked teeth again. "And no denying it sells papers. I'm in this for the money."

"Not a crusader, huh?"

His eyes blazed. So, the man had a quick temper. "No, I'm that, too. But gotta make money to pay for ink and turn the presses. Can't do much to help folks if I'm in the red, right?"

"But you must be doing pretty well for yourself," Brinke said. "That breezer of yours looks brand new. And expensive."

The reporter blinked. "Breezer? Come again?"

"The convertible you drive. You know, your pretty new car."

"Oh. Yeah, it is new." He frowned. "Don't draw any conclusions from that, okay? I mean, I'm not doing all that well. What my car boasts, my house lacks."

Brinke thought, *So do your wardrobe and teeth.* Quite the lady-killer, this one.

Mike said, "Really, I'm not rich."

Brinke stifled a smirk, figuring Rogers must be getting the impression she might be some flavor of gold-digger. Time for a course correction. She said, "Awful, what he does to these women. The Clubber, I mean."

"He's a monster," Mike said flatly. "A fiend."

"But I don't get it," Brinke said. "Fires set here, then women murdered over there. How do you know both are the work of this... monster?"

"The police," Mike said. "They say it's so. They're the professionals. So it must be true."

"And...?"

"And they are the police, like I said."

Yes, not a watchdog journalist, this sorry excuse for a reporter. Brinke bit her lip. "Sometimes police are wrong. Lots of sometimes."

Brinke came on sultry, all bedroom eyes and her chin propped on her palm, giving Mike a better look down her T-shirt. "What do you think, Mikey? What are your theories about these crimes? Seasoned reporter like you, you've been around. Man of the world that you clearly are, you've been some places and seen some things. Must have some theories of your own. Maybe a theory as good as or even better than those of the cops."

"Things were quiet here for years," the reporter said seriously. "We never had stuff like this happen. Then that big fire swept the Key in twenty-three. More fires soon followed. Then the beatings ensued, the rapes and murders. Gotta be the same guy doing this stuff, 'cause it came all at once."

Brinke nodded. "Yeah. Sure. Makes sense, when you put it that way. 'Scuse me."

She dipped her head and grabbed her purse, headed toward the restrooms. Brinke could feel his gaze on her legs, on her hips. She turned around and caught him looking. Mike grinned awkwardly, blushing. Brinke said, "Back in a jiffy, tiger."

Brinke turned the corner into the narrow corridor for the restrooms. Mike could no longer see her. She slipped out the back door of the restaurant, running down an alley and then crossing over to a side street and back onto Duval. She slipped on her black sunglasses and tied a scarf around her head to hide her hair, just in case Mike came looking.

She thought about her chat with the reporter and shook her head.

Fruitless. A dead-end.

Hector was wearing his single warm-weather suit and a black nylon tie. He'd picked up a clipboard at the general store for under a dime.

Paw-Paw Stryder had lectured him years before, in one of the few lessons of its strange kind that stuck, "Look confident and carry a clipboard and all doors will open to you, sonny. Nobody will ask you why you're there or what you're doing. They'll just try and stay out of your way, hopin' you're not there to take their jobs away. A clipboard and attitude are the world's wickedest and simplest skeleton keys, kiddo."

Hector stood scribbling on his clipboard now, frowning and looking annoyed.

The mortician, who doubled as Monroe County coroner, arched wormy gray eyebrows above thick glasses. "I confess I didn't get a good look at your credentials, Mister ah—."

Hector continued busying himself scratching away at his clipboard, apparently taking furious notes. "Stowe. Ronson Stowe, state regulator."

"Regulator?" The old man scowled. "What's that mean, exactly?" The man wet his lips.

"I suppose it's another word for inspector," Hector said. "Sorry, but state regulations are strict, albeit quite new. And that's why I'm tolerating all your increasingly tedious questions while I'm trying to take notes." Hector sighed deeply. "Okay. I'll explain it once more. All mortuaries in the state of Florida are under intense and rapid review for recertification. Everything is very much on the double-hurry. Something the state legislature stipulated after that dreadful mess in Tampa."

"Tampa? Dreadful mess?" The mortician mopped at his forehead with a graying handkerchief. "What in the Lord's name happened in Tampa?"

Hector sighed again, acting as if he'd just about run up against the limits of his patience. "It was kept from the papers, lest the whole bottom fall out of your industry. The consumer backlash against Florida funeral homes and mortuaries could be, well, profound just doesn't quite get there in terms of a description. Let's just say I'm here to assay the disposition of all your current cases. To account for the bodies, don't you know? See they're where you claim they are. And also that they haven't been, how to put this politely? Interfered with. And I must do all this quickly. I have other stops today. Working my way back up to Miami, on the double quick."

The mortician, still looking confused, said, "There's just the two right now. Bodies, I mean. The one badly burned in a fire last night. She'll be buried day after tomorrow. Then there's the rape victim who was found in her home."

"Rape?" Hector made a face. "I see. How terrible. And that deceased's name is…?"

"It's confidential. We're keeping it from the papers until next-of-kin can be found."

"I'm not the damned press as we both know," Hector said, all sarcasm and impatience. "Please, I am already sorely pressed for time. Don't make me go over your sorry head."

The man flinched; his cheeks reddened. But he caved: "Her name is—er, was—Caprice Boothe."

Hector nodded. "C-a-p-r-i-c-e B-o-o-t-h-e. Right. And this lady's cause of death?"

"Asphyxiation."

He arched a dark eyebrow. Hector said, "You mean from strangulation?"

The mortician shook his head. "To my mind, strangulation implies some business with hands, or a garrote. Her throat was slit. She choked to death on her own blood. And that's just as well, I'd say, given the post-mortem beating she endured."

Hector looked up again from his notes. Raw-voiced he said, "Beating? Tell me more."

"She was beaten with a ball bat. The killer left the bat at the scene. An authentic Louisville Slugger. Guess he couldn't leave the scene carrying a bloodied bat. There's been a lot in the press lately. This isn't the first crime of its type. Police think we may have some kind of what they call a *pattern killer* loose on the island."

"Seems just as risky that the slayer would come to the scene with a baseball bat in hand, given what you've shared with me," Hector said.

"Cop named Dixon, one of the good ones, maybe the only good one, thinks maybe the killer hides his ball bats near the scene of his intended crimes," the mortician said. "You know, he puts 'em there in waiting."

Hector nodded; he had to struggle to suppress a shiver. "Let's see your paperwork on this Boothe woman. If we wrap this up in the next few minutes, I may even be able to squeeze in a piece of your island's famous Key lime pie. Least do something to feel like I was here on your island for more than this morbid damned business. Those Tampa shysters, they did us all harm, brother."

# 15

Hector slipped off his jacket and tugged off his tie. He un-tucked his shirt, unbuttoned it, then collapsed onto a chair to pull off his shoes and socks. Brinke turned the radio down on "What'll I Do?" She handed Hector a shot glass of bootleg rum. "Learn much?"

"Nothing I likely couldn't have simply surmised without digging," Hector said. "You?"

"Ditto."

"What was your take on the newspaper reporter?"

"Inept," Brinke said. "He's a one-man band. Reporter *and* publisher. Very stretched by both and not particularly good at either." Brinke arched an eyebrow. "Yet he's driving a brand new convertible."

Hector nodded. "That flivver is some kind of payoff, you're thinking?"

"Maybe," Brinke said. "It's the obvious enough thought. What about the mortician?"

"Just what he appears to be," Hector said. "And far out of his depth with these killings."

A rap at the door. Hector shot Brinke a look, said, "If it's that damned sheriff again…"

Hector rose and pushed his fists against his back until his spine cracked. He opened the storm door and then grinned. He said, "I'll be a sorry son of a bitch!"

Hector fumbled with the catch-and-eye hook of the badly hung door. He finally flipped it loose and opened the screen door. Brinke rose and stood behind Hector.

The old man at the door was a tall, slender, silver-haired echo of Hector, Brinke thought. He wore a seersucker suit, white with thin blue pinstripes, and clutched a Panama hat in his big left hand. Hector hugged the old man and said, "Means the damned world to me, you coming here on short notice. Means everything to both of us, Paw-Paw."

The old man kissed Hector's forehead, then bear-hugged Hector back. Beau Stryder said, "How old are you now, boy? Twenty-four, twenty-five?"

"There abouts," Hector said.

"So you ain't a boy no more. Peers, that's what we are now, kiddo. Enough of this Paw-Paw nonsense. We're both well and soundly past sentiment. And, hell, just makes me feel more the geezer and makes you sound the childish fool. You call me Beau, now. Right-o?"

Hector blinked, said, "Okay. Sure… Beau." He furrowed his brow. "So what do you call me?"

The old man wrapped a big hand around Hector's scruff and shook him, staring him in the eye. "Call you same as I always have. I call you Mase."

Brinke stepped out from behind Hector, extending her hand to the old man. He smiled at her—dimples either side of a thick white moustache. She said, "Why not call him Hector?"

"'Cause I hate that cussed name," the old man said, still smiling. "Told Mase's father that when they settled on that handle for our boy, here. Hec's middle name is Mason, after my mother's side. So he's Mase to me. And your name, honey? Brinke, ain't it?"

She smiled, nodding. "Brinke Devlin." She held out her hand.

Beau looked at her offered hand, shook his head, and spread his arms wide, simultaneously tossing his hat to Hector. Brinke stepped into Beau's embrace, turning her head to offer her cheek. The old man wrapped his right arm around Brinke's waist, his fingertips pressing her to him, almost reaching to her tailbone. With his other big hand, Beau turned Brinke's head to kiss her on the mouth. He said to Hector, "So this is the mother of all my future great-grandchildren? Must say, Mase, I approve, and emphatically. Confess she's a dish, just like you wrote, kid."

Brinke smiled, actually blushing to Hector's surprise, and said, "Good voyage, Beau?"

"Fine, my pretty Brinke." The old man smiled looking her over. Brinke saw now where Hector got his blue eyes, all his features, really. Hector was undeniably Beau's descendant. "Brinke," the old man said. "Brinke Devlin. Now, someone of taste hung that handle on you darling. It's a damn fine name and it suits you."

Brinke smiled. "Thanks, Beau. And I've got to say, Beau Stryder is a great name, too."

"So give it to your first boy child," Beau said. "I'd be hurt if you did anythin' less." He looked around at their house. "Very nice. But smallish. How many bedrooms you have?"

"Two," Hector said reflexively. "We'll get you set up in the guest room and—"

Beau waved a hand. "Not at all. Already seen to myself. Saw a place downtown that appealed. Besides, you two are young and lusty and been apart a time it sounded from your wire. Whatever else age has done to me, it has not dimmed my hearin'."

Brinke was blushing again. Beau saw it and laughed. "I consider embarrassing you an early and telling victory, beauty. 'Spect it doesn't happen often, darlin'."

Still smiling, the old man pulled out an old pocket watch and checked the time. "Here's our agenda, children. Eight tonight, you look me up at Sloppy Joe's. I hear it's the waterin' hole on this rock. We'll find our trouble from there. Dinner tonight's on me. Let's establish that, up front. Good? Right."

Hector said, "Walk you back to your lodgings, Beau?" He smiled. "It's been a few years after all. We've got some serious catching up to do now, don't we?"

The old man smiled and clapped a hand on Hector's back. "Sure, Mase. Sure, we do at that. Let's ambulate." He paused and gripped the scruff of Hector's neck again. "You do have worthy hooch on this goddamn rock, don't you? Got me a hankerin' for some fine rum."

"I already know a few places," Hector said. "Good coffee places, too. Maybe after a belt or two, we could stop at the Star Coffee Mill. That place has been around almost as long as me. It's run by the Sanchez family. When the wind's running the right way, you can find it by the aroma."

Beau said, "Sounds a fine treat." He nodded and smiled at Brinke again, gave her a last long look, up and down. He winked at Hector, said, "Sonny, you are in so far over your head."

Then the old man stopped again. Beau pointed at the poles and fishing tackle against the wall near the kitchen. He took off his jacket and began rolling up his sleeves. "Hell with walkin', Mase. Let's fish a little! Dusk coming on as it is, somethin' must be bitin'. And there's a drizzle comin', too. Can smell it on the wind. Cool us off. Know some good fishin' spots, Mase?"

"It's an island, Beau," Hector said, picking up the tackle box and handing a pole to the old man. "You just walk until you hit water and drop your line."

"Brinke's a beautiful woman," Beau said, blinking back the rain as he cast again. Hector watched and smiled as the bobber plunked in and then surfaced about twenty yards farther out than his own best cast. It always went like that when they fished together.

"She may be the most beautiful woman I've ever seen," the old man said. "And yet, gritty and lusty, too. But Brinke don't exactly strike me as the barefoot and pregnant type. Confess I fear for seeing any of my great-grandchildren out of this marriage, however long it lasts."

"There's plenty of time for babies," Hector said. "And hell, you're too crooked to ever die."

The old man smiled and handed Hector his pole to hold while he lit one of his cigars. He offered one to Hector. He lit the cigar for Hector as his grandson minded the poles. Both men blew smoke rings and Hector handed his pole back to Beau.

"You're too unmoored for kids anyway," the old man said. "Neither of you is settled enough for that, based on what you wrote me about this woman last year. And those books of yours and hers? Can't spend your early mornings and late evenin's writing at the books with a baby in the house. Christ, the sleep and income your momma cost me during her first three years of screaming and bawlin'? You don't wanna know the lost hours I suffered. You really don't wanna know the lost revenue. Hell, I can't think about it, not even after all these years."

"There'll be time for kids later, maybe," Hector said.

"Sure, keep thinkin' that," Beau said. "Still, you only get one or two women like that through your life if you're lucky. I still grieve Samantha gettin' away from me. That Miss Crawford…" he waved a hand. "Anyway, what about you two right now? What about her? You both keepin' your noses clean? Staying out of trouble the way you two didn't do last year in Paris, France? No more of that silly stuff going on that you both got caught up in in Gay Paree, is there? Keepin' to the settled life this time, right? No sleuthin' around nor any of that sad quixotic tripe?"

"Funny you should ask," Hector said evenly.

"Holy Christ," Beau said, sour-voiced. "Better tell me everything before you two get yourselves and your pretty life here all balled up again. And for Christ's sake, Mase, spare no detail."

Beau sipped his black coffee. When the waitress came to check on them, he took her hand in his, smiling. He nodded at his coffee mug. "This stuff tastes a might familiar, luv. Star Coffee Mill? The Sanchez family?"

The hostess smiled. "Exactly!"

"The old man's nose knows," Beau said to Brinke, releasing their waitress' hand.

Brinke took the old man's hand and squeezed it. Smiling, she said, "Hector—*Mase*—has been frankly shy about sharing facts about you, Beau. We're going to be family soon, and I'm getting the increasing sense you know all about me. Perhaps from letters from Hec, and maybe from loose talk over fishing poles late this afternoon. But I know next to nothing about you, sir."

The old man stroked the back of Brinke's hand with a big thumb. He smoothed his moustache with his free hand. "Yonder comes the risk." A beat. "And don't call me sir."

Brinke said, "What do you mean about the risk, Beau?"

"The risk of maybe falling from your favor as you learn more about me," Beau said. "My life has been, well, let's use one of them fifty cent words you and Mase seem to favor so strongly. My life's been what you'd likely describe as picaresque."

She considered that. Brinke said, "What's your trade, Beau? Or what was it?"

"Oh, I'm not retired. Not by a long shot. Don't believe in doing nothin'. Nobody, but nobody, survives retirement. Can't retire from retirin', neither. You just turn up your toes and shutdown. Who the hell finds that prospect enticing?"

"So what is your trade?"

Beau squeezed Brinke's hand a little tighter, smiled and averted his eyes. "My trade is… Well, it's a tad bit abstract, you might say."

Hector sat back in his chair, sipping his own coffee. *Here it came.* He said, "Just tell her, Beau. Our Brinke here, she's plenty worldly. Hard to surprise. And almost impossible to offend."

"I live by my wits, pretty Brinke," Beau said, shooting Hector a look of annoyance.

Brinke smiled prettily back, furrowing her eyebrows. "I'm sorry. But I'm still at sea."

Beau's tongue tip traced the inside of his lower lip. "You could call me a man of opportunity," he said. "A man who creates his own luck, so to speak."

"I'm still confused," Brinke said.

Exasperated, Beau collapsed back in his chair, starting at the ceiling. "Oh, Gawd."

Brinke narrowed her eyes. "I'm so sorry, Beau, but I've been years abroad. Just cow-simple, I guess. Throw me a rope. Please, be direct."

"Ah, Christ," Beau growled, signaling their waitress. "Incremental won't do, that's too clear now." He held up the empty bottle and told the waitress, "This one is dead. Need a fresh soldier. Another bottle of rum and some Coca-Colas, all around, please. Sliced limes, too."

After the waitress had left, Beau leaned back in, still holding Brinke's hand. "No gloss, lovely. What Hector refrained to tell you, and what I'm calamitously loath to confess, is that I am a kind of a ruthless opportunist. Let's call it being an exploiter of the avarice of others. That sounds nice." A hopeful smile. "Doesn't it?"

Brinke rested her cheek on her free palm. She was all flirt, now. Hector watched it click for her. Wearing an expression that was something between a smile and a frown, Brinke said, "My God, you mean you're a con man, a bunko artist... a flimflammer, don't you?"

Beau ran his fingers through his white pompadour. "Those terms all sound so pejorative. They make me wince, and I mean down deep. And I select my targets with real care. Only the ones who can well afford to spare some. Never send 'em to the river, that's my motto. Never leave them with no options or prospects for a future. A mark's only truly dangerous when you leave him nothing."

"Sorry," Brinke said, "sorry if I sounded accusing, or harsh. I actually think it's fascinating in its way. And you shaped the man I love, according to Hector. Good can't come from bad. I truly believe that. I really do, Beau."

Beau said, "Some bookworm said, 'Reason, never, is the equal of feeling.'"

Brinke smiled and said, "My feeling is that you're a good man, Beau."

"He is that," Hector said. "A little slippery in some ways, but at base, just."

The old man said. "I really am very choosy in my targets. Never soak 'em to the point of suicide. And a mark can only be taken in direct proportion to his own greed. So I see the ugliest, most rapacious sides of people as I shake 'em down. I always make 'em complicit in their own fall. Spares my conscious, true. But maybe they learn a rough but needed lesson in the process. Or so I delude myself on the way to the bank with their money."

Licking her lips and sipping more rum and Coke, Brinke said, "How long have you been doing this, Beau?"

He shrugged. "Probably since my mid-twenties. Started about the age that Mase is now. Tried my hand on the other side of the so-called law before that. Had me a brief stint as a cop. But the corruption was so rife. Penny-ante stuff much of it, but just everywhere. I lost my stomach for that, pretty fast. And hell, I've maybe set more scales straight doing what I do to make my living these days than I ever would have playing flatfoot." He smiled. "There is also something very intoxicating about living by your wits. About going to a fresh town and knowin' you can make a fine wage with just your brains and your words."

Hector recognized Brinke's bedroom eyes. She bit her lower lip in thought, then said to the old man, "Okay, a hypothetical, Beau. You're here on Key West. You've seen some of the island now. Say you have one day before you're going to flee to Cuba, or up the other Keys to Miami. You want to make a few quick dollars in that single day. You crave walking-around money. What exactly would you do?"

Beau let go of Brinke's hand, leaned back in his chair and stretched his legs. He pulled out another cigar, lit it, and blew a few smoke rings. He was in performance mode now. Hector had seen the old man's act a thousand times, mostly put on for comely women like Brinke.

The old man said, "Island aspect appeals to me in a limited sense. Have to time the escape well though, or else face a world of grief. But like you imply, you can get off the rock and be gone before anyone can be warned further up the chain. So let's presume you two would be my confederates. You, and maybe three more grifters I'd recruit or bring with me."

"Okay," Brinke said, tanned elbows on the table. She sipped more of her rum and cola. "All those are givens. Six of us in total. What do you do next?"

Beau smiled. "Here's how we play the game. We slide into town with a trunk full of bogus, cheaply printed, gilt-edged certificates of canine pedigree. I usually travel with a stack of those. Our first stop is the local pound. We take turns picking out doggies. We get ourselves six of the oddest-looking mutts we can find. Next stop is any local body of water. In this case, like Mase says, we just walk until we hit the ocean. We shampoo those dogs in the Atlantic. Brush 'em out and force feed 'em ground Sin-Sin to mask their funky, post-pound dog breath."

Brinke was delighted. She said, "This sounds completely demented. Yet oddly fascinating. What happens next?"

"Then we disperse," Beau said. "Six of us with six dogs hit six different bars. Each of us six suddenly remembers an urgent business appointment. The six of us then pay six barkeeps ten bucks to watch our respective dogs chained outside for ten minutes. We never pay 'em that ten dollars by the way. You with me still? You followin' the thread?"

Brinke nodded, grinning. "I'm with you just fine. What do we do next?"

Beau puffed some more smoke, then said, "The half-dozen of us then run to the closest bar just vacated by one of our compatriots. We each do a spit take at the dog leashed outside the bar we've just run to and declare it precisely the rare breed we've been seeking for years. Now, me, I say aloud I want that pooch and I want him bad. I offer five-hundred dollars to the man who owns the dog. Across Key West, you other five do exactly as I'm doing."

Beau leaned forward, impelling Brinke to lean in closer to him. Beau said softly, "The barkeep speaks up then and says to me that the owner isn't around. The keep says something like, 'Why don'tcha check back in twenty minutes?' Me, the potential dog-buyer, then splits with a promise to return, with cash, within a quarter hour, my five-hundred in hand."

"Now listen close to this next," Beau said to Brinke. "The other five of us have done exactly what I was doing at my second bar, enthusing over the dog I'd just seen and want to buy. Then the six of us return to our first bars, perhaps passing our partners on the way and exchanging knowing winks. We snag a stool in our first saloons, looking crushed. Manifest message of our hangdog faces is the pressing business deal we each had has gone south with a bullet. Destitution looms.

"Now, greedy people being greedy people," Beau continued, "six barkeeps begin to commiserate and offer to help their respective ruined businessmen out by offerin' to take each dog off each newly-broke dog-owners' hands at three-hundred dollars a furry head." Beau paused, said, "This three-hundred dollar asking price is each Mr.-Newly-Destitute's bargain-basement threshold to unload his four-footed best friend. You see, Brinke? Still holding the thread?"

Brinke smiled. "I follow you. I get it."

Beau smiled back. "Excellent. So each of the six dog owners then demurs...for about a minute. Reluctant, riddled with self-recrimination, we bogus dog owners give in, each of us pocketin' three-hundred dollars. We split our bars then, shedding crocodile tears for our lost dogs. Six barkeeps check their watches. In ten minutes, each anticipates a two-hundred dollar profit from a five-hundred dollar sale. As they wait, six grifters split town, perhaps thirty minutes before the cops are called, and nearly two grand to the good. Respectable money for next to nothing, wouldn't you say, Brinke?"

She nodded smiling, infatuated. Hector figured if he were out of the picture, Brinke would lay his grandfather in a New York minute.

He could tell Beau was thinking that too. His grandfather smiled and squeezed her hand again. He said, "And the con-science-salving silver lining in this little short con? The dogs that didn't get kept at least would go to the gas chamber well-groomed and with pleasing breath."

Brinke scowled and slapped the old man's hand. "You nearly ruined it with that last," she said. "But still, I love it. The whole scheme and its execution is wacky and wonderful. All those greedy tavern owners getting theirs! Did Hector ever run such games with you?"

Hector was about to object but Beau raised a hand. "No, darling. I tried a bit to groom him, and the lad has the raw skill. Problem with Mase and the con is his damn writer's mind and mouth. He starts working his jaw and then gets all caught up in the scenario. Buries himself in the role. Mase starts jawing and just makes everything overly convoluted and muddies all the waters. Solo, he's probably fine, but in a team setting? Well, old Mase here and his big imagination is just too cumbersome to handle, even for a seasoned and steady hand like mine."

# 16

The man watched the trio at the table. The older man and the younger man were very much with the pretty, raven-haired woman.

The man shook his head, frustrated. The men with her were both tall and well built. Hell, even the old man with the white hair and moustache looked potentially formidable.

The man figured he might have to come up with some scheme to get that pair out of the house to ensure the woman would be alone.

He watched the dark woman, licking his lips as he did. She was gorgeous, like the last one, Caprice. But this one was even prettier somehow. Had longer legs, which he didn't think possible, and full, firm high-riding breasts. And, God, that smile of hers? She had that thing—did they call it charisma?

But the trio looked like they were in for a long and leisurely night.

Cursing, the man settled his bill and walked to his car. He took a baseball bat from the trunk and slipped into the front seat. The neighborhood was quiet and dead looking. The house in question was unoccupied for the moment. It was dark enough for his needs. He'd stash the baseball bat in a shrub out front of the Devlin woman's door. Have it in place for his eventual *strike* against her.

No, that didn't work as a joke or a pun: After he'd had her, the bat would surely make contact well enough. Anyways…

He'd bide his time. Hell, Brinke Devlin was more than worth a little wait.

# 17

They walked arm-in-arm along Duval, Brinke in the center. All three were fairly lit.

Brinke said, "You're a delight, Beau. So, will you give me away, good sir?"

Beau closed his hand over her hand gripping his left arm. "What about your own parents?"

"Quite don't know about them," Brinke said thickly, suddenly serious. "They failed me, Beau." Brinke's voice cracked a little on that last, piercing Hector, even though he already knew the story.

Beau squeezed her to him. "Enough said then, child. I'll happily and proudly escort you up the middle aisle."

Brinke kissed his cheek. "Thank you so much, Beau."

The old man said, "It's my pleasure and more, my privilege, dearest Brinke. You know, I've read a few of your books, too, I'll confess. Read one makin' the Gulf crossin'. The ones you wrote under the name of Connor Templeton. Having spent so much time in your head, via your novels, I mean, I feel as though I truly know you. They are wonderful books. Fine time-passers."

"Thank you again, Beau."

"I also read our boy here's first novel a few weeks ago," the old man said. "Loafed out by the ocean with that sucker. Actually sat on the seawall several nights before the sun sank, reading that tome."

The old man leaned forward to get a better look at Hector. He squeezed his grandson's knee. "It was a great story, Mase. I don't read much of that what I guess you call *fiction*. You know that. Really not read anything like that at all, until your books. But yours was wonderful and I flat loved it. I'm very proud of you and of your writin'."

Hector, surprised and genuinely touched, said, "It really means something, coming from you."

The old man nodded. "Much money in your line of work?"

Well, here it came, from the other direction. "We're doing just fine," Hector said.

The old man nodded. "Good. That's good." A beat, then, "How fine?"

Hector sighed, said, "Fine enough for us. Good enough to live well enough in this place."

Beau laughed and shook his head. "This place is no place. It's like El Paso with water on all sides. But maybe even more lawless if that's possible. At least seems so based on what I've been reading in the papers. And based on what you were tellin' me out to the pier earlier."

Brinke started to talk but Beau said, "And here's my hotel. Come up, you two, have a brief nightcap. We'll talk more about Key West and how dangerous it is. I mean, if you're not at your libational limits."

"A last drink sounds great," Brinke said. "And Hector has no limits, so far as I can tell."

"Often feared that, too," Beau said. "Regardless, we'll drink in my rooms."

Hector winced. "Rooms plural?"

"You know me, I like my space, Mase. Like to sprawl." Beau hesitated, then split a smile between them. "Oh, in front of the staff and such, please don't call me Beau or Mr. Stryder, okay?"

Hector shook his head, smiling. "Of course. Who are you tonight, Pap?"

"For the purposes of the hotel staff and management, I'm Cornelius Astor."

Brinke, grinning said, "You mean of *the* Astors?"

"I haven't confirmed it to them that's inside," Beau said. "But I haven't denied it, neither."

Hector walked around, whistling, low. Beau seemed to have the run of roughly half of the upper floor of the just-opened hotel. Hector stepped out onto a balcony and looked out over the rooftops of Key West, staring out at ships at sea, their lights glowing and swaying in the darkness. He heard the cry of gulls overhead. He searched the island for signs of fire, but it seemed a quiet night. Hector slipped back inside and sat down on the bench by a baby grand piano. He played a few bars of Stephen Foster's "Old Kentucky Home."

"I didn't know you play," Brinke said, delighted. She sat down next to Hector.

"If you call that playing," Hector said, taking his hands from the keys. "This room, rather, rooms, are beyond posh," he said to his grandfather. "How much have you paid this place so far?"

"Zilch," Beau said. "It's all on credit and presumed last name for the moment. They think I've got more money than God, so they haven't asked for any of it just yet. Perception, as always, is reality. That said, a marriage, sooner rather than later, would help the cause. That cause being me not paying a cent to this place, not ever. I'm a man with an eye always on an exit or a road. As I indicated earlier, islands cramp my style in that way."

Brinke nodded. "Day after tomorrow soon enough for that ceremony?"

"Perfect," Beau said, beaming. "Who else will be there?"

"Just us three, a priest and maybe an organist," Brinke said. "Some rummy or two Hector says he'll pull out of a bar just before the time to stand witness. Isn't that romantic?"

Beau shook his head. "Jesus, what a motley ceremony it promises to be. You should have a proper audience. *Alas.* Just leave me the address and time I should show up."

"Done." Brinke sat down on a satin covered couch. Beau's cowboy boots clunked hollowly against the Saltillo tile as he walked to the bar to mix some drinks. She said, "You mentioned Hector's been telling you about the crimes here."

"That's right," Beau said evenly. "The fires. The so-called Key West Clubber, too."

"And what do you think about all that?"

Beau handed Brinke a whiskey soda. Hector rose and looked over the selection and poured himself three fingers of tequila. Beau sat down with his own tall whiskey and soda and sipped some. "I think you two should not go back to bad old habits and try and poke around this thing. Not like I hear you did in Paris, dear. That said, I figure you're both in too far already and not to be dissuaded. Particularly not since a friend's blood's been spilled. So I aim to see this thing wrapped up nice and neat before I head back to Texas to await word for my next Florida visit. Say, for a christening. That'd be a sufficient and worthy reason to return to this sweltering sand heap."

Brinke smiled. "Indeed. You said you worked under color of authority for a time, Beau."

"Texas Ranger for three years," Beau said. "Did some private work for Pinkertons—for about five minutes—before I found my *conscience*. So I know some things about how to go about this stuff. If I want to go at it straight, that is. Hector's also told me a good deal. Now you tell me some stories, Brinke."

An hour later, Beau said, "I'm not buying this phantom killer—this sometimes rapist, sometimes arsonist, and his years' long crime spree. Doesn't make sense to me, not a lick. And an arsonist, short of a professional, is always a compulsive criminal. Firebugs can't control themselves, and they get the itch worse over time. After that 1923 fire you described, the subsequent fires seem almost insignificant. And the attacks against the women? That doesn't make sense to me, neither. Not a lick. Again, rapists and repeat killers are creatures of habit and compulsion. They go after targets of opportunity, likely as not. And usually they go after fallen women. They favor working girls and barflies. Women on the margins who won't be easily missed or likely avenged."

Brinke nodded. "You've figured it about as Hector and I have. So what's your theory?"

Beau shrugged. "Haven't gotten me one of those, yet. Not really. But sex aside, at bottom of almost every other crime, there's always money to be had in the end. Someone's turnin' a buck on these bad doin's, somehow. Even these rapes. That's my instinct. Give me the mornin' to do some of my own nosin' around. About noon, let's aim to reconvene. That little coffee shop on Duval Hector tells me you both favor sounds good and private for a rendezvous. Let's meet there." He checked his pocket watch. "And God Almighty, look at the time. Way past my bedtime."

Beau hustled up to his feet and took Hector's and Brinke's glasses from them. The old man deftly slipped Hector's discarded blazer over Brinke's bare shoulders. "It's gonna be brisk out there by now," he said, urging them to the door.

Hector narrowed his eyes; what the hell was this rush out the door about?

Beau had always been the consummate night owl.

They said their hurried goodnights and Brinke and Beau exchanged a brief kiss. Hector opened the door to find a petite, dishy young Cuban woman on the other side, her hand poised to knock. She looked surprised and a little fearful to have been seen.

Clearing his throat, Beau said, "Brinke, Mase—this is Consuelo. She works here."

Hector could have guessed that. The woman indeed had a hotel uniform, but it was on a hanger and dangling from her crooked finger. The woman, maybe Hector's age or even a bit younger, was currently wearing a strapless black cocktail dress and black heels. She sported bright red lipstick. Some brand of heady perfume clung to her curves. The dress, the makeup— they all looked fresh. A small duffel bag was slung over her bare shoulder.

Seemed to Hector that Beau had quite an evening ahead of him.

Before Brinke could try and say something to smooth the awkwardness between them, Hector took Brinke's arm and stepped past Consuelo into the hall. Hector said to Beau, "Later Cornelius. We'll leave Consuelo here to see to your needs... to your *suite's* needs. Do try and get some rest, buddy."

As they rode down in the elevator, Brinke smiled crookedly at Hector and shook her head. "For God's sake, don't take this wrong, Hec, but I think I'm jealous of that woman."

"Hell, I'm jealous of Beau." Brinke shot him a look. Hector said, "C'mon, you saw her."

"Beautiful and saucy, yes," Brinke said. "Think she speaks much if any English?"

Hector laughed. "If not, she'll know all kinds of new gringo terms comes the dawn." He paused and added, "At least some Latin, at any rate."

The man sat in his Ford with the engine off, watching the house. He cursed softly when he saw the woman return; when he saw the tall young man holding her hand and watching the streets warily.

The man ducked down when he saw how cautious the woman's escort was. When he heard the front door of the house slam shut, the man sat back up in his car. He watched lights go on and off inside the house.

He waited a few minutes, then the man cranked his car's engine. He looked at the shrub to the right of the porch a last time, the one in which he had hidden the baseball bat, then drove off to find himself some place to drink.

# 18

It was nine in the morning: Beau's first stop was the Last Key Realty office Hector had mentioned off-handedly while recounting his first movements on the island, as he had spoken to Beau of the dangerous atmosphere of Bone Key and elaborated about the crazy real estate market of Key West and greater Florida.

Beau wore a black suit and matching homburg. He had a starched collar and carried an ebony walking stick with a heavy silver head.

It was all very Old World. All very calculated for effect.

The man with slicked-down hair parted in the middle—the one who had talked to Hector when he had been idly perusing the plats and houses for sale—leaned out again. The real estate agent said, "Interested in some property, sir?"

Beau smiled, squinting up in the morning sun. "Vigorously!"

Just before ten a.m., Beau stopped at the telegraph office. The clerk pulled out a form. "Where bound?"

"This goes to Corpus Christi," Beau said. "By that I mean Texas."

Eleven-thirty a.m.—a knock at his door. Beau pulled a sheet over Consuelo, naked and softly snoring on the bed in the noon heat. He closed the bedroom door, shrugging on a paisley robe. He opened the door on a sweaty man with crooked teeth. Beau said, "And you are—?"

The man said, "Mike Rogers, reporter for the—"

Beau closed the door in the man's face, yelling through the closed door, "Sorry lad, I don't grant interviews."

It was shortly after noon. Beau sipped his coffee. "Superlative." He looked his grandson and Brinke over. Both had slightly wet hair that still showed comb tracks; ruddy skin from their showers. Or, more likely, their shared shower, he guessed from their equally damp hair. Hector wore khaki shorts and a white T-shirt. Brinke sported white shorts and a black T-shirt that was too big for her—one of Hector's, Beau figured. Both looked half-focused, groggy and sated from devouring one another.

Damn grandson—so much going on of moment and Mase was full-gone sex-struck. Well, he'd have to just work Mase's carnal distraction into his calculations, to make allowances.

"Children," Beau said, "we may need distance from one another in the days ahead. At least when it comes to visible public contact."

Brinke looked up from her Cuban coffee. "I'm not sure I follow you, Beau."

"He has no trouble seeing us at his place, or perhaps even at ours," Hector said, "But I think he means we won't be taking anymore coffees together, or strolling Duval and hopping speakeasies."

Brinke looked to Beau. "Is that it?"

The old man nodded. "Mase is essentially correct. Oh, I'll be there for your wedding of course. After all, that's a controlled environment and invitation only. Now, apart from that, it causes me pain to say some space is needed between us if I'm to do what I need to do." Beau sipped more coffee, then rose. "So we start now. If you do come callin' at the hotel, you do so under the pretense of sellin' your house to me, understood?"

Brinke nodded uncertainly. "Okay…?"

Hector said, "Where are you off to now, Beau?"

"I'd have you both blissfully ignorant of that next stop," the old man said.

"Generally then, where are you headed?" Hector stared back at him, clearly expecting some illumination.

Beau sighed. "Seed money is needed. Thus, I've got to see a man about a dog. Several dogs, really."

Brinke and Hector watched Beau strode back out into the sun. She shook her head, smiling. "What in God's name is that man up to?"

"Please don't pursue it," Hector said. "Don't try to figure it out. Neither of us, even together, has enough imagination. Trust me on that. Beau goes his way, and we go ours."

Brinke squeezed Hector's hand. "What is our way, Hec?"

"Still thinking of details. But in terms of broad strokes, figure we act as if we're still on our own."

# 19

Brinke sat in a chair by the front door, fanning herself; a thin sheen of sweat coated her forehead, cheeks and chest.

Hector was on the front porch, struggling with the hinges of the crooked screen door. "Just a few more turns," he said, leveraging against the screwdriver. "Thing has been driving me crazy for days, ever since I broke in myself a few days ago. Way things are now, I want this place to lock up good and tight. Serenity of certainty, to borrow one of your terms."

Brinke extended her long, bare legs, fanning herself more vigorously. "So it comes to this. We start looking over our shoulders and living in dread. Is that it? If it is, I don't like it."

Hector cursed as the screwdriver slipped. "How long have you been carrying that gun, sweetheart? Some would say buying a gun lets slip the fact none of this caution will be new for you."

"Touché." Brinke rose and stretched. "I want to swim, down at our place. You know, from the first day we were together here. Get your tan evened out like mine."

He dragged his arm across his forehead; blinked sweat from his eyes. "Sounds a great idea. Just another turn or two of the screws." He lost his footing then, nearly tumbling off the porch into a shrub. Hector grabbed at the door jamb with his free hand. Brinke reached for Hector's flailing other hand— the one clutching the screwdriver. She caught his wrist. Leaning back, Brinke hauled Hector toward her, steadying him.

"You are some kind of strong," Hector said, kissing her cheek. "And lucky thing you caught me. That shrub would have been a goner, otherwise."

The man in the Model-T watched as the tall man left the house. The woman—"Brinke"—kissed the tall man at the door, then locked the screen door and storm door as the tall man waited to see she did that.

Damn their precaution. But the neighborhood was still too busy anyway, too alive with late afternoon bustle.

The man in the Model-T would wait a bit longer. Early evening would bring quiet to the street. It had every night he'd sat vigil outside Brinke Devlin's home. He'd just have to hope the tall man didn't return first.

Hector sat in the Cuban café he'd adopted as his writing place. He sat at a corner table away from the hot glare through the window, writing in his notebook and sneaking pours of whiskey from a silver hip flask, spiking his cups of strong black coffee.

A shadow fell across Hector's notebook. Hector glanced up. A man, roughly Hector's own age and build, stood over the writer. The man looked familiar, though Hector couldn't quite place the face. The stranger said, "Join you please, Mr. Lassiter?" The man put out his hand and Hector saw the man's middle finger was missing.

Hector remembered then that it was the cop who'd stood behind Sheriff Melvin Hoyt on Brinke's front porch the other morning, the underling cop who'd looked ashamed of his superior's surliness. The junior cop said, "I'm Jack Dixon." The cop held a cup of coffee in his good hand. "May I join you, please?"

Hector nodded and closed his notebook. "Take a load off, Dix. You're out of uniform and the day ain't that young. Why the civilian threads?"

"My day off."

Hector arched an eyebrow. "Tuesday is your day off? Some-one must not like you. When's your other day off? Monday, Wednesday?"

"Sunday."

"Split days off," Hector said. "Someone must really detest you, brother."

"Might well be so," Jack said. He sipped his coffee with his ruined hand.

"You're off duty, you said." Hector held up his flask. "Give that coffee a boost for you? Or do you enforce and support the Key West version of the Volstead Act?"

Jack frowned. "You mean prohibition? Screw that." The cop held out his coffee cup and Hector poured in some whiskey. "World's too dark a place to face it without a stiff drink."

"You're shaping up to be my kind of police," Hector said.

"Guess maybe you'd know, having gotten to know some cops elsewhere, I mean," Jack said. "Cops in far-flung places."

Hector's stomach rolled. "What's that mean now, Dix?"

"My boss… Well, you're a kind of a preoccupation of Sheriff Hoyt's of late."

Not good news. Hector said, "What do you mean by that?"

"You came on strong against Hoyt. Stepped up against his intimidation. Nobody else does much of that on this island." Dixon smiled. "So he took notice. Hoyt began to research you."

Hector's blue eyes narrowed. "Did he now?"

"Yeah. All the way to Paris."

Hector made a face; his spiked coffee suddenly tasted bitter. "That so?"

"Found some French police, a man named Simon," Jack said, watching Hector for a reaction. "Figure he's some kind of Frenchified inspector."

Hector smiled. Good old Aristide—a born detective. Hector said, "Yikes. Oh, boy."

"Simon spoke well of you, Mr. Lassiter. Vouched, I mean. Said you helped him out with two or three things back there in France. Said you might have made it in his profession." Jack smiled. "I guess that is to say, my profession."

"Simon overstated," Hector said. "The part of Paris, where I made my home, well, it was like here, kind of. I mean very American. Probably twenty American expatriates for every authentic Frenchman sticking it out in the quarter where I lived. So I was more of a go-between with the Yankee expats and that French cop and his officers."

"Right. Either way, it rattled my boss' cage, hearing you did some work with police back there in Paris. 'Specially when he heard some of the things you did and were doing to help that French cop."

Hector nodded. "And so Sheriff Mel sent you by here to rattle my cage back now, is that it?"

Jack shook his head. "Not at all. No, Sheriff Hoyt would fix to shaking my cage, and I mean meanly, if he knew I was here talking to you like this."

Hector bit his lip. "Do say?"

"I was the one who conferred directly with that French cop," Jack said. "I heard a good bit more from Simon than I shared with the sheriff. The more I learned, the more I thought you'd be a good man to know."

"So why exactly are we talking now, Dix?"

"Thought you might be a good person to know, like I said, Mr. Lassiter."

"Hector. And did you? Think we could be useful friends, I mean?"

"Yes. You and your wife. Brinke Devlin. Who, I might hasten to add, French Police Commissioner Aristide Simon seems to believe is dead. Murdered 'by parties unknown,' as the Frenchman put it."

Hector shrugged, a half smile on his lips. "Well, Dix, that's a story for another time. A hell of a tale unto itself." Hector poured some more whiskey in the cop's coffee cup. "You didn't, well, disabuse Commissaire Simon of that notion he has regarding Brinke's fate, did you?"

"No, Hector. Figured you and the lady have your reasons for the subterfuge. You and the Missus. The two of you. Whom, parenthetically, according to Monroe County Court records, have a marriage license but haven't yet tied the knot. Like I said, guess you have your reasons. For that, too, I mean."

"And you've got your own reasons for jawing with me now, Dix. Don't you?"

"That's right, Hector. There are bad and bloody things going on here on Bone Key. Stuff like I can't fathom or abide."

"Things with your boss, maybe?"

Hesitation, then, "Maybe."

Hector smiled. "Well, we do need to talk more, that's clear. But somewhere more private. Somewhere we can get a real drink."

"Sounds good," Jack said. "I know a place. Let's go there now."

"Let's do that, brother," Hector said. He paused. "Say, you got plans tomorrow around noon?"

"I could take a long lunch for the right reason," Jack said. "What's up?"

"That wedding you alluded to. I could use a witness. A man in uniform will class things up. Give the ceremony some, you know, gravitas."

Jack smiled. "Don't know what that last word even means, but I'm game. Got yourself a best man, Hector?"

"Nope."

The cop put out a hand. "You do now."

The man got out of the Ford, stretched and looked down both sides of the lazing street. Not a sign of the tall man returning.

His time.

At last.

Howdy-do, Brinke Devlin! Shake hands with the Devil.

The man hesitated—another man turned the street corner, an older, stoutly built man.

A knock at the door. Brinke reached for her gun. She hesitated, then checked the clock. Seeing the time, she put the gun back in a drawer. She opened the front door.

A man standing outside said, "Miss Devlin?"

Brinke smiled. "Hello, Father. You're very punctual."

The priest smiled and stepped into the cool of the front room. "One tries. And the prospective groom? Is he about?"

"He's usually quite punctual, too. Should be here any second." Brinke hesitated, then said, "Something to drink while we wait, Father?" Blushing, she nodded at the bottle of French red wine she'd forgotten to stash.

The priest was bleary-eyed; gin blossoms at nose and cheeks. He smiled and shrugged. "I really shouldn't."

Brinke smiled back. "Well, I'm truly sorry if I offended—"

The priest quickly held up a hand. "I shouldn't. But that doesn't mean I shan't."

# 20

B rinke tipped her head back into the warm wind that whipped the rooftop of Beau's hotel where the trio sat on the patio, awaiting dinner. Hector nodded at the fourth place setting and said, "Consuelo will be joining us?"

"That's right," Beau said. "Go ahead and call me Beau in front of her. Told Connie it's a bewildering nickname. We'll keep things simple that way."

Brinke said, "Mightn't eating up here with us, in these posh surroundings, cause some trouble for her with coworkers? Some resentment?"

Beau smiled. "Might at that. But Consuelo will be moving on to another position quite soon. Something I'm lining up for her."

Hector said, "Well, of course. She's running late?"

"Not at all," Beau said, sipping wine. "Just thought we'd have some time alone to catch up before dinner. So, we have twenty minutes or so. What have you done today, Mase? Sleuth-wise, I mean?"

"Too little," Hector said. "I mean, other than befriend a cop, maybe a good one. He hates his boss, Sheriff Mel Hoyt. He thinks Hoyt is dirty. Dirty, and purposely fumbling the Key

West Clubber case." Hector smiled at Brinke. "By the way, my new friend will be standing with me as best man tomorrow."

"Beats a barfly," Brinke said. She sighed. "I mean, I guess."

"It's a close thing," Beau agreed. "Brinke, anything you have to report?"

"Zilch," she said. "I confess, I spent today stewing about tomorrow." Brinke was more than a bit ashamed of herself for that. Seemed like something someone else would do.

"Just jitters," Beau said. "Understandable. It's a big, life-changing day." He smiled and squeezed Brinke's hand. "Try to enjoy it. No fretting, now."

Brinke squeezed the old man's hand back. "And you, Beau? What've you been up to?"

"Keeping busy. Throwing out a few lines to see what perhaps nibbles back."

"And? No more to share, Beau?" Brinke arched an eyebrow. "Nothing more, really?"

"Nothing I'm prepared to share," Beau said. "Not at present. So, tomorrow Mase becomes one dead bachelor. What about it sonny, you got those butterflies?"

Hector shrugged and waved a hand as if to say, *Nah.*

"Anyway, we'll try to make it a gentle night," Beau said. "An early night. Can't have a lovely like this one tying the knot with tired eyes."

Brinke said, "Thank you so much again for coming, Beau. It means everything to us, having you with us. Having family here for it." She saw that made Hector smile. Brinke had to admit her life up to now had been a lonely one. She'd lived solo lobo in a way Hector never had.

"Wouldn't have missed it," the old man said. "Mase and me are all the family we have left. 'Til you join the clan tomorrow, darling. 'Til you raise a passel of little Lassiters."

"Right," Brinke said, her smile dimming a bit. She saw that Beau caught it. She hoped Hector didn't.

"When the time is right I mean," Beau said, backtracking. "When the damn sleuthing bug turns loose of you both."

The old man reached over and shook Hector's arm. "This is one of the rare decisions Mase has made I can support whole-heartedly. God knows there's been enough of the other kind. Runnin' off as a gangly kid. Lyin' about his age to ride with that bloody bastard Black Jack Pershing in pursuit of Pancho Villa. Getting himself shipped off to Europe for Wilson's mad folly of a war. Our Mase is goddamn lucky to have come back with all his extremities from that waste of life. Christ knows a lot of Texas boys like old Mase didn't come back all there." The old man sipped more wine. "Then he spent all those years living abroad, away from my sage counsel and boon companionship. Well, hell, at least doin' that he met you." Beau raised Brinke's hand to his mouth and kissed it. "That meeting between you two there in Paris, France, that was a blessing. I credit you with bringing my boy back to me."

Hector said, "Do you smell smoke?" Frowning, he tossed his linen napkin on the table and stood and leaned out over the railing, searching the streets. Brinke joined him. Something was on fire further down Duval. Hector said, "Back in five minutes, all. Gonna go see what's burning down up the street. You two carry on."

Hector shouldered through a crowd of gawkers. The building, based on remaining, charred signage, had been a mom-and-pop hash house. It shouldered up to a vacant lot with a Last Key Realty sign poking up through weeds.

Looking at the sign and the burning building next to the empty lot, thinking about Beau's assertion that all crimes come down to money, Hector felt this theory cohering.

Hector saw Jack Dixon. The nine-fingered cop, listening to Sheriff Hoyt, dipped his head a fraction to acknowledge Hector. Hector nodded back. He decided it best Sheriff Mel didn't see him hanging about another potential crime scene.

Beau's new friend, Consuelo, answered Hector's knock. She smiled and kissed his cheek. "*Hola*, Héctor."

"Howdy, Consuelo. You look absolutely smashing."

"*Muchas gracias*, Héctor." Hector hugged her. She did look sharp, and all but falling out of her metallic silver sheath of a dress, low cut and backless—all this enticing *café-au-lait* skin on display.

Goddamn Beau: Hector should be so lucky in love if he ever saw the age of seventy himself, a prospect that struck Hector as pretty unlikely given the way he seemed driven to live his life. Consuelo brushed long brown hair from her shoulder and said, "I'm to go downstairs and tell them to serve us now that you're here, Héctor."

"I'll mix you a drink for when you get back," Hector said. "What's your pleasure, darlin'?"

Over her shoulder, Consuelo said, "Mojito, *por favor*, Héctor?"

"Done."

Another woman was suddenly at the door, one of the desk clerks. The clerk pulled Consuelo aside. Hector heard the female clerk ask Consuelo in Spanish whether Hector spoke the language. Consuelo shrugged and responded that she didn't think so. In Spanish, the maid said, "He's back downstairs looking for you, Consuelo—Miguel. I told him you aren't here. You better not come down right now. I don't think he's ever going to let you go, Consuelo. And he's crazy to look in the eye. *Muy loco.* Crazier than you've made him sound. He scares me."

Consuelo glanced at Hector. He pretended not to understand, not to care about what the two women were talking about. Consuelo said, "Right. Please tell them we're ready to be served. I'll wait here to let them in. And thanks, Malú."

Hector said to Consuelo, "That anything important?"

"Just saying dinner is ready," Consuelo said. "I have to wait by the door."

Hector smiled. "Then I'll make those drinks."

As he mixed a couple of mojitos, one for his grandfather's new lady friend and one for himself, Hector eavesdropped on Brinke and Beau, speaking softly to one another out on the patio. Beau was talking:

"All those years alone living with those two warring boozers. I credit that sorry solitude, that need to escape into himself, with Mase's too-vivid imagination and skills at writing. But the price was maybe too high. Just that lonely little boy and those crazy parents of his. Make no mistake, I loved my Livia. She was a good girl, comin' up. 'Til she met that bastard Grafton Lassiter and ran off to Galveston to elope with him. That sorry son of a bitch. Those two ruined one another in jiffy increments. Escalating warfare with booze stoking the anger, both sides. Liv started catting around behind Lassiter's back, going around with one of Grafton's hired hands.

"He caught them in bed together. All three were drunk, but Graf had a gun. Mase heard the shots fired that killed Livia and her lover. Mase grabbed one of his daddy's other guns and ran to help his mother. Mase put one in Grafton's shoulder. Didn't kill him, though. State of Texas saw to that. That's this life's one real regret, sweet Brinke. I knew things were bad between those two. I should have pulled Liv and Mase out of that place. Should have put Liv in some hospital somewhere to dry out and I should have raised Mase up myself, years earlier than I ended up doing. You and Mase, you both got equally robbed on the parent front, sounds like."

Beau hesitated then. "God forgive me, failing Liv and failing Mase. A lot of wicked things come out of Tulare, but none of 'em quite so nasty as Grafton Lassiter."

"It's a terrible story," Brinke said. "Just the thought of that little boy seeing all that. But Hector had you."

"You flinched when I mentioned babies earlier," Beau said carefully. "I'm sorry if I hit some nerve. It's too soon for kids of course. You two need that time alone. I mean, if you ever even want kids."

Hector stood there, listening, the drinks sweating in his hands. He heard Brinke make a false start or two, then she said, "When I was a little girl, I was attacked. A man, a neighbor, well... They put him to death later. I wasn't his only victim, just the only one to live. Anyway, the doctor back then, he said probably I can't have children of my own, not ever. They said it maybe could even be dangerous to try."

"Maybe isn't can't," Beau said, "and forever is too long to get your mind around. But we'll talk no more of that. What happens, happens. You can always adopt if you want a child."

"Maybe I'll get lucky," Brinke said, "prove that old country doctor wrong. Cheat fate."

"It can surely be done," Beau said. "We can make our own luck, darling."

"You truly believe that?"

"Every day of my life." It was quiet then, and Hector deliberately bumped into a chair—made its leg make noise against the Spanish tile. Beau called from the veranda, "Mase? Connie? That you?"

"Just me," Hector said. He set Consuelo's drink next to her placemat. Brinke reached out and took Hector's drink from him. "Thanks so much, darling," she said. "That was very thoughtful of you."

"That's me all over," Hector said, returning to mix another drink for himself. He called back, "Something for you, Beau?"

"Bourbon, neat," his grandfather said. "What the hell's on fire down there?"

"A diner downtown is going up in smoke," Hector said.

Brinke asked, "Arson?" He could hear the frown in her voice. "Do I really have to ask?"

"I'll know for certain when I talk to my best man," Hector said. "But I'll hazard it was a torch job. Right up against the burning building is an empty lot from an earlier fire."

Beau blew smoke out his nostrils. "You wouldn't happen to know the realtor of record on that lot, would you, Mase?"

Hector nodded, taking the seat opposite his grandfather. "I would."

Beau said, "I'll take a stab at a guess before you declare. Last Key Realty?"

"Yes, but—" A door slammed behind Hector. Consuelo shimmied out onto the porch, trailing servers. "Dinner is served," she said redundantly.

# 21

Brinke had ordered Hector to Beau's hotel to change for the wedding.

"Bad enough luck for you to see me so close to the ceremony," she had said. "Besides, first time you see me in my wedding dress, I want it to be as I come up that middle aisle on your grandfather's arm."

There had been some considerable interval between Hector's rap on Beau's hotel room door and the old man's eventual answer. Probably the result of Beau scrambling to put on some clothes and stash Consuelo someplace in a pointless bid at sparing Hector's sense of propriety, or the like, he figured.

Ultimately, Beau had left Hector alone in the sprawling hotel room. "Have to fetch my tux from a shop down on Duval," Beau had said. "You relax here a while. Treat yourself to a last solitary drink or three as a bachelor. I'll see ya in church, Mase."

It struck Hector then that last time he and his grandfather had been in a house of worship together was probably when Hector was a little boy, at his mother's funeral. They hadn't marked Grafton Lassiter's passing with so much as a graveyard visit.

Hector poured himself two more fingers of bourbon and carried it with him to a floor-length mirror. He straightened his tie and then slipped on the jacket of his evening suit, a relic of his nightlife in Paris with Brinke. He looked at his left hand, at his naked ring finger. He asked himself if he had second thoughts, found he didn't. He savored the bourbon's quicksilver burn.

Hector splurged on a taxi to shuttle him to the church. It was already muggy and he didn't want to arrive for his wedding wet as a mop. A lone man sat on the steps in front of the church as the taxi rolled up to the curbstone. Jack Dixon was smoking a cigarette. He cast that down and snuffed it out with a twist of a toe. He stood and smiled at Hector. Jack said, "You're not quite late. Still time to bolt, brother."

"I'm just fine, Dix. Dandy, even."

"No second thoughts?"

"Nah. Hell, no."

"Quite a crowd in there," Jack said.

That threw Hector. "Shouldn't be more than a half-dozen in there, and that's counting the priest and the organist," he said.

"More like, say, six dozen," Jack said. "It's pretty much standing room only."

Hector ducked a head in, floored to see a full house. What the hell was going on? "This is very strange," he said aloud.

Jack said, "Saw you last night, hanging around the fringes of the fire."

"Yeah, what was that, Dix? Another torch job?"

"Utterly."

"Any clues? Anything useful?"

"Sheriff says not." Jack paused, "Best man… say, I'm supposed to buck you up or something, aren't I? Offer some advice? Something like that?"

Hector shrugged. "You ever been married, Dix?"

"Christ, no," Jack said.

"So what could you possibly say to me that would mean anything?" Hector slapped the cop on the back. "Let's get in there and get this crazy thing done."

Hector and Jack stood at the altar, scanning the crowd. Hector thought he recognized one or two of Beau's old cronies, a local merchant or two, but hardly anyone else. The crowd still baffled Hector.

The organist segued into "The Wedding March."

Brinke and Beau began making their way up the aisle. Brinke wore a white beaded gown that left Hector wondering how she could breathe. The dress bared Brinke's shoulders and emphasized her breasts and the brownness of her exposed skin. White silk gloves nearly reached her bare shoulders. Brinke's face was hidden behind a veil. Beau wore a dove gray tuxedo with a cut-away coat. His white hair was slicked back. The old man seemed unusually reserved—very serious. Or possibly just badly hung-over or sleep-deprived from his night before, carousing with Consuelo.

Brinke's veiled head moved side to side, taking in the audience and leaving Hector with the impression the crowd was a surprise to Brinke, too. Beau, on the other hand, was nodding and smiling now—sometimes even winking—at various men and women in the audience. The old man seemed to know everyone, pricking Hector's curiosity even more.

The bride-to-be and her escort finally reached the altar. Beau squeezed Hector's hand and grinned. Brinke smiled nervously at Hector. Through her veil, he read her lips: "Here we go…"

After the ceremony, Brinke, Hector, Jack, Beau and Consuelo, the latter a last minute addition as maid of honor, posed for pictures.

The congregation gathered on the front porch to toss rice on the newlyweds.

Beau pulled Hector aside at the curb. He pressed into Hector's hand a thousand dollars and a hotel key. "My rooms, Mase. Sorry I can't share the wedding lunch waiting there, but, well, I just can't. Place is yours until at least five. Fresh sheets are on the bed. Be nice if you returned that favor when you two are done wrecking said bed."

Hector nodded, sporting an awkward smile. "Thank you, Pap. Everything else aside, you just seeing this, and giving Brinke away today, I can't thank you enough for that."

Beau hugged him. "You want to choke me up? Now, you two do know what to do when you get back to the hotel, *oui?*"

"We've been practicing."

"Plenty, I'm sure. Now g'wan, kiddo. Scram. Leg it, Mase."

The crowd cheered as the Lassiters drove off in a gaudily decorated Model-T Jack Dixon had scrounged up. Jack followed in his cruiser, blowing the siren all the way to Duval.

As the two vehicles disappeared around the corner, Beau raised his arms, his demeanor sharply changed. Loudly, he said, "Folks, thanks again for your infinite patience. So sorry for the confusion on times. But we're ready to go now, if y'all just step back inside and grab a pew."

Murmuring, the crowd filtered back into the church and settled back into seats. Audience members fanned themselves with wedding programs and real estate brochures.

The priest pulled Beau aside. He said, "I have a few dollars of my own. I rather fancy some property."

"Clergy gets discounts," Beau said, smiling. He gestured at an empty space in the front row. "Grab a pew, Father. Take a load off. You can take a look at how you look from out here for once. Oh, and thanks again for the use of the space."

Beau slapped another man on the back, said aloud, "My associate, Barnaby Nash. He'll be running this auction."

Barnaby stepped up to the altar and began setting up easels. He then positioned enlarged property plats and architectural renderings on the array of stands.

When he was finished, Barnaby raised his hands, beaming. He said, "The Good Lord isn't making more dirt, so property remains the soundest investment of your dollar, brothers and sisters. Nowhere more so than Florida, and nowhere in the Sunshine State more so than here, on the Lord's last Key. Seventy plats are available for investment, all contiguous and all marking the footprint of Florida's most ambitious resort complex. We call it Buena Stella, a top-drawer, A-1 resort complex, mixing hi-tone retail outlets and sumptuous residential living. Now opening bids on plat number one!"

# 22

Hector fumbled with the front door lock. He finally got the key to turn and opened the doors. Brinke grabbed his arm. "Whoa, there," she said. "Bad luck, just going in like that."

"What?"

"The threshold, darling—you're supposed to carry me across," Brinke said, smiling. "You know? Sweep me off my feet? Carry me to our marriage bed and ravish me?" Hector wasn't sure he had any of that flavor of stamina left after an afternoon already spent at Beau's hotel ravishing Brinke.

"Right," Hector said. "How perfectly dense of me." Brinke wrapped her arms around Hector's neck and he leaned down and slipped an arm behind the backs of her knees and swept her up into his arms. Smiling, she kissed Hector and said, "Romantic, isn't it?"

"If I slip a disc it surely won't be." Hector turned a bit to edge through the door. As he did that, Brinke's foot bumped the shrub alongside the porch. There was a heavy clunk as the baseball bat fell loose from the branches of the shrub and bounced off the concrete step.

Brinke and Hector exchanged wide-eye glances. Hector said it for both of them, "Son of a bitch."

Voice cracking, Brinke said, "Does this mean what I think it does?"

"What else could it mean," Hector said, "but that you've been targeted?"

Hector scoped the street with angry eyes but saw no obvious spies in sight.

Brinke, also checking the street, said tautly, "Maybe you better put me down."

Hector, distracted, said, "But the luck." He carried her across the threshold of their house, then lowered Brinke to their living room floor. "Gonna go fetch that bat," he said.

Hector leaned out the door and checked the street again. He used a handkerchief to grasp the handle of the Louisville Slugger. He leaned the bat against a chair and passed the handkerchief to Brinke. "Take this," he said. "Use it to move that bat into a closet, or the attic. Somewhere safe for now. Just don't leave your prints on it. Then I want you to lock this door and sit waiting for me with your gun. I'll call out before I mount the step. Failing hearing my voice? You hear someone else put foot to that step? That happens, I want you to shoot through the door, high and low, no questions asked."

Brinke said, "Where are you going, Hec?"

"Hardware store. Won't be ten minutes. Then it will be about ten more minutes out on the porch setting up after my purchase. Meantime, don't take off that dress. That's still my job and I mean to relish it." Hector hesitated, then smiled and added, "I mean, *again*."

Brinke arched her back. She held her position, quaking, then settled atop him, her mouth at his throat and her ragged breath running counterpoint to his pulse.

"That might well have been the best ever," she said.

"The best to date," Hector corrected, short of breath. "Our marriage is still young."

"Don't edit my conversation," Brinke said. She lowered her head and nipped at his chest. She held up her left hand, the rings catching the lowlight through the window. "There's something very sensual, very intense, about being completely naked but for your rings," she said.

"Very," he said, holding up his own hand and contemplating the gold band there.

Cicadas, the sound of the oscillating fans; a distant dog baying at the moon. A soft, steady rain pattered on the tin roof. There was suddenly a sharp crackle, then the power dimmed. The fans slowed once, twice, then stopped. The radio cut out in the middle of "The Man I Love."

Brinke's nails dug into his arm. "No electrical storm to speak of and nothing to knock out the power I can think of," she said. "You don't think someone cut our electric connection, do you? That ball bat's owner, for instance?"

"Maybe him, but not like you mean." Hector slid out of the bed. "It's more likely a blown fuse or circuit," Hector said. He heard this strange edge in his voice. Hector sat there, listening: Had his crazy scheme truly worked? He slipped his hand under his pillow and pulled out his Peacemaker. "You wait here, darlin'."

Brinke scowled. "Like hell. And that gun was under the pillow all this time? On our wedding night?"

Hector paused, then shrugged. "Well, yeah. All these fires, these rapes and beatings?" Hector cupped her chin. "And because of that baseball bat you knocked out of that shrub. Thank Christ for your unending beautiful goddamn legs."

"Nicer than saying thank God for my big feet," Brinke said. She slipped her hand under her pillow and drew out her Colt. Sheepishly, she said, "It's catching, I suppose."

Hector smiled and extended a hand. Brinke took it and he drew her up to him. They cocked together. Nude, toting their guns, they padded quietly into their living room. Hector nodded and Brinke slid to the left of the front door. Hector drifted right. He fumbled with the lock on the storm door and then jerked it open, dropping to one knee and pointing his gun through the screen door. Nothing.

Brinke whispered, "You sure this blackout is something sinister?"

"Pretty certain."

"Why, Hec?"

"Bear with me."

Brinke wrinkled her nose. "You smell something? Like burned meat, maybe?"

"Like I was saying." Hector rose and now he could see the body on the porch. The man's hand was thrust into the shrub where the ball bat had been hidden. The man's eyes were wide open and rolled back in his head, showing mostly the whites. The stranger's lips were blue. His tongue was twisted out one side of his mouth. There was indeed a scent of burning meat riding the wet night air.

Brinke leaned out for a look, said, "What in God's name happened to him?"

Hector handed Brinke his Colt. Naked, he stepped out onto the wet porch and reached behind the shrub, groping around. He found what he was looking for and pulled. He felt the socket come free from the exterior electrical outlet. Then Hector jerked hard and the other end of the electrical cord came loose from its fastenings. Hector held up charred, exposed wires, then tossed the electrical chord into the house behind himself. Reaching into the shrub, Hector felt around, found the tube and pulled it from the damp ground. He wrenched it loose from the dead man's hand that was still tightly gripping the metal pole. Hector handed the piece of metal to Brinke, who scowled, looking at the hollow metal tube in her hand. Hector leaned down and felt the man's throat for a pulse. *Nada.*

"Stash our guns, darling," Hector said. "We both need to dress. Then I'm going to take a short walk and toss this electrical chord and piece of tubing into the ocean. After, I'll go find us a cop."

Brinke shook her head. "You deliberately electrocuted him?"

"Not so much," Hector said sourly. "I figured to knock him out. Didn't count on the rain. I think he parboiled from the inside out. Though I doubt the cops would see it as an accident." He pointed at the man's feet. "And he shed his shoes, which only made it worse. Guess he was hoping to be quieter once he got inside." The man's rubber-soled shoes rested on the bottom step.

Brinke winced, shaking her head. "You set a trap. So, it's over then, yes? You killed the Key West Clubber."

Hector stepped into a pair of shorts and then pulled a T-shirt down over his chest. "*Nah.* The Clubber may be dead, such as he was. But I don't think anything's over. Hate to say it, but I expect all we've done tonight is step up the pace of fires to come."

# 23

First, Hector replaced the blown fuse. Then he took the electrical cord, a length he'd cut from a cheap lamp bought at the hardware store, and shoved it into the metal tube. He closed over both ends with electrical tape to seal the cord inside.

Hector slipped on a striped, long sleeve shirt and rolled the sleeves up to the elbows. As he was stepping into sandals, Brinke returned, dressed in shorts and a fisherman's shirt and sandals. She held the baseball bat in her left hand, clutching to the grip with a handkerchief. Hector took the bat and said, "You going to be okay for five minutes or so? With that stiff still being on the porch, I mean?"

"He's past being of consequence," Brinke said. "And I've got my roscoe, remember? You pitch that pipe in the ocean, and I'll go find a phone. I'll call the cops."

Hector said, "I think I'll make that phone call, darling. With luck, I might draw our best man. Be better if we can see to it that Dix is the top cop on the scene. If he's the man in charge to see this thing gets handled properly, it'll go much smoother for us."

Brinke nodded. "Give me that pipe, then. I'll destroy that evidence while you scare up Dixon."

Hector nodded, stepping out onto the damp porch. It was still raining, though hardly more than a warm drizzle now. Hector knelt down next to the dead man and arranged the bat in the man's still stiff right hand, the one that had gripped the electrified metal pole. Hector rose and looked the scene over. "Is this convincing?"

"Is to me," Brinke said. "Some wedding night, huh?"

"It's far from over now," Hector said. "After we wrap this up with the cops, we still need to see Beau. Have to get him caught up on events tonight."

As they entered the hotel, Brinke snagged Hector's sleeve and nodded at the lounge off the lobby. Beau held court at a round table, entertaining several men. Suits and ties, all around. Hector recognized two of the men, and one of those was the salesman from Last Key Realty.

Brinke squeezed Hector's arm. "That man, the one with the thick glasses, I know him from the newspapers. He's the mayor, Winch Mills. What in God's name is your grandfather up to?"

"Nothing up and up," Hector said. "That tall man there next to the mayor? That's Barnaby Nash, one of Beau's old partners in the grift. Barn' specializes in Big Store cons. I've never liked him. Never trusted him. Always figured he'll eventually screw Beau."

Brinke reached out and turned his face toward hers. "Big Store? What's that mean?"

"Very large, elaborate and well-paying confidence games," Hector said. "The most dangerous kind in that they're so fragile and intricate. But when they come off, they're very lucrative. Also nearly always devastating to the mark."

"Well, it's a cinch we can't crash that party," Brinke said. She steered Hector toward the front desk. "Guess it's best you leave Beau a carefully couched letter."

"Right," Hector said. He asked the clerk for a pen and paper.

"And then we head home, I guess," Brinke said. She rubbed his back. "Confess I'm a bit wired after this dead man on our porch. My brain keeps turning over what might have happened but for me insisting you carry me into the house. I'm pretty edgy. And the cops are probably still all over our place. I hate to go home before they haul away the corpse on our stoop."

"Then we'll go to Captain Tony's," Hector said. "We'll have us a couple of deep drinks. Maybe Beau can catch up to us there. Doubt any of Beau's new friends will be dropping by that place for a nightcap. Not dressed as they are. He might even risk seeing us in public at this hour."

"Sounds great," Brinke said. She glanced back into the lounge. "Everyone's smiling and laughing, Hec."

"For now they are, sure. Few nights from now, only one who'll likely be laughing will be Beau."

"Golly, I sure hope that's true," Brinke said. She slipped her arm through his. "Let's take the air."

They waited and drank until past midnight, but Beau didn't show. Fairly drunk, Brinke hectored Hector into a moonlight swim. As they found their way in the dark back to their pile of clothes, Brinke, naked and slick from the sea, pulled Hector down on the sand and mounted him. Still drunk and slurring a little, searching his eyes, she said, "We need to be more careful now. You shouldn't come inside me this time."

"Will do," Hector said, hearing his drunkenness in his own voice. With all the liquor, he was a while climaxing. When he did, they were both so caught up in the moment Hector forgot to pull out.

Later, with her fingers still knotted in the hair at the nape of his neck, after another apology from Hector for his recklessness, Brinke said, "Hush. It's probably fine." She kissed him and said, "I so love our life here together. I want it like this forever."

Hector said, "You said forever is pretend."

Smiling, lips to his lips, Brinke said, "I've been wrong once or twice."

# 24

I t was a dark cool room, thick with cigarette smoke and the smell of hops. Mel Hoyt spat tobacco into an old coffee tin. "This goddamn Lassiter and his lying goddamn mouth. I don't know what Lassiter did, but a fucking young man like Karl Rush does not have a fucking heart attack."

Mayor Winch Mills said, "What else to say about that now? Doc Rourke says it could also have been electrocution. Maybe from the lightning during last night's rain, though I didn't hear any thunder myself."

"Lookit," Denton Stokes, the realtor from Last Key, said, "it'd be ideal to have the Devlin property, but it's a near-corner lot. We can manipulate the footprint to exclude Devlin's parcel. Maybe put something undesirable up against her property line, just temporarily, to leverage a sale later. What I'm saying is, we don't have to change our plans, not much, by excluding her lot. We took our shot, and now it's too risky to try again against Devlin."

The sheriff made a face. "Now there you see! That's another goddamn thing. That name Devlin. She told me they were already married. Maybe we could get 'em on a morals beef."

Mayor Mills waved a fat hand. "On this Gomorrah of an island? Dream on, Mel. This is Key West, not Boston. 'Sides, according to the papers, those two are legal now."

"I was there," said Barnaby Nash. "Got roped into fill out the wedding crowd. They're all married up now, nice and square."

"She's one thing," Sheriff Hoyt said. "Lassiter is something else again. I'm serving notice on you all now, that bastard is trouble for us."

Barnaby Nash cut off the end of a cigar and struck a match. "Why do you say that?"

"He's the type," Hoyt said. "I can tell. You can see it in that book he wrote. And the stuff my guy learned about Lassiter and what he did over in Europe? I'm telling you all, he can queer this for us and for sure. We need to shut his business down, and I mean yesterday."

"You tried yesterday," the mayor said.

Barnaby Nash blew a smoke ring. "Let me see to Lassiter. I'll assess his threat. Hell, I've got more to lose than any of you at this point. If I think he can queer our pitch, I'll deal with Lassiter, clean and fast. And I swear I won't deploy any gimps or screw-ups with bad tickers."

"You best watch your mouth," the sheriff said, pointing a finger at Nash. "And what of the woman? What of this Devlin? Or, now I guess, Mrs. Lassiter? We really going to cede that property?"

"It was our own fault," Stokes, the real estate agent, said. "It was our own inattentiveness that cost us that parcel. Face it, Devlin slid in and bought that house out from under our noses with the help of goddamn Rose. But that's done. I say we leave her be. Best take Rush's death as an omen. 'Ticularly in case it was some kind of act of God."

The mayor snorted. "What the hell, Dent, you changing your way of living now? You gone off and found religion this late in life?"

"I'm just saying we took our shot and something very screwy happened," Stokes said. "Something went really haywire. So I say that as regards the Devlin parcel, we cut our losses."

"Hell with that," Sheriff Hoyt said. "I'm thinking on the matter of her some more. I'm thinking hard on the issue of that leggy bitch."

# 25

Hector overslept and consequently broke his early morning writing routine. He awakened alone in bed. The sheets were kicked off and his head hurt from a mild hangover. Hector figured he must have been fairly drunk. Hell, he'd even slept right on through the clarion, morning screams of the island's fighting cocks.

He heard the screen door slam, then, a few minutes later, he smelled coffee. Hector heard cupboards open and close. When it came to noise, rusting hinges from all the salt water were a universal issue on the island. Brinke slipped into the bedroom with a serving tray. She lifted her own coffee cup and a dish containing a couple of chocolate-filled croissants and sat them on the table along her side of the bed. She passed the tray to Hector. "The rest is all yours. Have the morning papers, too. You look like hell, by the by."

"Might have been better to let me escort you on your shopping trip, particularly given events," Hector said. "Still, this might be the best breakfast ever."

Brinke shrugged off her purse. She reached in, pulled out her Navy Colt and slipped it under her pillow. "I can usually handle myself. You know that." Her dark eyes narrowed playfully. "You're aren't going to be the hovering kind of husband, are you, Hec?"

Hector held up a hand, "Sorry." Brinke pulled folded up newspapers from her purse and threw them at the foot of the bed. As Hector settled in with his coffee and croissants, Brinke shucked off her shorts and shirt. She slid naked between the sheets, plumped her pillow, and put on her reading glasses. She began pouring over the paper between bites of her pastry and sips of coffee. She groaned. "Oh, God, can you believe this?"

She read aloud:

Police Doubt Dead Man
Is Key West Clubber
By Mike Rogers
Staff Writer

Sheriff Melvin Hoyt is contradicting other sources within his department regarding the mysterious death of a man last night and that man's possible ties to the crime wave attributed to the so-called "Key West Clubber."

Karl Dale Rush, 28, of Miami, was found dead on the porch of a private residence on Green Street at eight p.m. Wednesday night.

Rush was found sprawled on his back, a baseball bat clutched in his right hand.

Coroner Paul Rourke said Rush apparently died of cardiac arrest, though the coroner allowed, "Mr. Rush's age argues against such a cause of death."

Rourke also noted the state of Rush's body might also indicate the man had suffered exposure to a severe electrical charge. "It was raining which would have enhanced conductivity," Dr. Rourke said. "It could have been an isolated lightning strike."

Brinke rolled her eyes. Hector sipped some more coffee, said, "So far so good, as far as I'm concerned. Better to let the bastard's death be perceived as an act of God."

"That's not the most annoying part," Brinke said. "It goes on to say Hoyt's more or less writing off Rush's connection to the Clubber crimes. The sheriff claims he has reason to believe Rush is at best a copycat."

"That's certainly bad news for this island's women," Hector said. "That means the bastard is trying to keep his options open. After the way the arsons and rapes have been coupled by the cops and the press, they can't afford to retire their bogey-man."

Brinke scowled. "Who is 'they' to your mind?"

"I do have a theory about that," Hector said. "I have this notion elected officials, realtors and that reporter are in cahoots, and I mean down deep and dirty. Maybe not even above killing to realize their aims."

"Okay," Brinke said. "In cahoots to what end?"

"Gelt. Bloody money from shady land development."

"I'll confess now I've had similar thoughts," Brinke said. "And, I guess, given his guests the other night at his hotel, so clearly does Beau."

"Seems so," Hector agreed.

"Three of us deducing the same thing breeds confidence, in terms of the rightness of our conclusions," Brinke said. "But I don't like Jack Dixon's prospects for holding onto his job." She hefted the second newspaper. "Not after his quotes given to this competing rag. Dixon directly contradicts his crooked boss in this article. That's salutary, but it's not at all politic."

"That said, Jack should be runnin' the show," Hector said. "He should be sheriff. Let's make a note of when the next election for county sheriff is. I'm no political animal, darlin', but even I'd campaign for Dix."

"We really need to knuckle down, Hec," Brinke said. "Beau's leaving us in the dust."

"We've had other tasks," Hector said. "Not to mention taking that bastard out last night on our porch."

"Well, I thought that last was some kind of accomplishment until I read this article Rogers has put out there," Brinke said. "I was looking forward to quitting looking over my shoulder. But now? Now I think there's still a killer out there, just like you said."

"They won't try anything here again, not right at our place anyway," Hector said. "I don't care how far the fix is in. Having Rush turn up toes on our stoop, and then having something *else* happen at our home? It's too much to explain away, even with the local law and newsman working hand-in-glove."

"So my question stands, darling. What next, Hector?"

"It is a might tricky," he said. "We don't want to do anything that could ball up Beau's gambit, whatever the hell that might be. Wish he'd let us in at least enough to know where not to tap around."

"But he won't, and so here we sit, cooling our heels," Brinke said.

Hector drained his coffee and reached for his cigarettes. "Know what I really don't like? That reporter buddy of yours, Rogers. As long as he's out there to color and twist the facts to push Hoyt's and the town fathers' line and lies, we're just going to keep banging our heads against a wall. Beau is right, darlin'. Perception is reality."

Brinke thought about that. "The reporter's a slimy little worm, don't get me wrong. But at bottom, Rogers is pretty harmless. He's no killer."

"He certainly is a killer of the truth," Hector said. "That fragile thing he's murdering brazenly. Since he's a journalist, it's so much more the atrocity."

"What do you propose, then?"

"Rogers is the voice of record, bought and paid for," he said. "This other newspaper, the one Dix is quoted in, it seems okay?"

"Seems independent, if that's what you mean," Brinke said.

"Great. Get yourself a contact point for the editor of that other rag."

Hector slid out of bed, heading toward the bathroom. "I'm gonna grab a shower, then go see about getting to know this scribe Rogers, the bought-out son of a bitch. It's past time to shut that man's business down."

Brinke slid into the shower with Hector. "You're not going to really hurt the poor wretch are you, Hec? Not going to rough him up too much? I loathe him, too, but he's a milquetoast."

Hector slathered soap on Brinke's bronzed back. "Won't hit him with my fists, if that's what you mean. And I'm certainly not going to actually kill him. You should probably have some coffee at the ready for when I get back, though. This is going to take some drinks, and I do not want another hangover tomorrow."

Brinke took the cake of soap from Hector and went to work on his scarred back. It was her first good look at them and the pattern of wounds made her shudder. It might have been her, if the world had turned differently. Still, she said, "This wifey thing is just not going to stand."

Hector rubbed water from his eyes. "What do you mean?"

"This implied scenario that Brinke sits home and brews coffee while Hector goes about his nefarious drunken business and old Beau Stryder does whatever it is Beau Stryder does."

"I didn't mean to make you feel like a prop," Hector said. "I'm just groping for an angle here, and you're already known to that reporter. You know he's probably still bitter you snuck out on him. Son of a bitch is probably nursing a grudge."

"Maybe. And, anyway, I want to go at Hoyt," Brinke said.

Hector bit his lip. That prospect he didn't like at all. He said, "Define *go at Hoyt*."

"I'd just talk to him, as a concerned citizen," Brinke said. "Brace him, but subtly. I'd engage him in the guise of a woman very scared because a neighbor who lived two-doors-down and who looked very much like me got herself assaulted and killed a couple of nights before a baseball bat-toting stranger turned up dead on my front porch."

"I don't like the notion of you alone with that bastard," Hector said. "It's crazy."

Brinke was adamant. "And that's too bad. You said it yourself: the risks are too high for them to come back at us directly. And I'll call at his office during business hours. I'll hardly be alone with Hoyt. Chances are, your new best friend Dix will even be there."

# 26

M ike Rogers was sufficiently drunk that Hector could finally nurse his own liquor.

After five or six tequila shots, Rogers was convinced Hector was his spiritual brother. Playing to that notion, Hector wrapped an arm around Rogers's shoulders. He said, "Mikey, you can pay a bunch of money, trying to finesse one of those women at the bar into your bed, or you can cut to the chase, pay much less gelt and get a far better return on your investment from what we'll call a carnal professional. You simply need to embrace the concept of fair exchange of trade, buddy. You can put up a good deal less money than those women at the bar will cost you in the long run and get a little professionalism in the proposition."

The reporter scowled. "Christ's sake, you mean hire a whore, don't you?"

"That's very crassly put," Hector said, an edge in his voice. "C'mon, Mike. Place I'm thinking of ain't far at all. Don't be a stick in the mud. It's a house on Whitehead Street. Let's go there now." Hector rose and grabbed the reporter's arm. "Gotta get on your feet, to get off your feet, Mike. Trust me, *amigo*. Bliss awaits. Hell, this could well be the night that changes your life."

"Are you calling my men incompetent, Mrs. Lassiter?"

Brinke sighed. "Not all of your men, Sheriff." Brinke was suddenly sorry not to be carrying her Colt. She said, "Jack Dixon, for one, strikes me as reasonably effective."

Sheriff Hoyt was set seething by that assertion, barely containing his rage. "And you, in your expert judgment, think that because Dixon's quotes to some of the local newspapers line up with your beliefs? What else can you base your opinion on?"

Brinke said, "If by my beliefs you mean what I've deduced based on known facts and proximity of violence to my home, then, yes. Absolutely."

"We're finished here, Mrs. Lassiter."

"Devlin. My last name is Devlin."

"Missus—or is it Miss, then?—Devlin, we're done now. But you could carry word back to that friend of yours—husband. Whatever he is to you. That Hector Lassiter. Tell that man I've got my eye on him. You tell him that unlike some French policemen, I won't tolerate civilians messing in official police business. You tell all that to Lassiter."

"I'm frankly more concerned about police business messing in my life and my husband's life," Brinke said.

Hoyt narrowed his eyes. "And just what are you inferring?"

Brinke rolled her eyes. "I imply. You infer."

"Guess you'd know that, you being a writer and all. You know all that useless stuff. Cipherin' and parsin' and the like. Most people get by fine without all that nonsense."

"You leave us alone, Mister," Brinke said. "I'm telling you this just once. Leave us the hell alone."

The cop snorted. "Or else what, you crazy twist?"

"Cross me again and you'll soon enough find out what I mean."

Hoyt rolled his eyes now. "I'm shaking, ma'am. There's the damned door. You just show me that fine rump of yours on the way to it and out."

The radio was cranked up to cover their conversation: "Hard Hearted Hannah (The Vamp of Savannah)." The Cuban madam fanned herself and shook her head. "I detest him, *Señor* Lassiter, make no mistake on that point. I can think of at least three stories that man Rogers has printed that have cost me business and sleep. Even lawyer fees, once. But what you propose?" She made a face. "It's maybe actually evil, even by my standards."

"And it's surely my doing." Hector patted the woman's arm. "You just stand by and look glum," Hector said. "And then you can have all the cash he's carrying. It's my play and so my sin to carry. My cross to bear. My soul will be the one to take any hit, here. You just collect the money he has on him and forget us both. For you it's just business as usual."

The woman's eyes narrowed. "How much money?"

Hector patted down Rogers' slack body. The reporter was snoring. A drool trail was sliding down his right cheek.

Hector pulled out the reporter's roll. "I count three hundred dollars," Hector said. "Less twenty dollars for his ticket across the Gulf." Shaking his head, Hector thought out loud, "Three hundred clams. That's a lot of walking-around money for a reporter." The bought-off son of a bitch.

"You can have that car of his out front, too," Hector said. "It's a nice one and brand new." He smiled. "Hell, if nothing else, it'll class up your parking lot. Maybe draw a better breed of customer than the likes this sorry bastard would on his own."

Scowling, the madam said, "You brought that one here. And you swear you'll cover for me if this doesn't come off?"

"It won't go wrong," Hector said. "But yes, I swear. Now I just need one of your girls, one who can play dead whatever happens. Whatever this guy says, or maybe even screams when he comes to. And I'll need some black coffee. I'll be needing you to step up when this reporter starts talking about cop friends who might help him out of the jam he finds himself in. You'll nod and confirm that the girl is family of Sheriff Hoyt's. That'll shut him up. Until he comes to, if you could, I need your bouncer Felipé to take this twenty and go to the docks and smooth the grooves with some steamer or shrimp boat skipper. Once we convince this sorry bastard he offed one of your girls, we want him on the first boat to Cuba. We want him pointed one way, and we wanted him headed out across the Big Blue River very fast and then gone from our lives forever."

# 27

Wrapped in yellow rain coats, Hector and Beau stood at the pier's end, blinking back the rain and catching glimpses of the bloody sunrise through the storm clouds.

Hector recast his saltwater rig. He said, "All right, Beau, I've determined we've both concluded that all of this, every dirty thing happening on this island, is linked to real estate and to development."

Beau nodded, smiling. "So far, so good, Mase. But, sonny, it's far bigger than what I think you're seeing. And one hell of a lot more treacherous."

"I can take care of myself."

"Sure you can. But there's your pretty wife to worry after now, too," Beau said. "Though I doubt I really need to remind you of that."

That shut Hector up. Beau said, "Mase, this crazy island is wide open. There's more than one fortune to be made on this rock. Everywhere I look, I see another opportunity just begging to be exploited. Unfortunately, the sharks got to this Key first. Tell you, Mase, if I'd hit this sand dab along about 1920 or '21, I'd be this coral bed's beloved sovereign ruler."

"I do believe that is true," Hector said. "I don't doubt that at all."

"Well, the good news is there's still some wiggle room. You mind helpin' me with a side project?"

"What's that mean, side project, Pap?"

"You know boats don't you?"

Hector nodded. "A fair bit. Yeah, sure."

"You can steer a boat, yes? You could ask some intelligent questions about one?"

"Sure, I guess." Hector recast his line. "What's this about?"

"It's all about another opportunity," Beau said.

"Something you're into with Nash?"

"Barn? Nah, Nash is outside this one." Beau gave Hector a hard look. He said, "Mase, you've just never ever cottoned to Old Barnaby. Why exactly is that?"

"I don't know," Hector said. "Call it instinct. Maybe a longstanding, visceral dislike. That's all. Except I figure it for mutual."

"That's plenty," Beau said. "Barn's okay, Mase. We've been partners for years, you know."

Hector changed the subject: "So what's with these questions about boats and me?"

Beau smiled. "Little opportunity I have for you in the Saddle Keys. This enterprise stands to net you some mad money. It's just a couple of days' job, I promise. Just until I can free up Conrad Vogel to serve as pilot."

"I've always liked Conrad," Hector said. "Con's jake. This pitch of yours, can I say no?"

Beau frowned. "It would cost me a lot of money if you did. Not to mention the hurt feelings."

"You told Brinke I'm too gabby for the con," Hector said. "Too inventive to use in a game."

"Well, here you're going to be the surly sailor who can't string too many words together," Beau said. "And bring Brinke. She can be my…er, companion."

Hector frowned. "*Your* companion?"

"Just for show. Just for an hour or two here and there. Brinke will be arm decoration. A fetching and desperately needed distraction."

"What's wrong with Consuelo if you're looking for decoration like that?"

Beau waved a hand. "Well, Connie's not sufficiently cosmopolitan. Not sufficiently American to be on the arm of Gunther Walpole."

Hector laughed. "And you're Gunther Walpole? What happened to Cornelius Astor?"

"That's a separate affair, Mase. Cornelius Astor wouldn't dabble in boats. Astor's a real estate baron. Walpole is shipping czar and sports boat enthusiast."

Hector shook his head. "Aren't you at all concerned about spreading yourself thin, Beau?"

The old man scoffed. "Now, don't be like that, Mase. That's hurtful talk. You in, sonny?"

"Two days?"

"Three at most, cross my dark heart."

"Brinke and me—"

"Have this goddamn bloody Clubber thing, I know, Mase. Trust me though, things are quiet on that front. And they will stay that way for at least the next couple of days."

"Quiet by your design? Is that what you're saying?"

"Please, Mase, my modesty. Seriously, it's nothing of my direct doing, but I have good reason to believe the violence will be edging off, at least in the near term. So, are you two in?"

"I'll have to ask Brinke. I mean, I can't speak for her."

Beau snorted. "And, in that, ain't marriage just humbling as all hell?"

# 28

B rinke stretched her arms out along the warm brass rail of the boat's stern, the Gulf wind whipping her hair. Beau sat alongside her, tending his line. Speaking loudly enough Hector could hear from his perch atop the flying bridge, Brinke said, "Have to say, this has been a heavenly couple of days. What's this make it? Ten, twelve boats you've bought, Beau?"

"Ten," Hector said, turning their craft to head back in while they still had some sunlight to steer by. He called down to Beau, "What's next, Commodore?"

Beau smiled up at his grandson. "What's next is you two sleep on that last big boat we brought in yesterday," Beau said, sipping his whiskey soda. "Have a party. I'll handle the wrap up tomorrow. Then we'll have a good dinner and celebrate our success here."

"Our success," Brinke repeated. "I'm curious what form that takes. What exactly have we been up two these past couple of days? I'm in it—whatever it is—up to my neck, and yet I'm baffled."

Beau patted her knee. "All will be revealed and directly."

"You are truly something," she said. "All this living by your wits, making money simply by using your brain in these funny and strange ways…"

"Not just me," Beau said. "You do the same thing really. How else to describe writing fiction?"

They were sitting in the cabin of the forty-footer they'd taken possession of Saturday night. They dined on wine and fresh-caught amberjack. Hector turned down the radio on Ted Lewis and his Orchestra's version of "Show Me the Way (To Go Home)."

"This yacht club has been deserted for nearly a year," Beau said. "I rented it for near nothing a few weeks ago. You see, as The Fates would have it, I was actually headed down to the Keys before you two sent your wire inviting me for the wedding. I've been putting this operation together for a while. Timing is often a funny thing in this business. Funny, yet so critical. Call it a happy accident."

Hector said, "You mean this yacht club is all your stage-setting? That's incredible."

Beau beamed. "Yep. Great, ain't she? Just had to clean the place up a bit and hire me a few fellas to play waiter and doorman and the like. Had to find me a just-good-enough chef. Looks like a million dollars, don't she?"

"I was fooled," Brinke said.

"Anyone would be," Beau said. "This is a sweet touch. Maybe one of my slickest to date. Once I got this place secured, I started answering classified ads regarding boats for sale. I wired the owners to get them all down here one after another, bang, bang, bang. Well, you've seen how we're grinding them through, buying these boats, I mean."

Hector said, "But using what for money to buy these boats, exactly?"

"Stock certificates," Beau said. "Former owners'll all be paid out end of day tomorrow."

Hector made a face. "You're confessing you mean to pass off false title on all these rich marks?"

"The certificates are real enough," Beau said. "But near worthless. Or they will be tomorrow night. That's another story, unto itself, Mase. Ties back to another game I've got going. Roots of that one trail back to the oil fields of Texas."

"This sounds dangerous," Brinke said.

"Not a bit of it," Beau said. "By the time these fellas realize their stocks are worthless, the rafts will be in the hands of new owners and far away from here. The yacht club will be deserted again come Monday morning. And Gunther Walpole? That chap will be a vexing chimera."

Brinke smiled, shaking her head. "I should feel much dirtier about all this than I do."

"Hell, it gets in your blood," Beau said. "And anyways, none of these guys is going to miss their money. Ain't like we're bilking widows and orphans. That's not my style at all." He slipped the wedding band off his finger and passed it back to Hector. "Thanks for the loan, of the ring and of your lady."

Hector slipped back on his ring. "Brinke enjoyed it. I could tell she liked having a sugar daddy, even fleetingly."

She smiled at Beau. "Shameless as it sounds of me, it's true enough. Some sorry part of me has always yearned to be a kept woman. I've toyed from time-to-time with being some rich and attractive older man's pampered prize."

Beau stroked her cheek. "I don't believe that. But when it comes to the con, you're a natural, darlin'. Soon as you entered the room, the IQs among those boat owners sounded, and I mean down deep. Any scraps of reason they ever possessed fled."

Brinke said, "That's this con explained. What are you up to back in Key West, Beau?"

The old man looked around the cabin. "That might be a bit premature, yet. Too soon to talk, I mean."

"Give us the broad strokes, then," Hector said.

Beau thought about that. He sighed, then said, "I bought a few blocks in Key West. Well, me and some confederates did that. An even seventy parcels."

Hector said, "Again, I have to ask. Using exactly what for money? I mean, I don't care if you sold a thousand pedigreed mutts, that wouldn't buy seventy parcels of Key West real estate."

"Just bought options," Beau said. "We just bought options on partial payment. My investors have ponied up half-cost on those options. I don't have a dime in this thing, so far. Isn't that sweet?"

"Your investors?" Hector shook loose a cigarette. "Who are these investors?"

"The congregation at the church," Beau said, pulling the cellophane from a cigar.

"These investors were our impromptu wedding crowd?" Brinke looked stricken. "Beau, we're planning on living on that island. Key West is home now. You can't soak all those Key Westers in some land scam! Those are our neighbors, maybe our future friends."

"Soak?" Beau looked hurt; maybe even a bit angered. "I'm not going to see any of them Key Westers lose a penny of their investments." Beau held up his glass for Hector to refill. "Point of fact, those investors of mine will not end up with any land. But they will enjoy a respectable profit on their original investment."

Hector looked up from the bar. "And how is that exactly?"

"That may take some more explaining," Beau said. "May need to show you some things back in Key West to put the plan across. You two stop by the hotel when we get back. I'll explain the rest there."

"We're headed to Key West then?"

"Tomorrow night, I figure," Beau said.

# 29

The men were gathered in the back room of a shanty speakeasy on Elizabeth Street. Music through the walls: "There's Yes! Yes! In Your Eyes."

"The woman paid me a visit, couple of days back," Sheriff Hoyt said. "The Devlin woman, I mean. I give her credit for courage, coming right at me like she did. She's either got guts, or no brains. Maybe both. She's also quite the twist. God-damn walking wet dream. Hell, I shouldn't have farmed out that hit on her. Should take care of that cooze myself. Prettiest I've ever seen, anytime, anywhere."

Nash grunted. "She really came straight at you? To what end?"

"On face, she came to ask about the dead man on her porch, fishing after what I'd learned about him and such," Hoyt said. "She was playing the concerned citizen. The fearful frail."

"On face," Nash repeated. "What was the real reason?"

"To put me on notice, I guess," Hoyt said. "She expressed doubt in my crew. All but fuckin' Dixon, who she singled out for praise, that conniving cocksucker. Then she threatened me. Warned me to stay away from her and Lassiter." The cop leveled a finger, moving it from man to man. "I told you, all of you, this Lassiter is trouble for us. Her threat confirms it so far as I'm concerned."

"So it would appear," Nash said. "I've done some more checking. I'm starting to come around to Hoyt's thinking on this. We should kill Lassiter, and I mean yesterday."

Hoyt bellowed, "At last!"

Mayor Winch said, "My bigger immediate concern is our missing member. Where the hell has Rogers gotten off to? He's missed two editions of his paper. People are talking and that won't do."

Nash frowned. "Who is Rogers?"

"Owner and operator of the *Key West Tattler*, one of the local rags," the mayor said. "It's the newspaper we had a handle on. One we same as wrote ourselves."

Hoyt cracked a peanut shell. He tossed the peanut up in the air, caught it in his mouth. Chewing, he said, "That's a sideways way of saying Rogers was bought off. Reporter just cost us a new car. Some chump change here and there. He came relatively cheap. And Rogers helped us put over the myth of the Clubber."

"A valuable asset, indeed then," Nash said. "Too valuable to lose. The newspaper, I mean. This Rogers? He's missing long?"

"A few days," Hoyt said. "Rogers' house is abandoned. I take it as another bad sign."

"I know some newspaper folk back in Miami," Nash said. "Our kind of newspaper people, if you get my drift. Malleable, that is to say. I'll get one or two down here. We'll get our newspaper up and running again, Rogers, or no. Agreed?"

Grunts all around.

Nash slapped a palm on the table. "Righty-o, then!"

Mayor Winch said, "Word from my sources is the big man, Cornelius, has been scarce for several days, too." The mayor's brow furrowed. "Should I be worried, Nash?" The mayor pulled out a Cuban cigar. He offered another to Nash who accepted. "I ask," the mayor said, leaning forward to light Nash's cigar, "because Astor strikes me as reluctant to get too directly involved with us."

Nash took his time getting his cigar to draw, slowly turning it and sucking in his cheeks. It was maybe too much time, Hoyt thought. Finally, puffing smoke, Nash said, "You deal with me because Mr. Astor doesn't fancy himself anything more or less than a businessman. He likes to keep his hands clean. Mr. Astor doesn't face up to the fact that men like us, right here, are the ones who truly make things happen. We're the ones who really get things done. Men who aren't afraid to dirty their hands."

"Which doesn't answer the question of where Mr. Astor has gotten off to," the mayor said.

"Well, Mr. Astor fancies himself a lady's man, too," Nash said, smiling wickedly. "He's found himself some pretty young Cuban cooze. He's drifted north with that bimbo. Traveling on his boat, *Jolly Sally*, to spend some time with her. Our only concern about that, gentlemen, should be that randy old codger doesn't have a stroke or heart attack in the saddle, so to speak. Would be very bad to have him found dead, *in flagrante delicto*, right?"

Denton Stokes, the real estate agent, said, "What the hell does that mean?"

"Dead with a boner," Sheriff Hoyt said. "At least in this context. Why do I sense you're holding something back, Nash?"

Nash looked up sharply. "Explain yourself. I don't approve of your tone."

The cop lit a Lucky Strike. "That old bastard Astor—based on things the mayor and Dent have said—strikes me as squirrelly."

"It's no revelation that the rich are often eccentric," Nash said, checking his fingernails.

"Eccentric ain't the same as crazy," Hoyt said. "Stakes are too high for us to have some senile codger in the mix. What if, in some horny throes, that daffy bastard gifts his Cuban whore with a critical Whitehead Street parcel or two? What happens to Buena Stella, then?"

The mayor gestured at Nash with a cigar. "Blunter than I'd have put it, but then Mel's like that—direct, that is. That said, Mel speaks to a point of real concern we all share. The other night, in the hotel lounge, Cornelius struck me as, oh, let's call it a tad foggy."

"Foggy," Nash furrowed his brow. "Foggy?"

"Senile," Stokes said. "You know, dodgy."

"Point is," Mayor Winch said, "you're our man, Nash. The one we deal with, the one we see. The one we can confer with directly. And candidly. Presumably, you have contact with Mr. Astor's other backers back east. You have his proxy, so to speak."

"Don't beat around the bush," Nash said. "What are you asking?"

Sheriff Hoyt leaned forward, eyes drilling into Nash. "The question is, if Cornelius Astor died tomorrow, if his ticker broke while sticking it to his Cuban slut, or maybe if he just fell off his goddamn boat and was lost at sea, would life go on so far as we care? Would it queer our pitch in any way?"

Nash was evasive, eyes searching faces. "The short answer, under normal circumstances, would be no."

"That should be the only answer we need," Sheriff Hoyt said with a feral smile. He said, "Confession time, then. Rest of us convened early. Before you arrived, we reached an agreement, Nash."

Nash shifted in his chair, frowning. "What kind of agreement?"

Mayor Winch ground out his cigar. "Staying with our blunt talk, Mel is going to eliminate Astor. Astor is unstable. Old man is probably sliding into dementia. We have too much at stake to let him maintain a continuing role in this. Mel will see to Astor. You're going to see that Lassiter is taken care of. Then we're going to deal with just you on Buena Stella, here on out. We'll sweeten the pot for you out of Astor's end."

Nash wet his lips. "Perhaps you didn't hear me," he said. "I said Mr. Astor's needed participation would be expendable under *normal* circumstances. We no longer enjoy those happy circumstances."

The mayor frowned. "What about these *circumstances* makes me think you think things aren't normal now?"

Nash fidgeted with his cigar, unable to make eye contact. "I'd hoped to have a better handle on things before we had this discussion."

"I'm not liking the sound of this at all," the mayor said.

"There's been a complication," Nash said carefully.

The real estate agent leaned forward, brows furrowed. "What kind of complication?"

"Mr. Astor is a populist. Unbeknownst to me, this past Wednesday, Mr. Astor held a public auction. All of the lots in the Whitehead Street project are now under option by nearly six dozen new parties."

Hoyt looked on the verge of suffering his own stroke. "Astor fucking sold our land?"

Nash bowed his head. "That's essentially right."

The other men leaped back as Hoyt flipped over the table and hurled himself at Nash, getting his hands around the man's throat. The mayor recovered first. He pulled out a gun and pushed it up hard behind the sheriff's ear. "Stand down, Mel. Do it now, goddamn it, or so help me I'll lay you out cold!"

Seething, the sheriff threw Nash across the broken table. Hoyt snarled, "This fucker has sold us out! Shoot him!"

Nash was gripping his side, trying to get his breath. "I didn't know until my secretary processed all the paperwork and gave me carbons this morning. The options have been filed and notarized. This all happened before I knew about it to try and stop it."

"So what do we do now?" The mayor kicked over a chair. "What the fuck do we do?"

Nash struggled to his feet. "I have a notion about that. We buy out the investors. Pay 'em back their money and a little extra to sweeten the pot."

Stokes shook his head. "Against what they stand to make once we build that resort? They'd be crazy to sell."

"That's just it," Nash said, rubbing his side. "We cancel Buena Stella. We'll give these new owners some nonsense about the coral bed and our engineers' insisting it can't support structures of the height we envision. Those parcels have sat largely dormant since the twenty-three fire. Even with Florida's land boom, they weren't moving until Astor came in with his plan for Buena Stella. If those plans are canceled, these new investors will see the writing on the wall. They'll see that their new property will just sit there again, but now they'll be the ones paying the taxes on it with no income from the other direction. They'll sell, for certain. We pay some money now to buy up that land, get it entirely under our thumbs knowing we'll make it back, and much more, on the back end. That's our solution."

Hoyt was flexing his hands, wanting to hit something. "Back end?"

"When we have the properties secured under our exclusive ownership, we simply announce we're pushing ahead with Buena Stella, after all," Nash said. "Folks back east, the real money men, the fat-cat sports fishermen who'll pay us to live in that resort, the ones who'll underwrite construction, won't have to know any of this has happened."

"I don't like it anymore than you fellas," the mayor said. "But I don't see another way. We'll have to start consolidating resources, liquidating assets, getting the cash together. It'll be tight short-term, but once we get moving, we can have our own auctions, maybe. Infuse some moneys that way." The mayor chewed his lip. "Hell, we'll just dip into the city coffers to help cover losses in the meantime."

"See, this kind of shit is just what I feared with that crazy old man," Hoyt said. "Christ knows what he's doing right now, as we sit here jawing. All of which means, now more than ever, Astor has to be taken out. Are we at least agreed on that much?"

Nash rubbed his stomach. He nodded with the other men, said, "I'm forced to concur."

Sheriff Hoyt said, "Where is Astor? Where do I find this geezer and his boat?"

"He's returning to Key West shortly," Nash said.

"Good," Hoyt said. "And just to see there are no more screw ups, and to give you a bigger stake in a happy outcome of all this, you're the one that's going to kill Lassiter, Nash. I don't want you farming that hit out. I want a blood bond between us, to keep me thinking you're to be trusted.

Knowing you've got some to lose, something more than money? Now that's what I call peace of mind. So you kill Lassiter, personally, Nash. Agreed?"

"I hear you," Nash said, looking a little sick.

# 30

Brinke lay naked on the deck of the boat, sunning. Hector had pulled the craft a ways out to sea so nobody could just stumble upon them as they made love in the open air, or as Brinke baked herself naked in the morning sun. Brinke had a record on: "Why Did I Kiss that Girl?" Watching her from the flying bridge, Hector checked his watch. "Figure we have about two hours before Beau comes looking for us," he called down to her.

Brinke nodded. Because of her black sunglasses—all she had on other than her rings— Hector couldn't really read her expression. "I'm pretty torn, Hec," she said, rising to turn down the music. She stretched back out on the deck and smoothed on some more suntan lotion, glistening and brown in the sun. "Part of me wants to get back to our Key, to straighten things out there and make those bastards pay for what they did to Rose and all the others."

Hector smiled, aroused watching her. "And the other part of you?"

"The other part of me wants to live naked on his boat until I'm brown as a wallet and the money and the rum run out."

"I frankly like most of the last option better," Hector said.

"Me too, but the guilt about all the other is starting to settle in," Brinke said.

"Guess it's a good thing we head back tonight, then," he said. Hector climbed down the ladder and then slid off the cabin roof onto the deck. He slipped off his shirt and fetched a couple of cold beers. He opened them and then lay on the deck next to Brinke. Hector said, "What guilt, by the way? Guilt about not being back on the Key while it burns down around us?"

Brinke shook her head. "Guilt about this shakedown of Beau's, actually. This scam we're a party to. All these soon-to-be-swindled yacht owners."

Hector folded his hands behind his head and crossed his legs at the ankles. "You've seen the boats we're bringing in. They're rich men's toys. And likely as not, these boats are on the block because the owners already have next year's model on order. Beau's so-called victims probably aren't hurting."

"I suppose," Brinke said, sipping her beer. She stroked his leg with her calf. "And like I said, I hate to end this decadent idyll." She looked around them. "Maybe I should have bought a houseboat for us instead of that cottage."

"It is harder to strike at people lost out on the Gulf somewhere," Hector said.

"And there's no shrubbery to hide murder weapons inside," Brinke said. "Can't be ambushed on a boat. Yep, would have been perfect," she said.

"At least until hurricane season," Hector said. "Houseboats are great for lake or river living, but not here on the Gulf. The storms down this way are downright personal. September of the year I was born, across that way to Galveston? Hell of a hurricane." He shrugged, said, "Anyway…"

"Well, we need a boat of our own, Hec. The past couple of days have convinced me. I want to explore every Key. I want to get down to the Dry Tortugas. Want to tour Fort Jefferson. See where they held that doctor who treated John Wilkes Booth." She rolled over on her side and propped her head on her hand. "And I need to get back over to Cuba. Really need to soak up more atmosphere for my novel. I'm running too much on imagination, this book. Need to see some of the seedy places I couldn't venture into without a strapping, Colt-toting escort."

"Maybe next weekend," Hector said, feeling drowsy from the sun. "Beau swears he'll have turned Key West upside down by then. He'll have run out all the rats."

"I'm still trying to figure out how that can be," she said. "Particularly without bankrupting all his investors."

"I pressed Beau again for more explanation," Hector said. "Beau swears he'll lay it out for us when we get back home."

"Yeah, home." Brinke reached over and stroked his chest. "Part of me feels like I should have been reading the papers or listening to the radio to see what's been happening since we left there. But I'm playing ostrich, instead, I guess. I used to live for this intrigue. Striving to mount some clandestine crusade to set something or other right. Then you walked into that church. We made those vows in that same place we made love. Now I just want to loaf and write and eat and drink and keep making love with you. That's all. That's all I want, all I want to do. Forever."

"In that order? Sex comes last? That could be a problem."

"I mean it, Hec. I don't want to do this other anymore, the sleuthing I mean. Or I don't think I do. Maybe I'm deluding myself with all this. You know, wanting a house, being a wife and maybe having a child with you. Maybe I'm running some kind of confidence game on myself with all that." She sighed. "Yet it doesn't feel that way to me, not at all."

"You started it up again here, the sleuthing, if you'll recall."

"Right," Brinke said. "So I'm stopping it."

"Really?"

"I really do mean it. Time to invent my fiction again, like I did when I started."

"Great. Then let's close cases when we get back to our Key. We'll let Beau do his thing, and we'll bow out. Live that quiet life until they throw dirt over us."

"You can really do that, Hec? Just be a quiet, solid citizen? You can leave the rest just to the written page?" Brinke sounded dubious.

Hector said, "It's never been my way, this thing you do. It's been your life and the fuel for your fiction, honey. If it hadn't been for you and Gertrude putting boots to my backside, I'd never have poked my nose into that bloody affair in Paris last February. I still rue doing that and have the scars crisscrossing my back to prove it. And Molly? Well, Jesus Christ. But for the fresh wounds on my back about this time last year, maybe she'd be alive still." He sighed. "So, yes, let's just be like the rest. Let's be stay-at-home types. Lazing during the afternoon heat. Let's leave the cops' sorry work to the cops."

Brinke said, "I bet it's cold in Paris tonight." She smiled. "Or I guess it's mid-afternoon there."

"But probably still cold enough," Hector agreed. "Probably raining, too. Or sleeting."

Brinke suddenly pressed her palm to Hector's cheek. She turned his face toward hers. Her coal black eyes searched his pale blue. "Something I really should have told you long before this. I don't think I can have children, Hector. It might be dangerous to even try. It scares me to even contemplate rolling those dice. I guess I'm a coward that way. Too attached to myself." She pressed her forehead to his. "I know it's late to be admitting this. Selfishly late. But it's the way things are. Does that matter to you? Not having children of our own, I mean? Because, if it does, I do understand. I'll let you go if so, and you can find—"

He pressed his fingers to her lips. He said, "The two of us is plenty."

"We could adopt, Hec."

"If you want to, sure. But all I need is you, Brinke."

"Really?"

"Truly," Hector said. "I swear it's so, darlin'."

# 31

Beau surprised them with his announcement they would be returning to Key West in one of the boats he'd swindled from its owner.

"I'm holding onto this sucker," Beau said, pointing at a small, but opulently appointed yacht christened "Jolly Sally."

"I don't remember this one having that name," Brinke said.

"Well, of course given events here, terms of purchase and what not, it had to have a new name," Beau said.

Hector said, "Isn't it bad luck, renaming a boat?"

Beau waved a hand. "No room for worry. Couldn't keep it without a new name. So this is it. Stop trying to borrow trouble, Mase. Worry is a waste of the imagination. Now get in there and steer. I'm going to watch you play pilot. Have to pick up some of these seafaring skills to use my new boat. Going to be useful for visits with you two living across the Gulf."

Hector checked the sky. It was black out there, and the storm front was rolling their way. "We really better get underway, pronto. Looks like we'll be racing a hell of a storm to dock in Key West."

"Thought it was looking ominous," Brinke agreed. "Can smell the rain on the wind." Hector's gaze lingered on Brinke. It was strange to see her in clothes. It felt strange to him to be wearing clothes and to feel long pants against his legs, their cuffs brushing his ankles. He'd been naked or in shorts since the wedding. Brinke was right—he was in danger of going native. Tan lines were a memory and Hector's hair had faded closer to auburn than it's usual chestnut.

Beau helped him cast off ropes, then Hector backed her out and idled away from the yacht club. The boating facility was dark now, empty again. A few of Beau's cronies had made off with some of the fixtures to pawn or sell for salvage.

Two boats remained in slips, the one Hector and Brinke had spent the day on and a slightly larger one. Hector said, "What of those two yachts?"

"Gone in an hour or two," Beau said, smiling. "Got plans for those boats."

"Wonder what will become of the club," Brinke said, watching the abandoned yacht club recede from them. "It is a beautiful place."

"It'll resume decay, likely," Beau said. "Posh as it is—was—it was a damn bad place to build a club like that. On Key West, it might well have thrived. But on that Key? No money and nothing to bring money there."

"Always with the money," Brinke said.

"Always," Beau said, as if it should be obvious.

Brinke thought about that, then said, "I don't think I can wait until we get back to Key West, Beau. I want to know what's going on with you and real estate back there. What's the rest of the plan?"

Beau went below and returned with a champagne bucket and some glasses. As he stepped onto the deck, the rain kicked up. Ducking low, he slid back into the cabin. Hector climbed down from the flying bridge to steer from inside the cabin until the storm subsided.

Brinke was already turning on lights in the cabin. She grabbed a blanket and sat down on one of the benches, wrapping up in the throw. Beau handed Brinke a champagne flute and then closed the door to the deck, shutting out the thrashing rain. He poured champagne for Hector and for himself, then Beau settled in beside Hector to watch his grandson pilot the boat through the storm.

"Children, here's the story on those seventy plats," Beau said. "I picked up first options, then before I had to pay a cent on those parcels, my people, led by Barnaby Nash, went out and recruited those investors who became your wedding party. They put up payments that essentially covered my payments for the plats."

"Right, so you said," Brinke said. "But now they own that land and you don't. I can't see how they don't get soaked, here."

Beau smiled and held up a hand. "You're getting too far ahead. Back up a second. The question to ask, is why would seventy people rush to buy those parcels from me? Parcels that have sat vacant and unpurchased since the 1923 fire. Why want 'em now?"

"Okay," Brinke said, "pretend I just put that very question to you. What made that land suddenly so attractive?"

"Buena Stella," the old man said. "That's the thing that turned the tide on that land."

Hector said, "And who, or what, is Buena Stella?"

"Five years back, in Galveston Bay, they built 'em a beautiful and swanky resort area," Beau said, "big hotel and surrounding shops and apartments. I watched that sucker go up. Watched the excitement and the domino development effect it had on that portion of the Bay. And it's a beautiful piece of architecture. Stunning. Set my mind to working all kinds of ways, watching that unfold." Beau paused. "And then a notion occurred to me. What happens to all the renderings? The schematics? Blueprints? Not just elevation drawings, but the wiring and plumbing schematics, all the detail work? Is it just filed away in some county office and forgotten? Stuck in some architects' portfolios, pieces and parts?"

"You bought up all the blueprints," Hector said, "didn't you?"

"For a song," Beau said. "Then I found myself someone to slightly doctor 'em. To change that Galveston resort's name to Buena Stella on all the paperwork and renderings. Been holding 'em in reserve for just the right opportunity."

Brinke said, "So you used these drawings to hook the people back in Key West, using these very real blueprints that look like a million dollars."

"Two million, actually," Beau said. "But yes, I used them to hook and then to land those crooked city fathers, to get me some breaks up front on those seventy parcels and to sway them, and those Key West investors who now hold options on the land."

"So how do these investors get their money back?" Brinke sipped her champagne, then held the glass up for a refill. "How do they get that money back, plus interest, as you promised?"

Beau shoved the bottle back in the ice bucket, then sat down and tipped his chair back, swiveling around to face Brinke. "Here's where I address Mase's earlier and frankly unworthy concerns about whether I'm spreadin' myself too thin."

Hector glanced over. "Pray, tell." The boat was beginning to pitch as the sea roughened.

Beau lit a cigar. "My activities here make me necessarily absent back on Bone Key. My being missing, by now, has caused consternation. Particularly since, by this time, the city fathers will have learned the land that Buena Stella will sit on is now under the control of seventy or so members of the Bone Key's unwashed masses."

Brinke's brow furrowed. "Won't that make those city fathers at least a little bit angry at you, Beau?"

"They'll be murderous, sweetie," Beau smiled. "Particularly since our last night together back there—me and the Key West Cabal, as I call 'em—that last night out with them, I acted decidedly *non compos mentis*."

"So how does that play out?" Brinke asked. "I mean your feigned senility and the fact that all that land the cabal has been killing to make available is now out from under their thumbs?"

"Firstly, I have a confederate among the vipers," Beau said.

Hector winced. "Holy Christ, not Barnaby Nash? Please say it isn't him, Pap."

Beau scowled at Hector. "Mr. Nash, Brinke, by now will have confirmed for the Cabal that I'm slipping. And, consequently, he will have sold me down the river."

"Sold you out how, exactly?" Brinke licked her lips and stretched an arm across the back of the cabin window to steady herself against the boat's roll. "You really think they'll be murderous?"

"They will want me dead, no question of that," Beau said. "To recover Buena Stella, the Key West Cabal is going to have to pony up serious cash to buy out those seventy options."

Brinke said, "And why would those seventy investors sell? I mean, why should they do that for anything less than a small fortune?"

Beau said, "Barnaby and our confederates have quietly gone to those investors in advance of the cabal's word of my dementia and informed them my deteriorating mental condition has undermined any prospect of Buena Stella reaching fruition. By the same token, he's warned them against the fire sale you hypothesize. Told them to settle for no less than their original investments, plus twelve percent. My apparent death will further destabilize the development."

"And the Cabal members think they'll recoup that sum they pay the Key Westers via East Coast investors and rents levied against rich tenants," Brinke said. "I get it now."

Beau smiled. "Those East Coast investors are where I make my money. The operation here, such as it is, what with seed money, and hired help and paying out those local investors, well, that's break-even stuff, at best. I'll make my money on those Fat Cat bluebloods back east."

Hector, getting a bit worried about the weather, said, "And this bit about you ending up dead?"

"Human nature being what it is, the Cabal will be wanting me killed before I can engage in any other demented whim that threatens their bank rolls." Beau waved a hand. "Take a good look around, my children. Figure this time tomorrow, this pretty craft will be kindling."

Hector swiveled around. "What in Christ's name are you talking about?"

"There've been wires flying to and fro, my boy," Beau said. "Transmissions between that Key we left and the one where we're bound. Sheriff Hoyt means me dead, sonny. He's personally going to see to that when I get back to Key West." Beau looked at Brinke. "Or so Barnaby, who our Mase doesn't trust, kindly warns me."

Brinke sat up straight. "So how in God's name do we protect you, Beau?"

"You don't," Beau said. "Hoyt's going to succeed in slaying me, children. Or he'll think he has. When you run a game of this scale, often as not, you want to leave the playing field with yourself presumed posthumous. It neatly negates retaliation. To that end, I may need to take you up on that guestroom for a couple of days. Need to stay close to the action, but safely out of sight once I'm a corpse."

Brinke said, "And Consuelo?"

"Would you mind her moving in with me?" Beau smiled crookedly, blushing for the first time in Hector's memory. The old man said, "I mean, having Connie think me dead, that would just be cruel, wouldn't it?"

Hector said, "Cruel, yes, very. So, done. You're both in. What's the next move?"

"Someone obviously has to die in your grandfather's stead," Brinke said. She turned to the old man. "Isn't that so, Beau? Sheriff Mel's going to demand a body. So somebody has to die."

"They do and they don't," Beau said.

"Now you're just being a tease," Brinke said. She worried the old man might have something planned that would make her hate him, that Beau might actually kill somebody else to furnish a corpse.

Beau smiled. "Not a bit. No worries about the body, sweetie. I'm no killer."

"I'm going to miss that great hotel room of yours," Brinke said.

"Hell, me too. And I suspect Connie will miss it as well," Beau said, frowning. Then he smiled. "But I won't be paying that damned grandiose bill. Not a stingy penny. By now, hell, the tally must be beyond obscene."

"I don't like this," Hector said. "What if Hoyt gets lucky or doesn't play to your timetables? What if he decides on something other than taking you out while you're on your boat?"

Beau waved it away. "Got my man on the inside, I told you, Mase. There will be no pesky surprises."

# 32

Barnaby Nash cast a cigarette off the pier. "God, I hate this goddamn island," he said. "The heat and the damned humidity. The bugs. I thought Texas was one step short of hell, but this place?"

"Ain't all that different from Corpus or Galveston," Conrad Vogel said. Vogel was tearing up slices of bread and tossing them in the water, watching the gleaming tarpon feast on the morsels. "So how exactly does this play, Barn?"

Nash said, "I don't have direct access to all we need. Not yet. I have no firm grasp on all the strings in terms of the off-island investors. So at first we do things to plan. We let Hoyt blow up that boat. That puts me in the catbird seat with the local yokels, just as Beau has planned."

"Let the con play out, you're saying?"

"For a ways, sure," Nash said. "Then we put a gun to Stryder's head in a place of our choosing. Somewhere we can be persuasive as we need to be. We'll get what we need to take over the game and collect the cash from the big honchos back east and leave Beau's body for the Feds. We'll give 'em their dead legendary con man to brush off the heat and we'll retire in style. Let Beau's undoing be a first feather in J. Edgar Hoover's cap, maybe."

"What about the boy, Mase Lassiter? He's never liked you, Barn. Mase gets any sense you double-crossed Beau, and he'll come after you. After us. You know that. He'll slay us."

Nash took a breath, looking down at the swarming tarpon, he said, "I'm going to see Hector dead. I have to now anyway, as part of the con. I have to gain face by killing Hector."

"You've never killed anyone, Barn. You don't have the stomach for more than the jaw work," Vogel said. "You're not muscle, and you're sure as hell not a killer."

"That's why I need you to do it for me," Nash said. "Or at least to help me. You've always been the muscle in Beau's operation when it's been needed."

"Which is to say next-to-never," Vogel said, clearly angry.

"This is our one shot," Nash said. "We're never going to get another score like this one. I don't have the facility or the knack for planning the Big Con, and neither do you, pal. And Beau's getting old. He sees this as his last big touch, the one to go out on. Where does that leave us? I'll tell you exactly where. A year from now, we'll be selling fake lightning rods and bogus paint jobs in Dogdick, Texas, just like we were when Beau found us back in ought-eight. We'll be running the Pigeon Drop in El Paso and scrambling for nickels with roofing scams. That'll be our fuckin' sorry excuse for lives. Short games and chump change."

"But Christ, Nash, killing Beau? Little Mase?"

"Nah, we do this, Con," Nash said. "We have to. And you can get close to 'little' Mase like I can't. He's always liked you like he's never liked me, just as you pointed out. You'll get Hector out for drinks. I'll join you when he's a bit tight and maybe at least a little amiable. That's one thing in his favor – Hector has never been a mean one in his cups. We take Mase out before we make our play for Beau."

"What?"

Nash said, "We take Mase somewhere and put him down. We'll haul what's left of him out in a boat and drop him overboard with some lead in his belly. Wire an anchor into his torso to keep him down while the sharks and jewfish finish what's left."

"That'll be your contribution, then," Vogel said. "I ain't guttin' that boy. Hell, I've known Mase since he was just a tot. I like Mase, I like him fine. I've been like an uncle to that lad."

Nash leaned into his companion. "So you're out? Is that it? You know I'm right, Con! We don't have futures if we don't hijack this operation while we have a window. It's the last big score and I say let it be our score, not old Beau's. Hell, this game is close to collapsing under its own weight, anyway. Beau's playing too fast and loose across way too big a canvas. Nobody's ever dared a game this large and rambling. We need to get it reigned back in and the best way to do that is to give the big boys here on the Key just what they only think they're getting, one dead old rich man. We leave *Astor* blown to hell on his new big boat, so far as they know." Nash took a slice of bread from Vogel, tore it in half and tossed the two pieces in the water. "Hell, you don't see that old geezer gettin' us no big boats from that other game he's running, do you? Where's Beau's loyalty?"

"No, no, he surely hasn't done that," Vogel said. "This with Mase, though—I don't want to shoot him, and I ain't cuttin' Mase's throat or belly."

"Won't have to," Nash said. "I don't care if Mase does hate me. I watched him come up, too. I like him good enough, even if it isn't mutual. I don't want to slaughter Hec. I'm not cruel." Nash reached into his jacket pocket and pulled out a vial. "That's why we'll use this. It's a poison. Stuff is very fast, and not so painful, I'm promised. Mase'll think he has appendicitis or something, for about three minutes. Then it will be over. What passes for a mortician on this island here? He won't find it before he plants the boy."

Vogel shook his head. "Can't believe we're going to do this. Us and Beau, we go back, near on for all time."

"A long ways to be sure," Nash said. "So long that there's no prospect of any forward, anymore. Not with Beau. You know that's so. That's why we do this."

"Hell of a way to part company after all we've shared," Vogel said.

Nash stared at Vogel. "You're not up to this? Even after all I've said?"

"I'm fine," Vogel said bitterly. "Like you say, I've always been the muscle. The scale-tipper when a play queered. My hands ain't been clean in decades so don't fret about my conscience becoming a thing. It's you I'm worried about, Nash. I fear you losing your belly for this."

"Don't sweat it," Nash said. "I know the way it is. This is the last big score. This is our last good shot to make real money. The stakes are far too high for you and me to let this one pass us by."

# CRAZY FROM THE SUN

*"I suppose it is much more comfortable to be mad and not know it than to be sane and have one's doubts."*
—G.B. Burgin

# 33

Miguel checked the wall clock: half past nine. The sun should be long down. He massaged his temples with dirty-nailed fingers. He struggled up out of bed and then stood up, nearly falling over from the ensuing head rush. Groggy with sleep, he carefully parted the blinds.

*Darkness.*

*Thank God.* Light, any natural light—any at *all*—triggered paralyzing headaches. At least that had been true since last Christmas. Since he fell drunk and banged his head on the urinal behind Frankie's Saloon. He didn't remember the accident himself. Ones who saw the fall filled him in later, laughing and slapping thighs.

When he'd come to, the sun had been rising and they figured he'd been out at least five hours. None of them had thought to fetch a doctor as he lay there. They were too busy drinking and celebrating Christmas. He'd awakened with a knot the size of a softball on the top of his head, dead center, about four inches back from his hairline. A hell of a night for certain. He'd had his eye on some recent island arrival. A tall, black-haired beauty named Brinke or Twinke. Something like that. The booze was flowing with all that island Yuletide cheer. The cooze had been *so* fetching.

Had it been worth it?

Not since he'd taken that fall, he didn't think so. Not since he nearly bashed in his own skull because of some *puta* he never even gotten to touch.

The headaches began the day after the accident. Pain beyond description and the inability to long sustain a coherent thought. He'd lost his job at the cigar factory inside a week. Miguel couldn't abide the morning-into-afternoon light that seemed so harsh and that sparked such pain. The noise of the newspaper reader was like a hammer in his head as his once-sure hands fumbled with the tobacco leaves.

By week two, he'd begun to figure out that shifting his body-clock, staying up nights and away from the goddamn sun, gave him marginal relief the island sawbones seemingly couldn't. But that schedule shift cost him. Yes, it took plenty from him. It put him out of phase with the rest of the world and made a standup job impossible.

The head injury cost him Consuelo, too. She said he had changed. She said he'd gotten dark and gotten mean. She said he scared her.

He remembered the night Consuelo left him and what she said to him. "Something terrible's happened to you Miguel. You need to see a real good doctor. Better doctors than you can get here. We need to get you up to Miami before it's too late to fix."

As if he had the money for that. So Miguel lost his job and then lost his pretty woman.

There was no other thing for it now; he found his only relief in the dark.

And there were other women, the island was lousy with them. The women who lived on Bone Key, and the ones who just passed through as gawkers and loafers on holiday. Women he couldn't stop looking at as they sat in open-air speakeasies, wearing next to nothing and getting tight; wandering back to their hotels in weaving throes of giggles while supporting one another.

Those women had stalked his dreams since last Christmas. In those fevered dreams, the women took Miguel home with them, but things always seemed to end badly.

That threw him. Before the accident, Consuelo swore he was the nicest and gentlest man she had known. Of course she'd never noticed his wandering eye. She had never known about Miguel's tendency to follow that straying eye from time to time. Meaningless affairs, that's all they'd been.

But his dreams since the fall? His dreams were now always limned in blood.

Then Miguel began finding cast-off newspapers, browsing over them by candlelight. As he began to follow the articles regarding the Key West Clubber, Miguel began to sense how he must be spending his unremembered days, the time he thought he spent unconscious behind shuttered windows.

Miguel had an old baseball bat stashed in his closet. The bat was a relic from his days in Cuba when he, like every young Cuban boy, dreamed of going to America as a baseball player. For many nights after reading about the Clubber's latest crimes, Miguel sat with a candle, carefully inspecting his bat for traces of blood or flesh, maybe a tooth or bone shard imbedded in the scarred ash.

*Nada.*

So Miguel could only *assume* that he—the Key West Clubber—was more circumspect by day than Miguel seemed to be by night. By day, Miguel, *the Clubber*, apparently took the time after each of his attacks to clean his bat.

Miguel figured that each night he went out on the darkened streets looking for a woman—for Consuelo, probably, who else?—but settled for any poor woman he could find. He raped that unlucky woman, then he beat her to death with his club.

That must be how it was, terrible as it was to consider. He must be doing these killings.

And Consuelo: What had become of her? Miguel'd called a few times asking around after her, but nobody seemed to know where she was lately. She'd quit her job at the hotel they claimed. They said she no longer returned home to her mother's house. None of that was good.

But the bigger mystery plagued Miguel: Precisely what kind of monster had he become?

Miguel checked the clock. It was getting closer to ten. If he waited too long, the raucous Key West streets would quiet and then empty on him. The search would be longer and harder. And it would be that much more dangerous for him, toting that bat around as he roamed the night searching for luckless women to slay.

Resigned to his fate, Miguel sighed and rose. He picked up his baseball bat, reconciled to his presumed fate and that of some doomed woman he'd yet to meet.

# 34

They'd split up, for a time. Brinke and Consuelo sat on a restaurant's rooftop patio, watching tipsy tourists stagger through Mallory Square, all of them sweating copiously in the afternoon heat.

Beau was at a near-abandoned old dock, sitting vigil on his doomed boat. The old grifter was alone, awaiting Sheriff Hoyt's attack. Hector had insisted he stay with Beau, to guard his grandpap's back, but the old man adamantly ruled it out. "This ain't something new for me, Mase," Beau had said, looking a bit hurt by his grandson's concern. He'd added, "I've got death and resurrection down cold. Had me more lives than a litter of bastard cats. And I've outfoxed far worse than this Hoyt fella. He's a mere thug. It's the smart and quiet ones that can surprise you. Those are the ones you never want to risk sending to the river. Don't fret after me on account of this one, Mase. It's frankly insulting."

Brinke couldn't shake the look of fear that had put on Hector's face; put there by the prospect of the old man alone on that boat. It was the first time she'd seen Hector visibly afraid.

So, still-worried Hector was closeted at their home. He was feverishly working over his manuscript and trying to make up lost writing time to distract himself from the threat to Beau. In the late afternoon Hector was supposed to meet for drinks with an old crony of Beau's, a man named Vogel. Vogel was one of the old man's criminal confreres for whom Hector maintained some affection. As Hector had described Vogel to Brinke, the man was something like a half-assed uncle to Hector—having looked after the young Lassiter when Beau was taken to and fro in the world by some or another "Big Store" confidence game.

Left at solitary ends, Brinke had reluctantly accepted Consuelo's invitation for brunch. Their day together was something Brinke figured Beau was at back of because it solved several problems for the old man. First, it kept Consuelo out of the way but also under the protection of Brinke's gun she now carried with her always, hidden at the bottom of her purse. So far, Brinke had no sense that Consuelo was in-the-know regarding Beau's grand machinations.

Brinke also had no sense that Consuelo was aware of Beau's impending "murder" at Hoyt's hand. So Brinke was left to steer small talk in other directions.

Brinke and Consuelo tapped sweating mojito glasses and sipped. Brinke said, "I'm way too fond of these. They're Cuban, aren't they?"

"That's right," Consuelo said, sipping her mojito. "They're even better there, made with more sugar. A real threat to the figure." Consuelo pinched her own wasp waist.

"Any more of that stuff and I'd be bouncing off walls and big as a house," Brinke said. She patted at her mouth with a napkin. "You were born in Cuba?"

"Yes," the younger woman said. "We came over when I was twelve. It was getting too dangerous. If ten years pass without a revolution there, then someone gets to thinking it's time they started one, whether it's needed or not. And it's always reckless and sloppy. More civilians end up killed than anyone else. Most often women and children, slaughtered on the streets by pitched bombs and dynamite. The men very much like their explosives back home. *Muy macho.* Or so they think."

"You don't miss it, then? Cuba, I mean."

"I do, in some ways," Consuelo said. "Havana is quite beautiful in its own way. The old architecture and the dance clubs at night are wonderful. Maybe it's just my child's memory, but the women all seemed lovely back home. All of the men dapper and distinguished." Consuelo sipped more of her mojito. She shrugged bare shoulders and smiled sadly. Brinke was struck again by Consuelo's unselfconscious beauty. She didn't seem to take pains with her looks unless Beau directed her to, Brinke thought.

Consuelo said, "It probably is just my memory, because I look at the Cuban women in the cigar factories here on Bone Key, working in the coffee shops or back at the hotel, and they all seem haggard. Tired and sad. I wonder if I look like that. Or if I soon will."

"Never," Brinke said. "You don't. You won't, not ever. You're very, very lovely." She hesitated. "What are your plans? Has Beau spoke of anything once this other hush-hush business he's got going wraps up?"

Consuelo stared into her drink. "It's crazy, isn't it? Me and Beau, together? He could be my grandfather, easily. Yet he seems so vital, so full of life. I have a hard time thinking of him being the age he truly is." So did Beau, Brinke figured.

"I can understand it well enough, your attraction to him," Brinke said. "I find him very appealing. Quite attractive. I could fall for him. Has Beau talked of a future together?"

"He wants me to come back to Corpus Christi Bay with him," Consuelo said, half-smiling. "I'm thinking about it, though my mother argues against it. Because of Beau being so many years older than she is, of course. Older, even, than my father is."

"What are you going to do, then?"

"Go to Corpus Christi Bay anyway, I think," Consuelo said. "Beau's convinced this will be what he calls his swan song. He swears he'll make enough money from this enterprise of his to carry him the rest of the way in style, as he puts it. He wants to settle down." She blushed. "He even talks about a baby. He's still smarting from what happened to his only child, to Héctor's mother. He says it's almost insupportable to outlive your child. Beau credits Héctor with keeping him 'above water' after what happened to his daughter—that is to say, to Héctor's mother. Beau says every man goes to his grave more peacefully knowing he's left at least one child to carry on after him in the world."

Brinke nodded slowly, licking her lips. "You want that too? A baby?"

"Of course. I would like to be a mother, and many times over at that. But I worry about Beau being around long enough to help me raise a child, let alone children."

Brinke said, "Hector swears longevity runs on that side of his family. The Lassiters don't last as long—they tend to burn out rather than fade away. But Beau's father lived until just short of a hundred, a vital man almost to the end, according to Hec. The Stryders sound damned near immortal."

Consuelo said, "I bet it would distress Héctor, though, his *abuelo* becoming a father this late."

"Hec'd survive," Brinke said. She smiled. "Funny, Hec'd then have an uncle a quarter-century or so his junior. And I'd have something to tease Hector about from here to forever."

Consuelo wrinkled her nose, then smiled. "That would indeed be…strange. Well, either way, I am seriously thinking about going away with Beau. His home there sounds rustic and beautiful. It's right on the ocean. And with you two here in Key West, we'd have reason to visit, often. I'd still see my family back here."

Brinke raised her glass and they tapped drinks again. Brinke said, "To family, then."

"To that." Consuelo wet her lips. "I want to leave this island soon for another reason, too. Before Beau, I used to be engaged to another man. He was a good man, until he hurt his head. The wound changed him. I could never get him to the hospital to be treated properly. He was stubborn, like men from back home can be. Thought himself indestructible as Cuban men too often think they are."

"Not just Cuban men," Brinke said. "Is this man giving you some trouble?"

"I think he could, soon," Consuelo said. "Some friends back at the hotel say he's looking for me. He's asked after me there several times the past few days. Called at their houses. He was back at the hotel just last night, I'm told. My friends there told him I'd quit my job. Malú, thank God, had the presence of mind to say she thought I'd left the island. I've warned my family to tell Miguel—that's his name, Miguel Sanchez—that I've taken work in Miami, in order to build on her lie. If I'm lucky, perhaps he'll go there looking for me. Maybe he'll leave this place behind. It's terrible how he's changed."

So Consuelo was running another little con game of her own against this deranged ex, Brinke thought. Maybe the flimflam bug was catching. She said, "Have you told Beau about this man and about how he's looking for you?"

Consuelo ran her fingers through her thick hair. "No. Partly because I didn't think Beau would want to hear about any prior loves. Men never do, though they seem to delight in telling us about theirs. Partly, too, because Beau has so much going on right now. He doesn't need to take on my distractions."

"Beau needs to know," Brinke said. "Just so he can be prepared. So he might take precautions. If this young man is a serious threat, Beau needs to have an edge. Wouldn't do for this ex-flame of yours to run into you two on Duval Street or to cross paths in some speakeasy when this Miguel is in his cups and maybe that much more out of control."

"Put that way, yes, you're right of course." Consuelo signaled the waiter for two more drinks. She opened her own purse and Brinke saw a sheaf of bills. Beau seemed to be keeping Consuelo in high-tone style. She said, "These next two are on me, Brinke." She counted out some bills and then put her empty glass atop them to keep them anchored as the balmy wind whipped their edges. "I'll tell Beau soon. Thank you again for letting us use your place for a night or two. I hope it won't be an intrusion."

"No intrusion at all," Brinke said. "We're same as family."

Consuelo smiled, fanning herself. "Especially muggy today."

"We should go for a swim after this."

"I don't have a suit handy."

"Won't need one," Brinke said. "I know a place."

"You're sure? It's private?"

"Been no problems so far, which is to say, for months."

"Okay," Consuelo said. Suddenly she added, "It's not like Beau goes around unarmed, you know. He has this little gun up his sleeve. Tiny, but he says it gets the job done, 'in close.' It's attached to some mechanism that makes it come out if he raises his arm quickly."

"A derringer," Brinke said. "A holdout or gambler's rig. That's very...Beau."

Consuelo smiled. "It is, isn't it? He's seen to my protection, too." She glanced around, then opened her purse wider to show Brinke the revolver inside. "Beau gave me some lessons down at the beach this morning. Told me to point it like finger, to lay my index finger along the barrel when I point and pull the trigger with my middle finger, and to shoot for mass whatever that means. He was scared for me, he said, after reading this morning's papers."

"I haven't seen the papers yet," Brinke said. "And I think that mass means for the heart in this case." She had resisted looking at the newspapers, preferring to maintain the veil of ignorance she'd so come to enjoy while they'd been away from the Key, while they were running their crazy game against rich boat owners. "What's happened, Connie?"

"Three women were attacked last night," Consuelo said. "Two of them are dead. The other is in the hospital. They don't know if she'll ever wake up to tell them anything about who attacked her."

"How were the others killed, Consuelo?"

"Beaten to death with a baseball bat." Consuelo paid their waitress for their fresh drinks. "You know, the Key West Clubber again. So I have to suppose that dead man on your porch really was innocent, just like Sheriff Hoyt said in the newspaper."

Brinke held her tongue, wondering at the brazenness of Hoyt and the others to resume their old tactic of hanging their development-driven plans on some baseball bat-toting bogeyman.

# 35

Crouched behind a stand of mangrove, Sheriff Hoyt lensed the cabin of the Jolly Sally with a smallish pair of binoculars. There were two men in the ship's cabin. The man that Hoyt took to be Astor was seated and had his back to the window. The other man inside the cabin kept moving, not giving Hoyt a clear look at him. The other man clutched a broad-brimmed Panama hat and wore a white jacket. Because the other man was standing, Hoyt couldn't get a look at the man's face through the low-set cabin windows.

As Hoyt spied on them, the other man raised his Panama hat, a sign that he was evidently at last leaving. The stranger briefly blocked the cabin window. When the man moved, Hoyt saw that Cornelius Astor was still seated, though he'd turned a bit in his chair.

The other man left the cabin, his head dipped low and face hidden by his hat's brim. The man closed the cabin door, then, head still down, held a cigar up to his face and began turning a match at the cigar's end as he strode down the jetty and back to shore. The man in the hat strode jauntily enough; he moved like a youngish man.

The sheriff waited until the unknown man had disappeared into the trees, headed back toward the downtown, then Hoyt lensed the cabin again. It looked to him as if Astor was still sitting in a chair, his back to the window.

Hoyt slipped his small binoculars into his pants pocket. He picked up the two, heavy, sloshing cans of gasoline he'd hidden behind the shrubs. Crouching low, Hoyt moved toward the Jolly Sally—that silly ass name was stenciled on the stern of the boat facing the shore.

The sheriff's plan was simple but its results should be devastating, he figured. There was only one way in or out of the boat's cabin and that was through the single door opening onto the deck. The windows and portals were too small for a big man like Cornelius Astor to squeeze through, even if the old bastard was spry enough to try.

But Hoyt planned to set that door and the surrounding deck on fire, trapping the crazy old rich man inside to burn alive. Or, perhaps the geezer would still have enough lingering presence of mind to breathe deep and force himself to succumb to smoke inhalation before the flames reached him. Either way…

Apart from the two, five-gallon drums of gasoline and some gas-soaked rags, the sheriff had also brought along a flare pistol and a couple of flares. He'd use those to ignite the gasoline and set fire to the door. If the old man tried to make a break through that fiery door, then Hoyt figured to shoot at Astor with the flare gun. He'd fire on the rich bastard at pointblank range and incinerate him where he stood.

Hoyt figured any insurance investigators who pushed on beyond Hoyt's own inevitable investigation would be forced to conclude the demented old man had inadvertently discharged his flare gun into himself and the gas cans.

Boaters lived in fear of fire. Boat fires spread quickly and burned the hull down to the waterline with appalling speed, more often than not claiming the lives of the owners. That was particularly true if the fire occurred any distance from shore.

Hoyt had caught a break in that the old man's boat wasn't moored close by any others that might also catch fire. Hoyt had seen authentic boat fires leap craft-to-craft, spread by floating sparks, burning jetties or spilled and ignited fuel on the water.

The sheriff crept out onto the decaying pier and poured gasoline onto the Jolly Sally's deck, sloshing it toward the cabin door. The stench of gas was strong and Hoyt feared the old man might smell it and react before the sheriff could get the fire really going.

So Hoyt hefted the second gas can and slung it at the cabin door. He took aim with the flare gun and fired at the gas can laying on its side up against the cabin door.

The resulting explosion blew Hoyt off the pier and twenty yards out to sea.

When he surfaced, cursing, Hoyt's face and hands were stinging. Hoyt saw the boat was fully ablaze. He saw the silhouette of a burning body through one of the cabin windows. The old man had never even had a chance to stand up. The man in the boat's cabin was a charred blackness—a briquette in a hat. Hoyt figured Astor was likely killed by the initial explosion's concussion.

Plumes of black smoke twisted up into the sky, threatening to draw gawkers and eventually a fire crew.

Hoyt's ears were still ringing as he staggered onto shore. Gulls were reeling overhead. Hoyt realized he couldn't hear the birds. He couldn't hear the crack and pop of the yacht fire. He puts his hands to his ears. When he took them away his fingers were slick with blood. His face hurt and his fingers stung where they'd touched his ears. He held out his hands; they were livid red and already blistering. He felt his face again. All of it hurt and the flesh felt puffy and blistered. He couldn't feel his eyebrows anymore. Hoyt's lungs burned as if he'd breathed deeply of that first blast of fire. His chest and throat hurt with each ragged breath.

Watching from behind the trees, Beau ground out his cigar and slipped off his white jacket and Panama hat. He raised the Peacemaker he'd borrowed from Hector, watching the sheriff. Hoyt was screaming obscenities and crying in pain. Hoyt's face was badly burned. Some of the burns looked permanently disfiguring to Beau's untrained eye. Hoyt's nose and ears were bleeding. His hair was scorched back at least three inches from his natural hairline.

Beau figured it would be sometime before the sheriff could risk showing his face in public. Even wearing a hat and sunglasses, his wounds would be conspicuous enough to spark difficult questions around the Key.

Hoyt kept pounding at his ears, too, leaving Beau to think Hoyt was left deafened by the blast, at least temporarily. Served the dumbass right, Beau thought. Spilling ten gallons of fuel and firing a flare gun at the puddle at pointblank range? How did *that* come to seem like a good idea to Hoyt? Bastard was lucky he wasn't atomized by the explosion. Hell, a pelican flapping high overhead had been killed by the blast's rising shock wave. The bird now lay dead and burning on the ship's flaming bow.

Beau sighted in with his grandson's big old Colt on the sheriff's forehead. He was sorely tempted to pull the trigger— to put the son of a bitch Hoyt flat on his back for all day. And godddamn, with the cocksucker's apparent injuries, it would probably be an act of mercy. Hoyt was on all fours now, spitting up blood.

As he'd assured Brinke, Beau was no killer. Seventy years of ducking, dodging and conniving had taught him that much about himself.

But he should do it this time, he thought.

Every instinct told the old man that.

Beau wished he had allowed his grandson to come along after all. Mase would shoot the son of a bitch, no question of that. Mase wouldn't leave one for seed—selfish thinking but true. That boy wasn't averse to spilling evil blood, not one lick. As Mase was given to pointing out, he'd been made a state sanctioned killer during the Great War. It was a dubious privilege Mase seemed sometimes loathe to surrender in peacetime.

Hell, it'd taken little Mase to put the bullet in Grafton Lassiter that Beau should have seen to delivering himself. Goddamn Grafton: another man Beau knew he should have put down but couldn't find the gumption or edge to engage when there was still time. That grievous hesitation or failure of nerve cost Beau his daughter and remained a haunting weight he would shoulder to his ever-closer grave.

Left alive, what might Hoyt still cost Beau or some other who mattered to the old grifter? Hoyt was a murderous son of a bitch the world would be well shed of, no arguing that.

Beau's fingers twitched against the trigger of the old Colt. His flesh was damp with sweat. Beau tried to will himself to pull the trigger, searching for his edge.

Hector had warned Beau the old Peacemaker had a hair-trigger. The gun went off, quite suddenly, and Beau flinched as he felt the trigger's tension change and the kick. A clod of sand sprayed up behind Hoyt. The sheriff didn't react at all. It was then Beau knew the dirty sheriff was left deaf by the boat's explosion.

Hoyt stood, staggered a step or two more, then collapsed. If he couldn't shoot Hoyt as he was standing, Beau knew he'd never do the job when the man was out cold.

And Beau couldn't risk being seen alive by Hoyt or the others who would surely soon make the scene, drawn by the boat fire and that big black plume twisting skyward in the sultry Gulf wind.

Beau looked at the sheriff a last time. Hoyt had fallen close to the tide line. Maybe the encroaching waves would do what Beau couldn't bring himself to do—drown the son of a bitch. Call it an act of God if it went that way.

That prospect was surely a faint breath of comfort.

# 36

Hector stacked his typed pages in a wooden box to the right of his typewriter. He lit a cigarette and poured himself a couple of fingers of Cuban rum and splashed in a little warm Coca-Cola. It was his reward for a good morning-into-afternoon's output. Hector heard a key in the door. He pulled back the drape and peeked through the picture window at the porch. Beau was fiddling with the lock. His grandfather looked a bit drawn, even flustered. Hector called out, "Ease up, Pap, I'll let you in."

He opened the door and squeezed his grandfather's shoulder. "You okay?"

"Sure, Mase. I'm fine." The old con man wasn't convincing this once.

Hector said, "And Cornelius Astor?"

Beau put his hand over his heart, trying to act nonchalant and full of bonhomie. "Gone to his reward, just as planned. A real honest-to-Odin Viking funeral."

"You leave a body to be found?"

"Also as planned," Beau said. "Wouldn't be convincing without a corpse, Mase."

Hector made his grandfather a rum and cola, extra deep. Hector said, "Too much to hope that Hoyt is standing in for the late Mr. Astor?"

Beau took a deep swallow of his Cuba Libre. He said, "Christ, Mase, you overestimate my skills this once." He drained his drink and handed it to Hector for a refill. "Hoyt is still alive, I think. He's badly burned from nearly blowing himself up trying to blow me up. Seems deaf as a stone, and maybe for keeps. But I left him out cold out at the tide line. Retching blood and having pissed his own pants. Hard and far as he was thrown by the blast, I suspicion Hoyt's innards are more than a might jellied."

Hector said, "Think he's still there?"

"Now don't you go and think like that, sonny," Beau said. Remembering, he reached under his white coat and pulled the big old Colt from his waistband and handed it to his grandson butt first. "Thanks for the loan of the Peacemaker. Wish I had the stomach to use it."

Hector said again, "Think he's maybe still out there?"

Beau shook his head. "Don't even offer, sonny. Don't dwell on it. I've done enough of that for both of us. Besides, if Hoyt goes missing or turns up dead, it might poison the game. That might send his friends for a loop. This way, if Old Mel survives, he'll at least look like a screw-up of the first water." Beau drained his second drink. "Hell, maybe his dirty buddies will take Hoyt out when they see how badly he bungled my assassination. Makes him seem positively butter-fingered."

Hector stuck his Colt in the center desk drawer. He said, "So who exactly is dead back on that boat Hoyt torched?"

Beau slipped off his jacket and hat. He draped them over a chair. "That guy you electrocuted out on your porch the other night? Well, Karl Dale Rush's cadaver went missing over at the county icehouse last night. I had his body stolen from the morgue. Old Karl's beyond caring and so he was my stand-in with a white wig. The new Cornelius Astor. You already burned Rush from the inside-out, Mase. This is just evening out the damage, in a way."

Hector said, "Won't Rush's body's disappearance raise a lot of questions?"

"No, I don't think so," Beau said. "And that's all thanks to you, sonny. That little act you ran by the coroner a few days ago, playing a state investigator looking into the state's funeral homes because of missing bodies in Tampa, that was a happy accident I could truly build on. Something I could use to my own ends. Lest he lose his license, that Key West mortician-cum-coroner is going to be like a clam about that missing body. And hell, based on what you've told me, I don't think he'll be sharp enough to recognize Rush when the body rolls right back through his place in a couple of hours, looking like a burned up log."

"Perfect," Hector said. "You're right, he can't say a thing. Very nice. Very deft."

Beau held up his empty glass. "That's me all over on a really good day. I could use another drink. Maybe after I clean up, though. Consuelo leave a shopping bag around for me?"

"Poke's on kitchen counter, by the coffee pot," Hector said, making himself another drink. "What's in that bag, anyway?"

"My new face," Beaus said. "And no jokes when you see it in a bit, Mase."

Hector smiled and crossed his heart, sipping his Cuba Libre.

Hector was laying in a hammock, reading a collection of short stories. Hector was fifty pages in when Beau emerged from the house. He was wearing a guyabera shirt and white shorts. Beau had shaved off his moustache. He'd also touched up his hair. It was now light brown with silver wings over each ear. Beau squinted at the harsh sun. He pulled on some black sunglasses. "I'll be damned if I'll be crawling into some hidey hole," Beau said. "Need to have some mobility, hence the new persona."

"Looks good," Hector said. "Really. Shaves off decades. I'll start introducing you around as my dad."

"Not older brother?" Beau shook his head. "Don't date me by assigning me an age, and don't call me kin around these parts. Not yet anyways. Not until this game is done. For now, I'm Jimmy Ray Gordon, man of leisure and gentleman beachcomber."

"You look the part," Hector said. He raised his sunglasses to squint up at his grandfather without their tint. "But you do need to get a little sun on that upper lip. Can't remember a time you haven't had a moustache, Jimmy."

"Not since Hector was a pup," Beau said. "No pun intended."

Hector rolled out of the hammock. "Take a load off, Beau. Rest up. I've got a date to keep."

"But Brinke's with Consuelo," Beau said. "You ain't already stepping out on my Brinke, 'cause that'd be crazy, given the one you've landed. And I'd surely beat you for it. Ain't doing that, are you?"

"It's not that kind of date." Hector handed the short story collection to Beau. "Here, take a load off and expand your mind."

Beau said, "One of yours?"

"No, a friend's book. Fella back in Paris."

Beau slipped into the hammock and stretched out. He looked at the cover. "*In Our Time*. Any good?"

Hector said, "Figure you'll tell me after you finish."

"Got any beer around this place, Mase? In this heat, beer's the only thing to hit the spot."

"Got some contraband Hatuey."

"I'll take two bottles."

"Done."

"Oh, and Mase, who are you meeting?"

"Your old pal—the one I like—Conrad Vogel."

"No kiddin'? You're meeting him somewhere out of the way, I hope. Vogel's still in the game, still playing a vital part. You remind Conrad he needs to be discreet and stay in character."

Hector smiled. "I'll hassle him to that end for you, no sweat."

# 37

Miguel sat in the bathtub with the door closed and the shades drawn.

Sacred darkness.

But the quality of the dark was different from that of night. His headache persisted in this blackness. He had drained and refilled the tub at least three times and scrubbed his skin raw, but Miguel figured if he could see in the dark, he would still see blood in the bath water. He just couldn't come clean.

He thought about the three women he had killed. He couldn't figure out why he could still remember the three from last night. Why could he remember every bloody, wrong detail and every stomach-knotting sensation from last night, yet he couldn't remember any of the women who had come in the weeks and days before last night's killing spree?

And his memories of the most recent three and how they'd struggled to stay alive and what he had done to them despite their pleas? Those memories were terrible, all but unsupportable.

When would it become fun again? When and where would he find the enjoyment he must have previously taken from his wicked work in order to have continued to do it for so long?

The baseball bat rested against the sink. He had brought it into the bathroom with the intention of cleaning it.

But now he thought differently. He'd let the blood linger on the bat. He wouldn't need it much longer, he'd all but decided that.

Tonight, when the true dark settled and the pain in his head subsided, he'd go looking for Consuelo.

Maybe he'd also go looking for that woman from last Christmas Eve, the one he'd had his eye on when he had his stupid accident. What was her name? Brinke? Twinke?

Anyways…

He'd look for those two, and take any others he happened across along the way.

After he'd done all that he could, he'd walk down the middle of Duval Street, bloody bat in hand.

He'd walk down that busy street against traffic until someone called the cops to come and the police cut him down in a flurry of lead. Put out the sorry light for keeps.

Sweet darkness.

# 38

"You do this a lot? Just like this? And nobody sees?" Nude, Consuelo floated on her back, stroking her way back toward the shallower water where she could stand. Her feet settled on the bottom and she was in the water up to her chin. Anyone who happened upon them might still think she was wearing a bathing suit. Consuelo smoothed back her damp dark hair.

"I do this nearly every day," Brinke said. "More often than not, since he arrived, I do this with Hector. Probably others do the same here, but I've been doing it since Christmas and haven't seen anyone. Or maybe this is just established as my time." Brinke treaded water, glistening nipples and knees rippling the sparkling surface. "And, as I say, nobody has ever happened by."

"It's a wonderful break from the heat," Consuelo said. "But look over there, that's a storm forming way out there. Coming this way, likely. We should probably dress and head back to your place."

"Storm's headed to sea I think," Brinke said. "Or is it that you want to get back because you're worried about Beau? I'm sure he's fine, Connie."

The young woman shrugged. "Maybe he's okay. What makes you so sure?"

"If Hec was willing to stand aside, I have to think Beau can see to himself," Brinke said. "Hector dotes on that man and would never see Beau put at risk. The fact Hector stepped back from whatever stands to happen today leads me to believe Hector knows that his grandfather can handle himself just fine."

"Logically, yes, that all seems true enough," Consuelo said. "But I'm also turning into one big brown prune being in the water so long. I'm going to go dry off while's there's still a little sun left to do the job. Hate to walk home in wet clothes."

Brinke said, "I'll follow you shortly." She rolled over onto her belly and began paddling farther out to sea.

Checking the shoreline a last time, Consuelo carefully made her way ashore, crouched low, her arms crossed over her breasts. The young woman stretched out on a grassy patch in the spotty shade of an old banyan tree. The sultry breeze was already beading the saltwater on her damp, brown skin. Consuelo began wringing out her hair in soggy lanks.

Brinke was a tiny shadow on the gunmetal horizon, just a hint of motion from elbows and feet now and then.

As the sun dried her, Consuelo squinted at a distant silhouette staggering in the sun. She picked up her clothes and began to cover herself. The figure dropped to its knees, then arms hanging loosely at its sides, fell backward onto the sand.

She finished dressing and slowly crept toward the body on the beach.

There was a rustle behind Consuelo.

Brinke said, "My God, I think he's dead."

"He looks terrible," Consuelo said. "I wonder what happened to him. Who is he?"

"Pretty sure he used to be the sheriff in these parts," Brinke said, arms crossed to cover her breasts.

# 39

"Have another drink, Mase."

Hector held up a hand. "Thanks, Con, but I don't drink like that anymore. And not for a long time. More than had my fill tonight."

"Was a time when you was a kid," Conrad Vogel said, "a time just before you ran off after that spic bandit with Black Jack, when I thought you might get professional with your elbow bending."

"Those were rough years," Hector said. "That whole period between about age eight and fifteen? A hard dark ride for a kid."

"You mean after your daddy and what he did to your Ma?"

"That," Hector said. "Sure. What else?"

"You had us though," Conrad said. "You had your grandpa and me. Three of us had plenty of good times as I recall."

"It was great when Beau was around," Hector said. "But Beau had his various women. And he always had his other… we'll call 'em enterprises. Looking back, I expect Beau likes to think he was around for me a good bit more than he really was. Hell, I saw much more of you, Uncle Con."

Conrad nodded slowly, his head bowed. "Yeah, you and me, we was the team." He ordered himself another drink, slammed it back. He said, "You didn't exactly race back from the wars to hook back up with your old Uncle Con, did you, Mase?"

"No, I didn't." Hector couldn't meet the old man's gaze.

"Why is that, exactly?"

"I knew what was waiting for me back in Texas, I expect," Hector said. That was the truth. "Didn't know what I'd find in France or Spain, but I knew in Paris I stood a better chance of establishing myself as a writer. There's not exactly what you would call a literary tradition in and around coastal Texas. And Paris was so cheap at the time. You could live fine on nearly nothing there. Writers need to find such places and make 'em their own."

"How's that working out for you Mase? The writing, I mean. Much money in that business now that you've got a book out there?"

Hector smiled. "Beau put you up to asking that question?"

Vogel ran his fingers back through his hair. "Nah, Mase. But he's wondered aloud a few times. Guess Beau's curiosity sparked my own. I read that book of yours. Good stuff. I like the fight scenes. Those, and the woman in there. That a real dame of your acquaintance?"

"Maybe just a bit," Hector said. He checked his pocket watch. "This was real nice, Con. But I should be getting back now. I should be holding down the fort in case there are any repercussions from the morning's events. You know, in case Sheriff Mel is feeling vengeful over nearly blowing his own fool head off and the like."

Vogel checked his watch. Goddamn Nash was running late. Conrad wondered if maybe Nash had gone yellow after concocting this scheme to murder Hector and Beau. He said,

"One more, Mase, what do you say? My whistle ain't quite wetted yet."

A voice behind them called, "Hey there!"

Vogel sighed, said, "Hey there back, Nash." The slightly older con man looked a little pale and rattled to Conrad's eyes.

"Hiya, fellas," Nash said. "Need to get us over to a little garage, to a blind pig I found, to meet Beau. Little place off Whitehead Street."

Vogel said, "A blind pig? What's that?"

"That's island lingo for a speakeasy," Hector said. "Though they don't do terribly much to hide 'em 'round these parts. Here, prohibition largely isn't." He made a sour face at Nash and said, "Trouble?"

"Just complications, as you always have," Nash said. "Some unintended consequences you always get spinning out of a complex game like this one."

"But Beau's okay," Hector pressed, "isn't he?"

"Fine," Nash said. "But he needs some hands. I know you don't like this stuff, Mase. Christ only knows you have no stomach for the grift, but we need a fourth man, pronto."

Hector stood and stretched. "For Beau and Con, I'm in. Where are we headed?"

"We can ride over in my car," Nash said. "One of you will have to take the back seat, such as it is." Nash looked at Hector. "You're young and spry. Probably the most nimble, Mase."

"Screw that," Hector said. "I'm also the tallest. I'd never get my knees in that son of a bitch."

Vogel said, "Forget it, Nash. Just give me the address. Mase can ride over with me."

Beau stood naked under the stinging shower spray, the water smarting as it drilled into his sunburned upper lip.

The old man stood lathering himself up and assessing angles. Considering contingencies and trying to find holes or weak spots where his con could go crosswise on him.

It was always in the last stages of the game, as matters reached consummation, that Beau's nerves threatened to overcome him.

Hector had told Beau what Brinke had said, late night pillow talk the two young ones had exchanged following Brinke's first meeting with Beau. Impressions informed by her superficial estimation of the old man's demeanor and further fueled by Brinke's rather shallow sense of grifters and sharpsters and their world that she, like so many others, seemed to see as merely quirky.

According to Hector, Brinke admired Beau's perceived air of unflappability and nonchalance. His "grace under pressure" and his seeming ability to drift through life "untouched by grief or drudgery," or the "tedium of a typical day job" as she had put it.

Beau had been left to shake his head at that. His grandson had said, "I set her straight of course. I told Brinke that old chestnut you trot out from time-to-time about trying always to be like a duck, 'all smooth on the surface and paddling like hell underneath.' I told her about your long and dark nights of the soul and the strain of never drawing an uncalculated breath. About the wearying drag of eternal vigilance and spotting every angle. Thrust and counter-thrust. Oh, and about your copious ulcers."

Beau smiled bitterly. *Untouched by grief.* If only saying it would make it so.

Pretty Brinke had evidently forgotten about Mase's mother. And of course Beau hadn't burdened Brinke with stories of a lost wife or two, women lost before his grandson's time.

Still, Mase had called it about right, Beau figured. Always having to think three moves out. Forever sweating a thousand details and evolving tropes and gambits for contingencies rarely played out. Those efforts ground a man down over time.

Beau cut off the water. He hitched a towel around his waist and looked in the mirror, searching his pale blue eyes.

Had he thought of everything? Had he covered every conceivable contingency?

Too late to dwell on that now. In a few hours, he'd know either way. His biggest score.

He held up his right hand, staring at it. Rock steady. He'd see how it looked in an hour or two.

See if he maintained his nerves through the dark and surely bloody night that lay ahead of them.

# 40

Nash had paid to rent the speakeasy for the evening.

Speakeasy? A garage, really. The place was close and dank. It was littered with some tables and chairs arrayed around a homemade bar. The rough-hewn bar was badly out of plumb. Light came from a single overhead bulb, dangling naked from a cord slung over the rafters.

Hector checked his pocket watch. "When is Beau due?"

"Soon," Nash said. "Very soon."

Vogel was mixing fresh drinks. Nash looked to his partner. Hector's back was to Vogel. Conrad held up the vial of poison and nodded. He stowed the bottle under the bar.

Hector said, "What's keeping Beau, I wonder?"

"Vagaries. Maybe some stumbled-upon quick buck?" Nash shrugged. "Hell, he's your grandpap. You know him."

Vogel handed Hector his drink. Nash and Vogel tapped glasses. "To Buena Stella," Nash said.

Hector shrugged and tapped his glass against theirs. "Hell, why not? Bottoms up."

❦

Hector was on the dirty floor, no longer moving. He was curled up, his hands clutching his sides, his legs drawn up toward his chin.

Nash was visibly shaken, actually looked sick. Vogel stared at Nash, flexing his hands and wanting badly to swing on his partner. "Fast," Vogel said, curling his lip. "You said it would be fast and not terribly painful. Shooting Mase would have been quicker. And *kinder*."

"That was awful," Nash said. He was unable to look Vogel in the eye. He said, "God, poor Mase, screaming like he did, kicking. All doubled over. Poor, poor Mase."

Vogel slung his shot glass across the room, whipping it by Nash's ear. Vogel said, "I got no stomach to hear this from you now, you sorry son of a bitch. Now what's the fucking plan for Mase's body? Or did you even have one?"

"I dug a grave out back," Nash said, a little fearful of Vogel's demeanor. "Grave couldn't be very deep at all on account of the water table. But I've got a couple of bags of quicklime out there, too."

"Least you did that much," Vogel said. He bent down and pressed his palm to Hector's forehead, almost lovingly. "We are surely going to hell for killing this boy."

"Let me help you get that out back," Nash said. "I'll get the legs."

"Don't you touch him," Vogel said. "I'll see to Mase. Owe him that much, and we're running behind schedule. You best get out front. You meet and stall Beau until I can get Mase out back."

Nash flinched. He heard pure hatred in Vogel's voice. Not that Nash hadn't foreseen Vogel's backsliding and regret. Nash had planned for that: another shallow grave on the other side of the island and another couple of bags of quicklime awaited Vogel.

It was going to be a back-breaking night, Nash figured.

"Don't cover him up yet," Nash said, grimacing. "I was thinking we'd use the same hole for Beau."

Nash shifted uncomfortably as he saw the expression that suggestion put on Vogel's face. Nash decided it was best that he wait out front, lest Vogel, in his mounting rage, put one behind Nash's ear.

He looked back a last time as Vogel struggled to get Hector's body into position to lift it. Nash thought, *A dead man carrying a dead man.*

# 41

Miguel toted the bloodstained bat in a long duffel bag. The sun was less than an hour down and he still felt twinges of pain at the top and sides of his head.

The streets were still too busy for him to begin work. Or was it that the terrible memories of the last three attacks were still too vivid, ambushing him relentlessly as they had been doing?

Up the street, two slender, dark-haired women were walking slowly, just ambling, really. From behind one resembled Consuelo; even her dress looked like one Consuelo owned.

Someone tapped Miguel on the shoulder. It was Malú, a young friend of Consuelo's, an employee at the hotel where Consuelo had worked. Malú smiled uncertainly. She said, "You look unwell, Miguel. You look scared. What's wrong?"

He shrugged and tried to smile. "My head, it's still a problem until it gets darker. You know, from the accident last year."

"Where are you headed, Miguel?" The young woman smiled. "You looked like you had some purpose."

"No, not really."

"I'm sorry you're not feeling well, Miguel. Can I help you to a doctor?"

"There's nothing they can do," Miguel said. "They're a waste of time."

"The ones here probably are, I agree, but Connie thought you should see someone in Miami," Malú said. "Someone with some real skills. Did you ever do that?"

He looked at his feet.

"You should go north then, Miguel. You should give the better doctors there a chance to help you. There might still be time to fix you."

"Maybe," Miguel said thickly. "I hear Consuelo is there. That could be a reason to go."

Malú averted her eyes. "Not the right reason, man. Look, Miguel, Consuelo went north because she was worried about you and your problems. She went to get away from all that, to lose herself in the city. I'm sorry, Miguel, but it's true. You know that's so. She was worried about you. Worried about your problems."

"Afraid of me, more like," Miguel said.

Malú shifted weight to her other foot. She said, "Listen, I'm going to church to light a candle. My cousin is very sick. It might be a cancer." She hesitated. "I'm going there before work. Why don't you come along? Maybe on the way I can talk you into seeing a real doctor."

Miguel looked up the street, searching for the two dark-haired women he had been watching, looking for the one who dressed and moved like Consuelo.

Vanished.

He gave Malú another look, a long one. She was pretty, in her way. Huskier than Consuelo; less there in the chest and shorter, too. But pretty enough. Why hadn't he noticed before now? She wore a silver crucifix that caught the light. The cross caused his head to hurt from glints of metallic glare.

Then Miguel flashed on a vision of himself raping Malú in the church. Humping her on some pew and then beating her to death with the bat. Sex in a church? What kind of sin would that constitute? Venial, maybe. Certainly a lesser one against actually murdering someone in a church.

Miguel didn't want to do that to her. And maybe he wouldn't. Maybe he would go to church with her. He could light a candle for his lost self. He'd do that, then he'd walk away from Malú. Leave her safe there, alone in the sanctuary of the church. Show some contrition.

Miguel felt sure he could do that. He nodded and shifted the bag with the bat to his other shoulder. "I'll walk you a ways, Malú," he said. "I'll give you a chance to talk some sense back into my poor battered head."

Brinke leaned out from the recessed door front. "It was a reflection in glass," Brinke said to Consuelo. "Are you *sure* it was your boyfriend?"

"Ex-boyfriend," Consuelo said. "And yes, it was him."

"Well, he's gone now," Brinke said. Music from inside reached them, "Charade."

"That was Malú that Miguel was with," Consuelo said.

"She'll lie for you, Malú, I mean?" Brinke searched Consuelo's face. "Will Malú lie for you?"

"*Sí*. She will. She knows what to say."

"Good," Brinke said. "Let's get home, then."

# 42

Beau dropped his cigar stub and ground it out with the toe of his boot. He nodded at Nash. "Evenin'. What's up, Barn?"

Nash said, "Thought we should touch base. See you survived the sheriff's attack and none too worse for wear for that. It was nothing too terrible, I hope."

"Not for me," Beau said with a tired smile. The old man suddenly seemed his age to Nash. Beau looked, for the first time ever, old to Nash. Beau was clearly weighed down, distracted. *Vulnerable.*

"You look good, Beau," Nash said. "Losing that moustache shaves years off, it does."

"Right," Beau said dryly. "So I've been told. Let's have that damned drink."

They moved inside the garage and Beau looked around with a sour face. "This is quite the shabby little hole you found for our rendezvous, Barn. A man would have to be a world-class juicer to hang out in a place like this one every night."

"It is a come down from that fancy hotel suite you've been slumming in," Nash said. "But it's not so far a cry from the dump where me and Conrad have had to bunk on this rock."

"You sound bitter," Beau said, narrowing his eyes. "I don't like the edge in your voice."

Nash thought he sounded angry, too. He needed to tamp that anger of his down, for at least another few minutes. "I'm just god-awful tired," Nash said. "Maybe gettin' too old for this work." He stepped behind the bar. Nash saw the poison on the shelf and reached for it. "What's your poison, Beau?"

"I've got a choice?"

"Rum, rum and whiskey."

"Whiskey, then. Up to hear with rum." Beau stretched out a leg and rested it on an adjacent chair. "Where's Vogel?"

"He'll be here, I expect," Nash said. His eyes flickered to the back door. He needed to watch that skittishness of his, too, he thought. Nash didn't want to tip the old man.

Beau said, "I'm exhausted, I have to admit. Three overlapping Big Stores. Plus that boat dodge. Don't expect anyone in our line of work ever took on this much at once. Certainly not at my age. Think I'm actually glad this is the last."

Nash put Beau's drink on the table in front of the old man. He raised his own glass. "To endings, then."

Beau winked without smiling. "They surely do come. And all at once, sometimes."

"And not fast enough, other times." The old man was reaching for the glass when he heard a revolver click.

"Put it down, Beau. No time for that now. Besides, you don't want that shitty drink to be the last you taste, not with your refined palate." Vogel had entered through a back door. He was aiming an old revolver at Beau's head. "You and your goddamn expensive tastes."

Smiling crookedly, Beau said, "You got one strange sense of humor. You always have, Con'. But age is makin' it stranger."

Vogel said, "Figure we all wish, one way or another, that this was just a joke. But it isn't."

Scowling, Beau put down his untouched glass. "What the hell is going on? As gags go, this one ain't in the least funny."

Stone-faced, Vogel said, "You tell how it is, Nash. It's your goddamn play. You tell Beau what's happening here."

Beau looked to Nash. "Speak your piece, Barnaby. What is this?"

Nash said, "You may want a slug of that drink after all before you hear this, Beau."

Beau extended a finger and flicked over the shot glass. The contents crept slowly across the rough wood.

Nash looked at the spilled drink, sighed and said, "Now it gets harder. Bloodier." He looked to Vogel and said, "Just please do it, Conrad. Let's not stretch this thing out."

"Man asked you a question," Vogel said. "You owe him an answer. You owe him that much. Tell Beau how it truly is."

Nash said, "Okay. We're taking over the game, Beau."

"Taking over the game." Beau's damp forehead wrinkled. "What does that mean, exactly?"

Nash slammed back his drink, unable to look Beau in the eye as he said it. "We're going to kill you, Beau. Conrad and me, we're going to put you down. All these years working with you, backing your plays, now you're going to make this crazy big score and bow out and go off somewhere to live like some fuckin' potentate. Where does that leave Conrad and me?"

"You get paid for your part of the job, like always."

"Exactly," Nash snarled. "Paid chump bucks, like always. Paid like mere employees. Paid not near enough for us to retire on."

"Little late to be complaining about wages," Beau said. "Time to complain was, oh hell, decades ago I expect, don't you think? I'm the one made the plans, took the big risks."

"Well, then you consider what's to come no more than measures taken to recoup back wages owed," Nash said. "Now, that's just about enough talk, Boss, 'cause I don't like this much at all." Barnaby pointed at Beau. "For Christ's sake, Con, just shoot the son of a bitch and just be done with it, won't you?"

Shaking his head, Vogel said, "No, Nash, I won't do that." He forced the gun into Nash's trembling hand. "Your plan, asshole, so you execute it. No pun intended."

Nash sprayed Vogel with some spittle. He said, "Con, goddamn it, you know I don't do this stuff!"

"You're sure as hell going to do this one," Vogel said.

Vogel looked at Beau. The old hustler's expression was something between rage and nausea. Beau put his hands flat on the table and pushed himself to his feet. "You ain't truly gonna shoot me, Barn...are you?"

His hand was still shaking, but Nash raised the Colt and pointed it at Beau's head. Nash said, "This where you figure to work that persuasive mouth of yours, Beau? This where you figure to grift a grifter? I don't have to remind you, I know you coming and going. I don't have to tell you that I know your act and tactics. You can't work your tongue on me like that."

"You just did remind me and twice at that," Beau said sourly. "For Christ's sake, Barn, put down the goddamn gun and bolt. Do it now and I'll even give you a decent start. I'll do that much for old and better times' sake."

His chin trembling, his hand shaking, Nash said, "Enough talk. Sorry, Beau, but it ends right here, and right now."

Flinching, Nash pulled the trigger, three times in quick succession.

The hammer clicked each time. Three dry fires. Nash frowned and examined the gun; he saw the empty chambers and cursed.

His chin trembling harder now, Nash said, "Conrad, what the hell? Is this your idea of funny? Is this revenge for making you handle Mase?" Wild-eyed, Nash looked to Beau. "Con killed Hector, Beau," Nash said, not sure why he was doing it. "Con poisoned your Mase."

Vogel said to Beau, "Still think this was a good idea, Skipper? Still think it was good strategy allowin' Nash here talk it through? Letting him hang himself with his own words and actions? Letting him take his three shots just so you could really be sure?"

Beau looked stricken. He said, "Maybe loyalty is overrated. Thought I had to see if he'd see it through. Had to hear it myself, God help me. Or I thought I needed to. To give me a push, you know? But I surely don't wanna hear no more. What I've listened to has made me soul sick."

The back door of the garage opened again.

Hector had his Peacemaker drawn and aimed at Barnaby Nash's head. He said, "Let me handle this one, Pap. I owe the backstabbing son of a bitch for that wicked stuff he wanted to put in my drink. He meant to kill me with that poison."

White and shaking, Nash sneered at Vogel. "You bastard! You son of a bitch, you sold me out!"

Vogel shrugged. "Just as fast as I could. If you'd shoot Beau, if you'd poison Mase, well, how long was it going to be before you'd murder me to avoid sharing the cut on this big score tomorrow?" Vogel waved a hand. "Honor among thieves is more than just a cliché for our kind. It's critical to the game and to the life."

Hector said again, "You two go. I'll take care of Nash."

"Like hell you will," Beau said.

"That's why Beau has me," Vogel said to Hector. "I do that bloody heavy lifting."

"Not this time," Beau said. "I fix my own mistakes. This is surely one of my biggest and letting it walk away isn't good policy or near enough just. As the poet said, 'A dead body avenges not its injuries.'"

Beau straightened his arm and the derringer was suddenly in his hand. "If you know any prayers, Barn, now's the time for 'em." Beau took a deep breath. He said, "Funny thing. This morning I had a gun pointed at Mel Hoyt's head. I hated that son of a bitch Hoyt, that killer hiding behind a badge. Yet I couldn't pull the trigger on even as low as Hoyt. But here I am, about to shoot a friend, and you know what, Barnaby? My hand isn't even going to shake."

Beau looked over at his grandson. "Is that what you writers call irony?"

Hector nodded. Raw-voiced, unable to watch, he said, "Expect it'll do."

"You still with me, Pap? Gonna be okay?" Hector handed his grandfather a deep glass of whiskey.

"I can't believe he hated me, resented me, so much as to do that," the old man said. He looked at Nash's body. "We need to do something with that. To hide it somewheres."

Hector said, "Old Nash never struck me as a poet, or as much of a worker, but out back, he dug his own grave, so to speak."

"Sorry to keep you in the dark, Mase," Beau said. "I mean, not filling you in until the last minute almost."

"Just kept me convincing, I reckon," Hector said. He drained his glass, smacked it down on the bar, then wandered over to the body. Hector said to Vogel, "Give me a hand? I'll get the feet."

Beau said, "This has been one goddamn unsatisfactory day."

Vogel huffed, getting Nash up off the ground. He said, "I do get Nash's cut too, right?"

"Sure, and that's for starters," Beau said, watching them haul the body toward the back door. "It's the last score and I always meant to do right by you and that Judas there. The miserable, greedy son of a bitch. Goddamn him anyway for making me do that to him. Goddamn him to hell and gone."

# 43

Brinke was sitting on the couch, holding Consuelo's hand. The younger woman was asleep. Brinke held a finger up to her lips to shush them.

Beau tossed his hat on a chair. "She okay?" he said softly, "What's wrong with her? What's happened?"

Vogel whispered to Hector, "That's the boss' new lady? She's awful young."

"Consuelo is her name," Hector whispered back. He opened his arms and hugged Brinke close. "What's up?"

"Just a long day," Brinke said to Beau and Hector. "Old ghosts. Less than a nothing."

"By the way, I think Sheriff Hoyt is dead." Brinke averted her gaze, drifting back in her mind's eye to the beach. "A man came across our swimming spot. If it was Hoyt, he was badly burned. Disfigured."

Beau shot Hector a look. Hector thought his grandfather had just about hit the end of his tether hearing this latest revelation. He thought about what Beau had told Barnaby about having Mel in his sights but not having the resolve to shoot him. He figured Beau would beat himself up to the grave after this revelation of Brinke's; if Hoyt *hadn't* been a walking dead man?

Hector said, "Where's Hoyt now?"

"On the beach, I suppose." Brinke searched Hector's eyes. "He's definitely past any help if that's really your thought."

Beau took in a deep breath, said, "Hoyt's body, it's still out there you say?"

"Unless someone has happened upon it," Brinke said, "but I don't expect that's too likely to occur before sunrise."

Beau licked his lips. "Hoyt disappearing would arguably be more effective than his body cropping up, particularly mauled as it is because of his botched assassination attempts. Tomorrow the net closes on his cronies. Would be good to have those fat cat locals off-footing and fulminating as the trap springs. Hoyt disappearing, after the reporter has also gone missing, would surely serve that aim. Give 'em something diverting to stew over."

Hector said to Vogel, "Let's you and I see to that. At least we know a place to put Hoyt's body."

"There was half a bag of quick lime left," Vogel said. That raised Brinke's eyebrows.

"I'll come lend a hand," Beau said.

"We've got it covered," Hector said. "Stay and keep Brinke and Consuelo company. Stand guard over them." He handed his grandfather his Colt, butt first. "Just in case," Hector said. He cupped Brinke's chin. Hector kissed her. "I'll be back fast as I can."

Beau locked the doors behind them. He said to Brinke, "What a ghastly day."

"Indeed. I need a shower," Brinke said. "Haven't had a chance to clean off all the salt from our swim, you know."

"Go, bathe," Beau said, his voice thick. "After, well, we'll talk. I mean, as the day's given me something new to brood over."

Brinke arched an inquiring eyebrow.

Beau said, "I speak of killing."

Brinke chewed her lip, said, "Frankly, I know something about that myself. Hector too, of course. The wars… the ones declared and otherwise."

"Today was my first," Beau said.

The old man suddenly didn't look so well to Brinke. She said, "I'll postpone that shower. Let's pour a couple of strong drinks and have that talk now, Beau."

Vogel tamped down the dirt with a rusty shovel blade. "What a terrible day this has turned out to be, eh, Mase?"

Hector wiped down his hands with a rag. "We've all surely had better."

"Hope Beau's gonna come through okay, after handling Nash, I mean."

"I know what you meant. And I hope so, too."

Vogel tossed the shovel aside. "You okay, Mase? After seein' it, I mean?"

"I've seen plenty to unsettle me worse, Con."

"But not like that, Mase. You've not seen Beau doing *that*."

"No, not that. But Beau had grounds, and the son of a bitch meant me dead, too."

Vogel gestured at the grave. "Funny, isn't it? I mean, old Nash spending forever with the law like that."

Hector shook his head. "That son of a bitch Hoyt wasn't any flavor of law I recognize."

Vogel grunted. "Then I guess it maybe ain't so funny after all."

Miguel shook off a chill as he waited for Malú to finish at the altar. The light in the church was low, but it still made his head throb. He closed his eyes and massaged his temples.

After a time, Miguel felt a hand on his shoulder, shaking at him. "Miguel, are you awake? Are you unwell?"

"The light," he said, "it hurts my head."

Malú said softly, "Light always hurts, since the accident?"

"Always. Almost any light. And I think it's getting worse."

Malú sat down next to Miguel and took his hand. "We need to get you to Miami. You need to see real doctors. Ones who work in hospitals and know things. You should go tonight. Leave while it's dark. You could ride in the dark on the trains and boats."

The notion appealed to Miguel, particularly since he'd all but decided to go there in pursuit of Consuelo. But he had no money; he'd already received several warnings from his land-lord that he was about to be set out.

She said, "Is there anything much to prepare?"

"Hardly anything," he said.

"Then you should go home now and pack. Do it while it's still dark. Get ready tonight. Arrange your passage, then leave tomorrow after sunset. That's how you should do it."

"Maybe, yes," Miguel said. He flashed on those three bloodied women and shuddered.

"What was that, Miguel?"

"Just a chill. No big thing."

"Then you'll do this, Miguel? You'll get yourself help? Please?"

"I think I will. But I have to scrape together some money first."

"I could lend you a little," Malú said. She figured when she told Consuelo she had talked Miguel into leaving the island, Consuelo could get some money from her new rich old boyfriend to pay for Miguel's trip. She said, "Go now, Miguel. Go home in the dark and pack. I'll try and get some money together and leave it at the hotel for you to pick up tomorrow night."

Groggy from the pain in his head, Miguel hauled himself up off the pew. His knees cracked and he saw spots. "I'll do that," he said thickly. "I surely will do that. And thank you." Resting hands on the backs of the pews to steady himself, Miguel walked down the aisle on shaking legs.

Malú saw the duffel bag under the pew where Miguel had sat. She reached down and grasped the bag by a raggedy strap. As she lifted it, the handle of the bat slid through a tear in the canvas. The grip of the bat appeared to be stained with dried blood. Malú shoved the handle back through the hole. She looked up and saw that Miguel was watching her. She wasn't certain whether or not he had seen her push the handle back through the hole.

"I almost forgot," Miguel said. "Thanks for remembering for me."

Malú forced a smile. "What's in there, Man? It feels awfully skinny." As cover went, she thought she had done okay.

Miguel said, "Fishing rig."

"You fish at night?" She almost winced. Idiot: The objective was to get away from Miguel now, not to badger or stir him up.

"Loaning it to a friend," Miguel said, watching her.

"I'm going to stay on here for a few minutes," she said. "Say another prayer for my cousin. Will you be okay to get home with that head of yours?"

"Be better when I'm outside in the air and dark," Miguel said. "And, actually, it's feeling a bit better now. Now that I have a plan. Thank you for talking to me. For convincing me to make the trip."

"*De nada*. I hope it all works out okay."

"*Adios*, Malú."

"*Adios*, Miguel."

She turned and walked back to the front of the church. Crossing herself, she knelt. She listened to his uneven steps, retreating down the tiled aisle. Malú sighed when she heard the doors close. She slowly turned around to confirm he had really gone.

Malú crossed herself again as she looked back at the empty church. She loitered a while, giving Miguel time to get back across the island. To pass time, she leafed through a hymnal, humming the tunes and fingering the silver crucifix hanging around her neck.

When she figured twenty or more minutes had passed, she gathered up her things. She walked down the aisle as quietly as she could and cracked the door of the church and peered out. There was no sign of movement, just a soft breeze and the trill of crickets.

She slipped out through the door and trotted down the steps, crossing swiftly to the other side of the street. She had hoped for other pedestrians, but the street was empty; the lights off in most of the houses.

Malú half-ran, half-walked to Duval Street where she knew there would be some bustle. She checked the clock in the window of the jewelry store. She had fifteen more minutes before she was to begin the night shift at the hotel.

The hotel lobby was quiet. Malú nodded at Kevin, the desk clerk. He said, "Everything okay, doll? You look flustered."

"Seems okay," she said. "Just need to change, then I'll relieve you."

The employee's changing room was located between the men's and women's restrooms. The lights were off inside the changing room. Malú frowned and groped her way into the room, feeling her way along the wall, moving her hand around looking for the light switch.

Malú felt a slight gust of air and then there was an explosion of light as she felt the bones in her face break.

Miguel said softly, "I'm so sorry, *chiquita*, but I saw what you saw. And I need money. First yours, then all the money your pass key to those rooms upstairs can get me." He raised the bat. "I always have liked you Malú. Please, believe, I wish there was another way." He swung the bat straight down, using both hands. He blinked back the spray of blood.

"I don't ever want to touch a shovel for that nefarious purpose again," Vogel said.

They were walking along Duval Street, passing a flask full of rum.

Hector said, "You planning on retiring like Beau?"

"Sounds like I could make enough tomorrow to maybe do just that. I live cheaply…not like Beau."

"So sit on your stacks of money and don't kill anyone else," Hector said.

"I'll give it an honest shot," Vogel said. He reached over and took the flask from Hector. "Retirement? Beau always insisted he never would go that route."

"There is retired and there is retired," Hector said. "Beau says he'll never run a Big Store con again. But the small opportunities? I have a hard time seeing him passing those by."

Vogel pointed at an open-air bar. "Keep hearing this place touted. Let's have a drink here."

"Not now," Hector said. "Sorry. After the day Brinke and Beau have endured, I need to get back there with them. Need to go home and pick up the pieces."

Someone slammed into Hector. Perturbed, Hector said, "Hey pal, it's a wide sidewalk. Watch your fuckin' step." As he said it, Hector felt for his wallet, checking to make sure it wasn't some hustle. Everything was where he had left it.

Miguel held up his hands, smiling. "Easy, *hombre*—my fault, entirely. I was distracted." A strange grin. "I'm happy!"

Hector looked Miguel over: a fairly well built young Cuban, probably about twenty-four or maybe twenty-five. The young stranger's eyes were crazed, Hector thought. Not drugs, and not liquor, he figured, but genuine dementia. The man was toting something inside a long canvas duffel. Hector said, "What do you have to be so happy about, *amigo*?"

"Going to Miami, to find my girl," Miguel said.

"Ain't she the lucky gal," Hector said.

Miguel's smile ebbed. "You being smart-mouthed? Looking for trouble?"

Hector waved a hand, dismissing Miguel. "I'm all troubled out for the day, really. Push on, pal. Have yourself a time up in Miami."

Hector watched the man go, then looked at Vogel. The old grifter had a hand under his coat, apparently prepared to draw if things had soured to violence. Hector said, "That necklace that fella was wearing, the crucifix, it looked like a woman's. And was that blood on the cross?"

Vogel let go of the butt of his gun and drained the flask. "Blood and crosses? *Feh.* They go together like winos and paper pokes."

Hector said, "Goddamn, Con, good looks and you're a philosopher, too?"

# 44

Hector had one foot braced on the porch rail, pushing the swing slowly back and forth. Brinke's legs were tucked up under her and her head rested on his shoulder. The swing's chains creaked and the tall old palms cracked and popped in the harder, warm wind. He said, "You've spent some time with him. Is Beau okay?"

"I believe he's more shaken up by what he seems to think of as Consuelo and I's near miss with Hoyt than anything he's done himself," Brinke said. She stroked Hector's hand. "He really cares for Consuelo, I can tell. We were in no danger. Though he was awful to behold."

Hector stroked her hair. "Hush. I don't need to know more." He really didn't. Hector had disposed of the body after all. He had some definite notions about what the explosion had done to Hoyt.

"Beau couldn't look me in the eye for quite some time," Brinke said. "He said if he'd had the courage to shoot Hoyt this morning, Consuelo and me, well, you know. We wouldn't have seen that. Could've, should've and if only."

"I surely get it." Hector tipped his head back and ran his fingers through his hair.

Brinke said, "You know, I'm famished, Hec. Got a funny metal taste in my mouth. Like I've been sucking on pennies or something."

He smiled, his fingers rubbing the soft down on the back of her neck. "You're always hungry, darlin'."

"True. But I have a killer craving now. And hunger pangs from hell."

"What do you crave?"

"Not sure," she said. "My taste buds will know when I see it."

"Or when it's on my plate," Hector said.

Brinke punched his arm. "I'm serious, I need to eat."

"Well, we best get going while there's still a few joints open on this wicked rock."

Brinke said, "As a dead man, it is wise for you to be out and about so much?"

"Hoyt was the only one of that so-called cabal who knew me on sight."

# 45

Beau was sitting in the porch swing when Hector and Brinke returned from their late dinner. He raised a hand in greeting. "Connie's sleeping." Sour-voiced, he added, "I couldn't."

"Would surprise me if you could sleep, Pap." Hector parked his butt on the porch railing and shook out a cigarette. "Might even worry me."

Brinke sat down next to Beau and patted his knee. She said, "You should really try to sleep, anyway. Big day tomorrow, isn't it?"

"Not for me," Beau said. "Had to slide someone in last minute to fulfill Barnaby's planned role, but tomorrow's more about big chickens coming home to roost for those crooked politicians, realtors and the like. Seems someone tipped the state attorney general's office that the mayor and members of his administration, and a councilman, here or there, have plundered the city coffers in the past couple of days to fund their illegal and self-enriching real estate speculations. They blew the city's funds in a big real estate boondoggle. The realtor from Last Key has also been turned into the state licensing boards. Off the books, so the money can't be taken away, your wedding 'guests' have all been issued their checks making them all whole on their original investments with more added in, just as planned."

"Paid back with their own tax dollars, it sounds," Hector said.

"At least they get the money back," Beau said. "Better they spend it than some goddamn politicians. They earned it. And you well know my mind on confiscatory taxation, Mase. Like you, I think less government is the best government." Beau closed his eyes and propped his boots up on the porch rail. "And in Texas and New York, my other endeavors, the schemes I stand to make real money on for myself, they reach fruition."

Brinke smiled sadly. "So it is over, then?"

"Far as I can tell," Beau said. "The so-called Key West Clubber—in all his parts—has been dismantled. Yeah, I think we're done here. Not bad for just a few days' work. Just need you two down at Mallory Docks tomorrow morning. Ten would do fine."

Hector raised an eyebrow. "What's that about?"

"It's a surprise, but a good one, I hope," Beau said. "Something I think you'll like."

Brinke said, "Can't wait. But now I'm exhausted. Don't you two stay up much later." She kissed Hector's cheek. "Particularly not you, Hec. We're newlyweds, remember?"

Hector slipped into Brinke's vacated seat. "You okay in your head, Pap?"

"What, you mean because of Nash?" Beau waved his hand. "Better'n you'd think, Mase. But in a way, he is at the crux of the way my mind is turning things over. Like I said earlier, I had Hoyt right there in my sights. A low bastard and killer who had just tried to burn me alive. Yet I couldn't pull the trigger on that son of a bitch. Yet, strangely, I could pull the trigger on Barnaby who I've known for, what, a quarter century or more? How could I do that to Nash but not to Hoyt?"

Hector lit another cigarette. "You really having trouble coming up with an answer to that one?"

"Oh, I've got a theory," Beau said. "I just don't like it and what it says about me."

"What's the answer you arrived at?"

"Ego," Beau said. "Nash hurt my pride, betraying me like that. He hurt my pride and I put him down. What the hell does that say about me?"

"You're glossing," Hector said. "Nash was going to poison me, and you too, before he settled on having you shot. I always hated that son of a bitch."

"That you did. Thanks for not saying I told you so."

"Wish you and I had some more time together," Hector said suddenly. "So much going on the past few days, feel like we've hardly seen one another." It hung there between them, unsaid: *How many more chances to be together like this are left us?*

"We'll have time. And, soon enough, we'll have the easy means to visit one another."

"Explain that," Hector said.

"Tomorrow. Then Connie and me, we'll probably head out about noon for home."

"So she is still going back to Texas with you?"

"So it seems." Beau slapped Hector's knee. "Don't worry about me, kid. I'm resilient. You know that. I always survive." Beau slapped Hector's knee. "You can knock off, Mase. Your lady's waiting."

"Yours too," Hector said. "You going to marry Consuelo?"

"You don't approve?"

"I've got no problem with it whatever, Beau." Hector smiled. "And would it matter if I did?"

"Well, I do incline toward marriage," Beau said. "Still got my health and my mind's sharp. She makes me happy, and the conversation's richer than I suspect you might think. How many more shots at good companionship do you reckon I get in this life?"

"I said I'm all for it." Hector heard sirens. He sat there grim-faced, listening.

Beau said, "Fire department?"

"Nah, different kind of siren," Hector said. "Cops."

The old man shook his head. "Coming across the ocean, I'd expected to find this a much quieter place."

"There's no end to the bar fights or the domestic strife," Hector said. "But at least thanks to you, there won't be any-more set fires. No women beaten to death with baseball bats in the name of commerce."

The old man shook Hector's knee. "You can be happy in this place, Mase? Really hasn't exactly proven itself safe, has it? No more than Paris did."

Hector put out a hand. "If you ever find a truly safe place, Pap, you make me your first call."

His grandfather took Hector's callused hand in his own big paw and Hector drew the old man up. He said, "Just us now, so I can say it the way I want to. Thank you Paw-Paw. Thank you for everything." Hector hugged his grandfather hard and the old man patted Hector's scarred back.

"I'd not have had you seen me handling Nash like that," Beau said. "But I am so glad to have gotten to see you again, even under these bloody circumstances. You make me proud and I do admire you so, Mase."

Brinke rubbed the side of her hand, trying to work out the teeth marks. "First time since Paris, and those thin walls there, I've had to bite my hand," she said.

"Good news that," Hector said. "It implies you've been chaste during our year apart."

"Doesn't necessarily mean that," Brinke said with a wicked smile. "Just means this is the first time since then I couldn't be loud during lovemaking."

Hector said, "Tomorrow you can be loud again. Loud as you please."

"Loud as you please, is more like it," Brinke said. She rolled onto her belly and kissed her way down his neck then bit at his chest. "But do count on me being very loud." She kissed the place where she had nipped at him. A long pause, then, "Where'd you hide Hoyt's body?"

"I was much more enjoying talking about sex," Hector said. He stroked her raven hair back from her face. "Fact is, he's in the ground. Let's leave it at that, just in case. Problem with Key West is you can't bury 'em deep. A hard rain comes along? Well, then it's best you don't know much."

"What's this surprise of Beau's?"

"Really haven't a clue."

"You sound so tired, Hec."

"Weary to the bone. You?"

"Same."

Hector urged her back up the bed to stretch alongside him. She rolled over onto her side and he pressed up against her, despite the heat, close up against her long back and the curve of her hips. He kissed between her shoulder blades and could tell from the lack of tension in her skin that Brinke was already asleep. He pulled her closer, pressing his lips to the back of her neck. Hector thought about the prospect of spending every night for the rest of his life with her, of never having to be alone in bed again. Together forever.

Smiling, he pulled Brinke closer.

# 46

Hector had somehow slept through the fighting
cocks again. Then he realized he heard rain and
figured the gray skies had kept the birds' screeching to a
minimum. The bed was empty, just a warm spot where
Brinke had lain.

The bedroom door opened and Brinke, dressed in her
short little Asian robe, padded in, ashen-looking. "I was just
sick."

"Virus? Maybe the flu?" That latter terrified him—as it
did everyone of his generation. There were points when more
of his fellow soldiers had died from flu than bullets.

Then he thought about what they had eaten the night
before. Well, really what Brinke had eaten. As usual, she'd
made short work of both of their meals. He said, "Food poi-
soning?"

"No, I'm okay now," she said. "Just a one-off event I
guess." Brinke curled into the bed and pulled the sheets up
under her chin. "Just need to lay here a minute until my stomach settles."

"You're sure you're okay?"

"I'm fine Hector. I'm just fine."

Brinke and Hector sat in the shade of a shanty bar, awaiting Beau and Consuelo. Hector ordered himself some coffee with Irish whiskey stirred in. Brinke declined liquor. "I don't think I should just now," she said, a look on her face that Hector couldn't read. When the waitress turned her back to them to make Hector's spiked coffee, he saw that Brinke massaged her breasts, a pained expression on her face.

"There you are!"

Beau was dressed in white deck pants and a white shirt. He also wore a yachtsman's cap.

The old grifter hugged Brinke and clapped Hector's back. Embracing Consuelo, Hector said to his grandfather, "Some dashing look you've got going there, Beau," he said. "Look like you're ready to run rum or smuggle immigrants from Cuba."

"Might could do just that," Beau said, grinning. He held up a bag and pulled out a second boating cap. He tossed it at Hector. "Here you go. Got to look the part now."

"I don't wear hats like these," Hector said, fussing with it.

Brinke, looking a bit more herself now—her color back—took the hat from Hector and adjusted it to a rakish angle on her own head. "What's this about, Beau?"

The old man wrapped an arm around Consuelo's waist and said, "Follow us."

They walked down the docks until they came upon two boats moored bows out. Beau said, "The name has been changed—hope you two like the new handle—but that's the boat you two enjoyed so much our last day up the Keys, running our little yacht scam." Beau handed a set of keys and sheaf of papers to Hector. "It's yours. Call it a belated wedding gift." He pointed at the other boat. "That one's mine. It's all packed, and Connie and me are going to break her in making a run back to Corpus here directly. This will make our visits to one another that much easier."

Hector was speechless. He looked at the stern. Stenciled there was:

DEVIL MAY CARE
Key West, Fla.

Beau grinned. "You like it, Mase?"

"We love it," Brinke said. "It's an extraordinary gesture. The best present ever."

"Hardly," Beau said. "You've got to keep up the payments on care and gas and whatnot. It's an expensive hobby I'm told. So you two best stow plenty of paper and your typewriters below decks. Gonna have to write plenty of books to keep her moving."

Hector started to say something and then saw Conrad Vogel tromping down the jetty. Con was waving a newspaper.

Beau said to Vogel, "What's up? Thought you'd be on your way, Con. Things not go to plan?"

"Everything went to plan," Vogel said. "Which is why I can't figure out this headline." He held up the paper with its boldface scream type:

CLUBBER KILLS WOMAN IN POSH NEW HOTEL

Brinke took the paper and pulled on her glasses. She began to read aloud.

Brinke hesitated when she read the name of the victim: "Malú Paz, age twenty-five."

Consuelo screamed, "No!"

Beau gathered her into his arms. "This doesn't make sense," he said.

Before she could check herself, Brinke said, "Miguel…"

Consuelo looked up, stricken. Beau caught it, said, "Who is Miguel?"

Brinke finished with, "So we saw Miguel with Malú yesterday, well, last evening, really. Couldn't have been long before she was…" The word murdered hung there in the air, implied.

"Important thing now is he's been looking for Consuelo," Hector said. "And Malú was attacked in that hotel where you both worked." Hector put his hand on Consuelo's shoulder. "Describe this Miguel to me. What's he look like?"

Hector listened then looked to Vogel. Hector said, "The guy who ran into me on the street last night, remember? He must have been leaving the scene of the crime. That bag he was carrying—it was long enough to hide a bat inside. And remember, he was wearing that necklace I said looked like a woman's, a silver crucifix?"

"Malú had one of those," Consuelo said. "Miguel never wore one."

"Well, he was wearing one last night," Hector said. "It was stained with blood."

Beau said, "Let's go hunt this son of a bitch!"

"No way," Hector said. "This is my territory. No schemes or glib tongues are going to carry the day in this crisis. He's hunting you two, now. You said that boat of yours is packed. You two get on it and get across the Gulf. Weather looks clear and you can get some real distance from here. You two go ahead on. I remember what this fella looks like and it's not a big island. Just need his last known address and some of his haunts, Connie. You give me those, and I'll see he doesn't bother you again. I'll see he doesn't bother or hurt any woman ever again."

Beau said, "Ain't my nature to run like this, Mase. Not and leave you holding the bag on this bloody mess."

"It's not like that," Hector said. "You see to Connie. She's in the greatest danger now. So you two skedaddle. I'm going to stop home and pick up my Colt and then go hunting. You in Con?"

The old man said, "Hell, why not? I'm rich and retired now and my time is my own. Sure, I'll ride shotgun, Mase. What this bastard did to that gal, it can't be allowed to stand."

Hector said to Brinke, "Don't go home, just in case, darling. Stay here on the boat. You should be safe here."

Brinke shook her head. "Actually, I've got a doctor's appointment. It's on the way to the house. You can see me safely there."

Distracted, Hector nodded. "Sure, we can do that."

# 47

Later, Hector found a note on the writing table next to Brinke's typewriter:

Darling,

I so hope you're okay. I couldn't bear just sitting here, waiting for something bad to happen.

So I've packed us a lunch and a dinner and bought some ice. I've stocked our boat with wicked goodies. I've also packed up some clothes (not much!) and brought your fishing tackle along so you can catch us breakfast. (You see to bait—*yuck*!)

I'm waiting for you on our boat.

Thought we'd take a long slow cruise.

Love,
Brinke

She was sitting in folding chair in the shade under the flying bridge, sipping iced tea and working over a manuscript with a pen. Hector unthinkingly vaulted over the side of the boat, setting the craft to rocking and making Brinke look up sharply.

Brinke was pointing her Colt at his head. She smiled sheepishly and put down the gun. "Given events, not a good thing, surprising me like that, Hec," she said. "I might have shot you."

"So I see now. Sorry."

She put down her drink and her manuscript and laid the gun atop the pages to keep them from blowing away. She rested her reading glasses atop her gun. Hector drew her up into his arms.

"Did you get Miguel, Hec?"

"No," Hector said. "He's gone. Fled the island, I mean. We looked everywhere. Eventually we learned he left late this morning, bound for Miami."

"He's hunting for Consuelo," Brinke said.

"Yeah. Better he look there than anywhere she really is." Hector kissed her forehead. "Few days, maybe I'll take the boat here and run up to Miami myself. Finish the job."

"God, I wish you wouldn't," she said. "I just want to have the life we planned when you got here, loafing and writing. No more of this blood and thunder nonsense. No more killing."

"I feel the same way, deep down," Hector said. "Though I did wire ahead to tell Beau how things stand. Wanted to let him decide on his own precautions. This man will kill Beau without thought to get at Connie, we both know that."

Hector thought about what Beau had earlier said about Nash. About not leaving an enemy breathing to stew and ulcerate, to try and kill again. To borrow one of Beau's phrases, Connie had, in her way, sent Miguel to the river. She'd left Miguel a sense of having no future, with no prospect for happiness, and therefore, no eye to consequences. For Miguel, anything was acceptable. Hector's strong instinct was to go to Miami and find the man and put him down like the rabid dog he'd become.

Brinke said, "Where's Vogel?"

"Off to Texas. Some plan about being the king of Galveston Bay or the like."

Hector drew Brinke out of the sun and deeper into the shade. He kissed her and said, "Go below, make me a drink and get that lunch ready, won't you?"

"What are you going to do while I play galley slave, oh, He Who Must Be Obeyed?"

"Cast off and put to sea pronto," Hector said. "Get a little distance between us and this bloody Key so we can finally really relax."

Brinke was astride Hector. Her back arched and she screamed, her nails digging into his chest. She hung her head, then slowly stretched out atop him, careful that they remained joined.

"That was a little reckless wasn't it?" Hector said, panting. "Not complaining, mind you. It's so much sweeter coming inside you. Beyond intense. But it's dangerous, isn't it?"

"My risk," Brinke said. "My gamble. Life is short and I don't want to leave this world regretting anything."

Hector's eyes narrowed. He remembered then that she had seen the doctor. His voice thick, he said, "Is everything okay, darlin'? Did the doctor tell you something bad? You're not sick are you?"

He waited for it.

There were tears in Brinke's eyes. She said, "He didn't die, Hec."

"Who? Who didn't die?"

"The rabbit."

Hector tilted his head, searching her wet black eyes. "You thought you were pregnant?"

"I did. I wanted to be, so much. Convinced myself I was.

Getting sick in the morning, those cravings. But I'm not pregnant. Just a virus, I guess.

Only cravings."

"But you wanted to be pregnant," Hector said softly.

Brinke smiled sadly. "Desperately. Maybe this time, after this just now, I will be. Guess that's selfish though, just keeping you inside me like this. Deciding for both of us. Don't you want children with me, Hector?"

"What I *don't* want is to put you at risk. You said other doctors told you that—"

"*My* choice, Hector. So can we try again in a little bit?"

"Sure," he said softly, feeling this knot. "Anytime you want." He cupped her chin in his hand. "But I want you to be sure. Because you are the one at immediate risk." He couldn't conceive of losing this woman, yet Hector couldn't take the dream of a child away from her. Not seeing now how much Brinke wanted it and would gamble to have her way.

"I've made my choice, whatever comes." Brinke looked around. "Made our choice, really."

"There's no hurry," Hector said.

"I'm over thirty, Hec, so yes, there indeed is very much of a hurry." Brinke looked around. "It's getting dark, darling. Can we sleep on this boat like this, out here?"

"Sure we can."

"I want to do that, then."

"All right," he said. "Anything you want. Anything at all."

# INDEPENDENCE DAY, 1925

*"Never's just the echo*
*of forever."*
—Kris Kristofferson

# 48

It was raining hard on Matecumbe Key and the rain pounded the roof of the church.

The confession was concluding. Margarita Pagón said, "Your voice sounds different, Father."

"I'm not who you think I am. Father Romano was called away. His sister is quite ill. I am Father Santiago. Now, you'll keep your promise? You'll follow through and tell this man the truth at last, *sí?* Lies, even little ones, murder parts of the world. The older they are, the more destructive they become. It's always their terrible way."

"I will tell him, Father."

Miguel waited until he heard the confessional door close, until he heard Margarita's footsteps on tile fade to silence. Then he stood up inside the confessional and finished undressing the priest whom he had murdered. Miguel had strangled the priest to preserve the priest's collar and coat.

As he tugged off the priest's vestments, Miguel almost second-guessed his plan. All that black clothing in the Key

West sun? It would be hot as hell. It was a good thing he lived by night.

Still, it was going to be an uncomfortable disguise, even at dusk. But a desperate man had to take the good with the bad.

Miguel let himself out of the confessional and moved quickly through the sanctuary, dashing from the low but painful light of the church's interior and into the dark balmy night.

"Father?"

He smiled at his last confession. Saucy Margarita Pagón was smoking a cigarette on the steps of the church. She was blond, busty. She said, "You're very young for a priest around these parts. They tend to send the old ones to the Middle Keys. Or it seems that way to me."

"You're very young, too," he said. "And didn't we just talk about smoking? About how you're trying to quit?"

"Still trying," she said with a sheepish smile. She hesitated, then smiled again and said with sloe eyes, "Would you like to go and get a cup of coffee, Father? My treat."

"I have to be pushing on," Miguel said. He tugged at his new, tight-fitting priest's collar. It nearly gagged him. How did the true padres tolerate the things in this damned tropical heat? "I have to get south," Miguel said.

"Where are you going? A new posting?"

"That's right," Miguel said. "In Key West."

"I've always wanted to visit that island," the girl said. Just a little innuendo in there, she thought. Just a tad—enough to maybe prompt an invitation, perhaps. It surely wasn't a sin if he—if a priest—wanted it, too. Or so she consoled herself.

"It's not so different than here," Miguel said. "Same weather, same trees. The same ocean and sky. And wherever we go, our problems travel with us. We live between our ears, *sí?*"

"*Sí,* but there are people there, too," Margarita said. "Real people, not like the ones here. There are streetlights and shops and entertainment. A movie theatre and pretty clothes on all the tourists who come from all over the world."

"Quiet and dark is very nice, too," Miguel said. "Maybe even better. You take what you have here too much for granted."

"I have to walk through the woods to get home," Margarita said. "It's very dark there, and after the murder last night—that woman they found beaten to death? Beaten to death and, well, *interfered* with? I'm more than a little afraid." The priest was very handsome and Margarita thought maybe she could steal a kiss from Father Santiago in her driveway, or better, somewhere in the woods where he could touch her, too. She sensed he was perhaps available in that way. There was something almost flirtatious in his manner, something she regarded as carnal.

She said, "You will walk me through to the other side, won't you?"

Miguel looked around, saw no one. He smiled and said, "Certainly. I will see you to the other side. That much I can promise."

# *49*

B rinke said, "I'm really looking forward to this. Holidays
haven't ever meant much to me. Not beyond Christ-
mas as a little girl. I can't remember the last time I celebrated
Fourth of July." She smiled and kissed them. "But there was
this past Valentine's Day…"

They were riding the streetcar to the docks. They shared
a suitcase filled with little more than swimsuits, shorts and
shirts. Brinke had packed a single dress and Hector dress
slacks and a sports jacket for dinners out. From somewhere,
Hector heard a banjo playing.

According to Beau's wire, he expected to anchor his yacht
at Mallory Dock by four. Hector and Brinke were going to
stow their suitcases aboard Beau's boat, then have dinner with
Consuelo and Beau ashore. Hector had booked them into
adjacent rooms at another of the Key's newer hotels so they
would be in short walking distance of the docks for an early
start.

Crack of dawn, they planned to set off for three days of
fishing, sunning and catching up on the Gulf Stream. An
idyll for savoring the quiet life they'd been denied in the days
before and after Hector and Brinke's wedding. And they were

celebrating another set of nuptials: Consuelo and Beau were two months married.

The sky was gray but doing little to dampen holiday spirits. Cuban boys in ragged shorts, their dirty faces and bare chests streaked with sweat, ran around, capering. They flung firecrackers at pedestrians and at fighting cocks. Red-white-and-blue bunting draped the Duval Street shops and their second-floor balconies. Old men waved little flags from lawn chairs as the streetcar passed them by.

There was a crack of thunder. The rain came suddenly in billowing gusts that tamped down the street dust and quickly overwhelmed the drainage ditches.

Brinke crowded closer to Hector, shivering in the sudden chill. He kissed her and said, "Are you sure about this? Days on a boat with your morning sickness?"

Brinke smiled. "Sick on a boat, or sick in a hotel or at home? What's the difference? And it's fleeting—the nausea, I mean. Let's talk about names again. You still haven't told me your ideas."

"I want to hear your thoughts on this," Hector said.

The doctor had confirmed Brinke's pregnancy the previous weekend.

Hector was still of two minds, delight and inchoate dread.

Based on everything he'd heard about Brinke's risk from carrying a baby to term he felt a little like their baby growing inside Brinke was some kind of lethal time bomb.

And deep down, he had to confess, he wasn't certain he was ready to be a parent himself. Brinke was right in some ways, Hector felt there was still too much kid left in him.

"I think if it's a boy, it's already a done deal," Brinke said. "We have to name him Beau, yes?"

Hector said, "It would mean the world to Pap. And I like the name well enough."

"Agreed, then. Beau Lassiter it is. So we just have to think about middle names for a boy."

"And if it's a girl?"

Brinke scooted a little further from the window. A chilly drizzle was blowing in through the windows of the streetcar, dampening their backs. "I had a grandmother on my mother's side I was quite fond of for a fleeting time," she said. "In a lot of ways, Grammy was more like my mother than my own mother was."

"What was your grandmother's name?"

"Dolores," Brinke said. It was the Spanish for "pain," but Hector didn't volunteer that.

"Then it's settled," Hector said. "Dolores it is. Either way it goes, one of our grandparents gets honored."

Miguel had run into Pablo in a bar on Miami's South Beach in late June. Three drinks in, Pablo, a bellboy at the hotel where Consuelo had worked, confessed that he and several others of the hotel employees had conspired to lie to Miguel about his lover having fled to Miami.

Seething, Miguel had continued to pump drinks into Pablo. Miguel was repaid with revelations: Consuelo had begged her friends at the hotel to lie to Miguel. She had convinced them she was certain Miguel would eventually kill her. Consuelo believed Miguel's violent streak since the accident had been growing stronger and more unpredictable each day.

Then came the most terrible disclosure: Consuelo had taken up with some old sugar daddy and run off to Texas with the old man to become the geezer's wife. Word had trickled back Consuelo was not only now married to the old man, but—and this last sickened Miguel—was carrying the wrinkled-up old codger's baby.

Miguel listened to the rest in a haze of anger and pain. While Miguel had roamed the darkened streets of Miami seeking a woman who wasn't even there, Consuelo had in fact been living it up on the far side of the Gulf of Mexico. Hell, to hear Pablo tell it, Consuelo actually had snuck back to Key West a couple of times, usually coming over for birthdays or to visit the old man's grandson who was now himself a noted Key Wester, some writer or something.

Sipping his drink, Miguel had taken it all in. Then, when Pablo rose on shaky legs to walk out back and relieve himself in an alley, Miguel followed. He throttled Pablo with his own belt and then cut out the man's tongue and slung it across his chest.

Two night later, Miguel began his slow, incremental voyage by night, south down through the islands, killing and stealing along the way to fund his passage back to the last Key.

Miguel had a vision. He'd confront Consuelo a last time. He'd rape her, then kill her while the old man watched. After, he'd cut out the old bastard's heart and show it him before the codger's eyes went dark.

After that?

Well, that was thinking too far ahead. Miguel tried to stretch his legs in the cramped confines of the steamer's hold.

The *really* nice thing about being a priest?

Hardly anyone denied you anything, not even last-minute, overnight passage to Cayo Hueso.

# *50*

B rinke held her hand up against sun, squinting at the yacht. Beau and Consuelo were sitting in deck chairs, fanning themselves. Beau was sipping sangria and tending a fishing pole. He had grown back his moustache and now had a goatee. He'd kept his hair tinted a light brown and maintained the silver wings above each ear.

Consuelo stood up and spread her arms. She said, "I'm pregnant!"

Hector and Brinke exchanged a look and Brinke, smiling and squinting against the sun, called up, "Me, too!"

Hector said to Beau, "That was supposed to be a surprise."

"Ours too," Beau said. He tucked the butt of his fishing pole into the seat cup of the fighting chair and extended a hand to Brinke. Hector wrapped his hands around Brinke's waist and helped her on board. Hector vaulted over the side of the boat and shook his grandfather's hand.

He said to Beau, "Get the hang of handling this fine craft?"

"It's pretty intuitive," Beau said. "And I have a new hobby as a result. Sport fishing. Ever try it, Mase?"

"Never," Hector said. "But I've wanted to. Wanted to try and land a marlin or two. Looks like real work."

Beau nodded. "I love it. Why haven't you taken it up yourself or paid for a charter? Is it just money?"

"Again with the money," Hector said. "That's not it. There's been no time. Not all of us are retired. I've still got to crank out five-thousand words a day."

"That for a novel?"

"Two thousand a day for a novel, then three thousand more or so for a short story a day. Send out six stories in a week, you usually sell at least three. And the magazines pay in a more timely way than the book fellas back east seem to."

"I don't know how he does it," Brinke said. "I struggle to do two thousand on a novel a day."

Beau pressed a hand to Brinke's belly. "You've got more going on inside you than telling stories. I'm delighted you're expectin'." Beau leaned into Brinke's ear as he hugged her. Hector figured he was making some inquiry after Brinke's health based on his reading of Brinke's lips in answer: I'm okay.

Hector said, "You two pick a place to eat?"

Consuelo shrugged and Beau said, "You're the island dwellers. Thought we'd leave that selection up to you."

"We know a good place," Brinke said.

Hector stashed their suitcase under a bunk in the cabin. He heard Beau say, "I hope this place of yours serves acceptable hooch. You and Consuelo may be occasional milk drinkers now, but me and Mase? Not even close."

Miguel knew the name of the boat he was looking for, "The Inside Straight." He simply wandered the docks until he found her slip.

As he was approaching the yacht, a tall man in a white sports jacket leapt over the side. He held out his hands and grabbed a slender, black-haired woman around the waist and lowered her to the dock. He did the same for a Latina that Miguel could now see was Consuelo. Then the tall man held a hand out for an older, equally tall man who lowered himself over the side of the boat.

Miguel could barely focus his vision in the scorching afternoon heat. His head was pounding and he felt like being sick. He turned his back to the quartet as they passed. He scented Consuelo's perfume on the sultry wind. Miguel watched them walk up the gangplank, then he leapt over the side of the Inside Straight to find a place to hide.

Brinke and Consuelo toasted one another with a couple of Shirley Temples. "We should do some shopping," Brinke said. "Clothes, cribs. Those sorts of things."

Consuelo said, "Yes. Absolutely. We must do all that and more."

Fifteen minutes later, they both excused themselves to the lady's room. Hector slammed back a shot of whiskey and said to his grandfather, "Christ, but our lives have gotten strange."

Beau smiled. "This time last year, we were two and pretty uncertain for the count. This time next year, we'll be at least six. It's good to have family, sonny."

Hector shook out a cigarette. "You were talking, not so long ago, about all the revenue Mom cost you when she was a mewling little baby. Ready for that next big wallet hit?"

"I'm retired and set for whatever comes," Beau said. "You know that."

"Really? You don't keep a hand in the grift, not anywhere?"

"Sports fisherman now, Mase." Beau winked. "Although I indulge in the occasional charter for walking-around money. I'll give you some pointers on that angle tomorrow. You could supplement your writing income with some of that, and I mean handsomely."

Hector rolled his eyes. "Bait, cast, reel 'em in. How hard can it be?"

Beau shook his head. "Holy Jesus. I'm *still* teachin' you."

Miguel checked his pocket watch. Midnight. He figured Consuelo and the old man had decided to room in town. Probably some joint with air conditioning, because it was still very hot on the boat. They probably wouldn't return before tomorrow Miguel decided, but when they did, it would probably be quite early. They seemed prepared for a fishing excursion. They'd want to leave with the dawn, if that was true.

Miguel stretched again, uncramping his leg muscles from the confinement of his hiding place in the engine compartment.

He figured if he returned by four a.m., he'd still be in plenty of time to resume hiding in order to position himself to strike at Consuelo and her geezer suitor after sunset tomorrow.

Settled on his plan, Miguel put back on his priest's collar and went trolling on Duval.

# *51*

"A t least now we can be as reckless as we want to be for a few months," Brinke said, crossing her ankles behind his waist.

Hector had one hand wrapped around the back of Brinke's neck and the other hand pressed to her tailbone.

"Can I ask one thing of you, Hector? Frankly, it's a big one."

Skittish, Hector narrowed his eyes. "What's that?"

"You're clearly worried something might happen with me like this, that something might go wrong," she said. "It's always in your eyes now, your concern. Of course, it's a possibility something could happen. You said it had to be my choice to try and have this baby, and it is my choice and I'm prepared to live with consequences. I know there were women before me, other women you had. If the world turns certain ways, there may be women after me, Hec. But I've always heard for every man, there's really only one woman. One great love. Do you think I might be yours? And if I am, are you prepared to tell me that now, while it would really mean something to me?"

"I'm not having this morbid conversation," Hector said, truly appalled. "I'm not going to invite bad luck mulling such prospects. I'm just not prepared to do it."

"Guess that means you can't say it."

Hector couldn't read her expression He couldn't tell if Brinke meant that, or if she was teasing him, playing some childish game. Though such games were admittedly not Brinke's style.

"I've married you, darlin'," Hector said. "I haven't done that before, not *ever*. Haven't even contemplated it with anyone else. So you can make of that what you will. I intend to stay married to you until they plant me, be that tomorrow or a hundred years from now. Unless of course you divorce me for some other man."

"Never going to happen." She smiled and bumped foreheads with him. "So, am I the one, Hector? Am I your one true woman? The great love of your life?"

"Now you're just being churlish. I'm never going to answer that one now."

"I mean it, Hec. I really need to know." Something funny there in her voice that reached him.

"But I mean it too, my love. Please don't jinx us with this stuff." Her desperate edge really made it feel like bad luck to Hector to answer.

Brinke's voice changed. "Something could happen. There is a medical risk."

"Hush," Hector said. "Really, just *hush*. Please. Don't borrow trouble. You're going to be fine, I know it."

"We're going to revisit this," Brinke said, moving with more urgency under him. "We're not finished with this topic. I *will* have my answer. I'm not going to let it drop."

"I'm sure that's too true," Hector said. If felt like bad luck to surrender and there was no wood close by to tap a knuckle on.

On the other hand, it happened to be the truth. "You're the one of course, Brinke," he said. "How could you even need to ask it of me?"

Miguel dabbed at his coat with a cloth dipped in whiskey. Thank "God" black didn't show much blood at night.

He took a last look up at the moon, stretched, then took a couple of deep breaths. He touched his toes ten times, then went below to his cramped hiding place.

Miguel hoped to hell he wouldn't suffocate as he tried to sleep through the day's July heat. But it he weathered that hot little hold?

If he didn't suffocate in there?

Well, come sundown, Miguel figured he would have himself quite the time.

*52*

B eau said, "Morning sickness. I'd forgotten."
Hector tossed his cigarette butt aside. He said, "Morning sickness. I'm just learning."

"The first of many strange lessons I'm afraid, my boy," Beau said. "Best just try and enjoy the rocky ride."

Brinke and Consuelo were several paces ahead on Duval, window-shopping twenty minutes after both running to a lady's room to be sick. The quartet had gotten a late start and they were slowly making their way to Mallory Dock.

Beau said, "You two are moving rather quickly with this baby thing, aren't you? Figured you kids would want a year or two together before a decade of distraction."

Hector said, "Brinke's a shade older than me. She feels time isn't on her side."

Beau smiled. "How much older?"

"Five years."

"I'd never have guessed," he said. "Or maybe you're just aging like a dog."

"Christ. Thanks, Gramps."

"Don't mean to depress you, Mase, but Brinke does look at least five years younger than you."

"Be sure to slip that in sometime in the next couple of days at sea. Not that you already haven't won her over ten ways from Tuesday." Hector lit another cigarette. "Brinke views time as a kind of predator."

"I'd say I understand the feeling," Beau said, "but I mean to live forever. I'm willing myself to never, *ever* die. Longevity runs my side of the family, as you know. Nearly all of us see at least a hundred. I mean to go even farther."

"I'm all for it." Hector held out his pack of cigarettes. "Want a smoke, Beau?"

The old man held up a hand, warding off the pack. "Christ no, those things will kill you deader than anything." He reached into his shirt pocket and pulled out a cigar. He slipped off the cellophane sleeve and then leaned into Hector's offered match.

"This retirement business," Hector said, "I'm not really buying it. How many marks have you stung since I last saw you?"

"Merely minor scores," Beau said. "Wee little hits for mad money. Walking around money. Hate to touch my principal from the great Buena Stella boondoggle and its attendant side stings. Hell, I hate to touch my interest from that score."

Hector squeezed the back of his grandfather's bronzed neck. "I knew you couldn't do nothing for long."

Brinke was looking at the chair bolted to the deck of the ship, at the leather harnesses affixed to the chair. They were about ten miles out. She said, "No offense, Beau, but you worried about falling out of your chair?"

Beau passed the wheel to Hector and said to Brinke, "Sit down in that." She did that. He fastened Brinke into the chair, then picked up one of the deep-sea poles and fitted its butt into the brass cup positioned between Brinke's bronzed thighs. He rested a hand on her shoulder and said, "What you have to imagine, darlin', is five-hundred or maybe even a thousand pounds of pure muscle on the end of that line, darting, diving. Makin' runs and sheerin' off at charging angles from the boat. If you weren't strapped into that chair, and if that pole wasn't secured in that retainer there, well, honey, it'd be like you were lassoed to the back of an outbound train with its hammer down. You'd be ripped off the back of this craft quicker than you can blink. We use the boat engines to wear 'em down. We run those big fish tired and bloody."

"And you really catch these monsters?"

"All the time. Hope to today."

Brinke thought about that. "And the meat? You can't eat anything that big."

"Not just the four of us," Beau agreed. "No, depending on which is closer, we'd run it back to Key West or over to Havana and sell it there. If we can beat the sharks. They've cost me a marlin and a tuna these past two weeks. Stripped 'em down to bone before I could make port. The Great Blue River is thick with sharks now for some reason."

Brinke quizzically repeated, "The Great Blue River?"

"What some call the Gulf Stream," Beau said.

Consuelo came out from the cabin with a couple of drinks she'd mixed for Hector and Beau. She said, "Next time to port, I think we need to buy some traps, Beauregard."

He sipped his drink. "Oh? What kind of traps? Why?"

"I heard some funny noises below," Consuelo said. "I fear we must have mice."

The day passed quietly. There were no hits from the big fish, so Hector and Beau used smaller rigs to catch sea bass and other smallish game fish, saving a few for dinner and throwing the rest back. They retained a particular couple of fish for bait.

Hector cleaned the fish they meant to eat and Brinke and Consuelo eventually went inside the cabin to prepare it.

Hector and his grandfather stood at the back of the boat, not anchored and just allowing her to be pulled along by the strong tug of the Gulf Stream. It was three in the afternoon and the sun was already getting low on the horizon, slowly sliding toward the curve of the sea.

Brinke made a face as Hector hefted the fish he had caught while Beau threaded a hook through the top of the fish's eye socket. "What is that?"

"Bait," Hector said. "But to what I take is your real question, it's a bonito."

"It's big," Brinke said. "If it's bait, what are we hunting for?"

"We're fishing for blue marlin," Beau said. "They can go ten to twelve feet and weigh five- or six-hundred pounds. They're strong as hell. If fishing for these monsters was another kind of sport, it'd probably be bull fighting. Men die in those fighting chairs sometimes, trying to haul in those monsters."

"This doesn't sound like a good idea," Brinke said. "If Hector can be hurt..."

Beau waved that away. "Me? I'd maybe be at some risk if I hooked a *really* big one, but Mase is a tough young buck. It's good sport. Don't fret for him."

Brinke still looked dubious. "I feel sorry for that bonito with that hook through its head. "Shouldn't you kill it before you put the hook in like that?"

Hector shook his head. "Huh-uh," he said, lowering the fish over the side. It squirmed in his hands, moving faster as it sensed the water close. "This thing will be alive for hours, still able to swim. Great bait for big fish."

"Seems cruel," Brinke said.

"It's a fish," Beau said. "Like the man said, never get too attached to animals other than dogs, horses and cats. Never name anything you might have to eat."

The bonito in the water, Hector took a seat in the chair. He said to Beau, "Sure you want me to be the one if we get a bite?"

"Hell, yes," Beau said. "Still somethin' I can school you on," he said. "Now let's get that harness on to spare your back and shoulders."

Hector belted into the leather harness. Brinke said, "Fetch you a beer, Hec?"

"No, gotta stay in the chair, maybe for some time, if we get one on the hook," Hector said. "There'll be no time for restroom breaks."

Brinke considered that. "How long a time?"

"Hours, sometimes," Beau said. He checked his watch. "Day's getting on—be good to get something soon while we will have light to fight 'em by. You stand by to pour water on Mase's arms and wrists as needed. They'll get sore sitting in that position waiting for a strike."

Beau moved around to where Hector could see him better. "Mase, you know what to do if you get a strike?"

Hector had been researching a bit. But before he could answer, Brinke said, "Hit him hard to set the hook, yes?" She smiled at Beau and said, "Hector's been giving me fishing lessons."

Beau smiled back. "This isn't like fishing off a pier. In this case, you give the fish some line and set the drag on, just a little. When he's on his first run, no line or rod or man on earth can contain that force. You haul back hard on the strike and you'll snap the line, lose the rod or help the fish throw the hook. Probably all three."

Hector wet his lips, said, "Slack and a little drag, right?"

"Right," Beau said, tousling Hector's sun-faded hair. "We chase him with the boat, let him sound, then start getting back line. Wear him out and break him. If he doesn't do that to you first."

# *53*

Thirty minutes later, there was high-pitched squeal as the line began running out. Hector whipped the butt of the pole into the chair socket, gave slack, then pulled back hard on the pole, setting the hook.

Beau was at his side, a hand on Hector's shoulder. "Good, that's real good, Mase. But not too much drag or you'll break the line or lose the pole. And maybe your arms, with it. That thing out there can wrench your arms clean from their sockets if you give it too much drag."

"That kind of talk isn't making me feel better about any of this," Brinke said.

Then the fish broke water, riding its tail and whipping its head side-to-side, trying to throw the hook.

"My God," Brinke said. The fish was dark in the sun, the fins darkest of all. The marlin's belly was a translucent white, its nose a gleaming sword. Brinke watched the big fish whip itself across the water on its tail two more times in an effort to throw the hook as Hector took in line. "What is it?"

Beau smiled at the changed tenor of Brinke's voice. He said, "It's a blue marlin, if it's anything. Easily five hundred pounds. At least ten-feet long. A real beauty, huh?"

"He's magnificent!" Brinke put her hand on Hector's shoulder, feeling the muscles taught there as he pulled back on the pole again, hitting the big fish again and slightly increasing the drag on the fishing line. Stroking and then massaging Hector's damp shoulders more slowly, sensually now, she said, "What happens next?"

Beau wrapped an arm around Brinke's waist. "Now those two duke it out. They try and break one another."

The marlin was out of the water again, whipping along on its tail, still trying to shake loose the hook. "Oh my God," Brinke said. "Look at him!" She squeezed Hector's shoulder harder. "God, he's beautiful."

There was a scream from below. Hector turned as much as his harness would allow. Consuelo was backing out of the cabin, sobbing. She ran to Beau's arms, pointing back at the cabin.

Hector scowled: a sweat-soaked, wild-eyed priest was in the cabin, clothes sweated through and collar askew. The priest was waving a gun and looking close to collapsing from heat stroke.

Brinke said, "My God, it's Miguel, Consuelo's crazy ex-boyfriend!"

Hector nodded, furious. "I remember his face. We have met, however briefly."

The marlin made another run then and Hector said quietly, "Hell of a time for this! We need to find out if Beau has a gun. I left mine at home, goddamn it." Hector jerked back on the pole again and took up some more line.

Consuelo said, "Miguel, I'm begging you to put down that gun. We'll turn around and head back in. We'll get you the help you need."

"You shut up, *puta*," Miguel said. "You just shut your lying mouth!" He squinted against the sun, aiming at the sound of her voice. He could hardly see in the harsh July sun glinting hard off the water.

Miguel pressed his free hand to his forehead. His hair was wet and there was a terrible throbbing behind his eyes. He had intended to wait until sunset to strike, but he couldn't stay in that hot little compartment any longer. It was hot enough all on its own, but when the twin engines had started up hard, the nearly unbearable space had become impossible to remain inside.

Looking back and fourth between the marlin and Miguel, Hector said, "What the hell's wrong with him? He looks ill." The marlin made another turn and Hector swiveled in the chair to compensate, increasing the drag a hair to slow the line going out. He braced his feet against the stern rail and jerked back on the pole, hitting the fish again. He gave it a second hard, backward pull, then loosened the drag a bit and gave the marlin some more line as it sounded.

Hector figured that soon someone would have to take the helm. Someone would have to maneuver the boat so the line wasn't cut as the fish swam under and maybe in front of them. Most importantly, the fishing line needed to be kept clear of the propellers. Hector said, "I ask again, what's ailing this son of a bitch?"

"The sun, the light," Consuelo said. "Since he hurt his head last year, Miguel can't stand light. It gives him terrible headaches. Pain he can't endure."

"I told you to shut up, Consuelo!" Miguel pressed his hand harder against the top of his head. "I don't want to hear your goddamn voice, not ever again, you traitor. You filthy, *puta*!"

"I gave you a choice," Consuelo said. "It wasn't like that, me being a traitor. You scared me. I told you I was leaving if you didn't get yourself real help, and you didn't. I gave you every chance."

Miguel fired at the sound of her voice. She and Beau both flinched as the bullet passed overhead.

Beau said, "What do you intend here, boy?"

Miguel snarled and took a step back, moving under the canopy of the boat into the negligible shade to be found there. He said, "I'm going to kill you, old man. I'm going to kill you and your wife. And I suppose, now, I'm going to have to kill these poor people with you."

Miguel shaded his eyes again and looked at Brinke. "Son of a bitch," he said. "You're that snooty bitch from Christmas! The one who laughed at me in the bar. The one who made me go outside where I had my accident! You *puta!*"

His stomach in knots, Hector said, "Rough language, from a fucking priest. And you can't fault a lady for having real taste."

"He's no priest," Consuelo said. She scowled at Brinke. "You *know* Miguel?"

Brinke made a face. "*No.* Only from hearing you talk about him About him, and his fall. About the blow to his head."

Miguel pointed his gun at Brinke. "Liar! You shamed me. You're that bitch—Twinke? Brinke?—who turned down my offer for a drink."

Brinke said, "You're nuts. I don't know you."

"Last Christmas, in the Cap'n's bar, you laughed at me, you filthy bitch!"

Consuelo said, "Last Christmas you were still with me, Miguel! So you bretrayed me long ago! How many times before seeing Brinke did you try to take up with other women and maybe even succeed? How many times did you betray me?"

Miguel kicked the wall of the yacht's cabin. "This isn't supposed to be happening like this! Damned sun, if it wasn't so hot? If my head didn't hurt so much? If I could just fucking think for one moment?" He slammed his fist into the cabin's door jamb. "Goddamn it, you people have to listen to me! I've got a fucking gun!"

Beau slowly lowered his hands. "What you really have, old son, is a big old problem. I don't think you've thought any of this through. Do you know even a little about pilotin' a boat?"

"Can't be that hard," Miguel said, one hand pressed to his forehead, shielding his eyes.

"You don't know where you are," Beau said. "No land in sight, and there's only so much fuel. You set off in the wrong direction, you'll end up adrift. If that happens, you'll probably die too, but slowly, from dehydration and starvation."

"I'm not afraid to die," Miguel said with a sneer. "But I'll kill you and your wife first. I really don't care about what happens to me after."

"I don't believe that," Consuelo said. "If that were true, you would have killed yourself already and not come here. You would have killed yourself before you killed poor Malú. Or, in guilt, you would have killed yourself, after killing our friend. But you didn't do either did you, Miguel? You care only about yourself. Now I see that is so." She nodded at Brinke. "Or, since you admit you dreamed of betraying me with her, I guess maybe the accident only made you more the bad man you *always* were. The man who always thought only of himself."

Hector checked the sky. Perhaps two hours before the sun sank enough to maybe give Miguel some desperately needed relief, some dangerous focus. Hector locked eyes with Beau. His grandfather chewed his lip and contemplated the fishing pole gripped in Hector's hands.

Miguel said, "I want you all to stand together there, where I can watch you at once. Give me time to get better, to clear my head to think."

Brinke moved to Beau's side. Miguel said to Hector, "You, in the chair, you get over there with them." Beau's eyes urged him to resist. Hector had already begun to grasp the old man's plan, mostly because it was his scheme, too.

"I just can't do that," Hector said. "Haven't you ever fished? I mean for really big fish?"

Beau stepped in then, eyes on Hector. "What Mase there is saying, Miguel, is that he's strapped to that chair, and that chair is bolted to the deck. That pole between Mase's knees is anchored to that chair in a brass socket. That's all so because on the other end of that line is maybe as much as a thousand pounds of blue marlin, a fish that's all muscle and has a sword for a nose. A real, honest-to-God man-killer."

"So cut the fucking fish loose," Miguel said. "Cut the line and get your ass over there," he said to Hector.

"Don't think you're hearing what the man said," Hector said. "A fish this big takes wire to catch, not fishing line. You can't just cut this cord. Hell, the three of us couldn't do that with the best of tools. It's made to resist cutting or breaking. It's made to haul in a damned whale."

"You don't know anything about deep-sea fishing," Beau said, "you don't know anything at all about it, do you, Miguel?"

Miguel pushed the heel of his left hand into each eye, blinking afterward. "How would I?" There was real hatred in his voice. "This is a rich man's sport," he said.

"Then let me tell you a couple of other important things about this rich man's sport," Beau said, holding up a hand to shush Hector and Consuelo. "We're dead in the water right now. There's nobody at the helm, and that's a really bad thing."

Miguel pulled at his priest's collar and the pressed his left hand to the top of his head again. "Why? Why is that so bad?"

"Because that fish, that giant damn fish, it's still moving somewhere down there," Beau said. "That's dangerous for us and for this boat. That fish is maybe plenty big enough to pull this boat *backward* if he makes a run to stern. Boats aren't made to go backwards, not at any real speed. Water comes up over the back here, well, then it weighs us down to rear. It'll upset the center of gravity and we'll sink, nose up. We'll all be in that water in under two minutes. Odds of bein' pulled out of the drink by some other passing boaters this far out is next to nil. Chances of rescue are so slim as to make prayer pointless, even if you were a real priest. But we wouldn't have to worry about drowning or dying of exposure in the water.

"Mase has been fighting that fish quite a while before you stumbled out of the hold," Beau glossed. "That fish is hurting inside. Probably hemorrhaging internally. Bleedin' from its overtaxed lungs. Even if his innards aren't compromised, his mouth is all torn up from the hook. That means blood in the water. Blood means sharks. This kind of fishing, you're always in a race with the sharks. And if that fish compromises this boat, then we'll be in the water with those sharks. I don't care how much you think you don't care about dyin', boy, you do not want to die from a feeding frenzy of sharks."

Miguel chewed his lip and slid a little deeper into shadow. "Maybe he won't run that direction," he said. "This boat has three other sides. Odds alone says he runs in one of those directions."

"Then we'd maybe be dragged sideways and swamped," Beau said. "We'd sink nearly as fast then." Beau gestured at the back of the yacht. "But any way he runs than off the back, he takes wire into our screws. Tangles the line in the propellers or bends the blades. Then we're dead in the water again, but for keeps. Then we just sit here, waiting to be sunk or to die of dehydration or exposure. You know, from the hot summer sun you can't abide."

Miguel hit the door jam with his fist again. "Then what's the point? How do we wrap this up with this damned fish?"

"You let us catch it, fast, before we lose the light you hate so much." Beau said, "Look, sonny, it gets dark, we lose the edge of eyeballin' the fish and trackin' his movements. In the dark, we're screwed all over again. All those bad scenarios come home to roost in spades."

Miguel said, "What do you need to do to catch this fish?" Miguel's voice was strained, Hector thought. But Hector supposed they couldn't be so lucky as to have the ailing Miguel black-out or become too incapacitated by the pain in his head to cease posing a threat.

"I need to drive this boat," Beau said. "I need to get us underway. Usually do that from the flying bridge, up top where I can see. But I can do it from below. You can sit in there in the shade with me, keeping that gun of yours trained on me. Consuelo can sit next to me, where you can see us both."

"And the other one?" Miguel waved his gun at Brinke.

"She needs to stay out here with Mase," Beau said. "That bucket by his feet is full of water. If that marlin gets himself in a real run, and Mase has to give him line, then Brinke needs to pour water on the reel there to keep it cool. Can't have the mechanism overheating and stoving up. But the most important thing, right now, is for me to get in there and get us underway. I need to use those engines to wear that marlin down. Need to steer us clear of the fishing line and turn us as needed to meet his runs."

Miguel seemed to Hector to be wavering, maybe prepared to go for it. Miguel just needed a firm nudge, Hector figured. So he wouldn't disturb the now-quiet marlin, Hector opened up the drag and carefully pulled loose a little line so there would be some slack. He saw that Beau saw what he was doing; the others hadn't.

Hector yelled, "Oh God, he's making another run!" Hector whipped back the pole, reeling in some of the slackened line, striving to make it look like he was working hard against fierce resistance.

Beau leaned over the back, peering out to sea, then turned around and said, "She's running from stern!" Nearly yelling, putting fear in his voice, Beau pleaded, "I need to get in there, right now, or we're all going in the drink with that fish!"

Miguel dithered a moment.

Hector said, "She's turning to starboard!" He swiveled in the fighting chair.

Beau said, "We'll lose our propellers!"

Miguel stepped aside and waved his gun at the helm. "Go!" He pointed the gun at Beau's head. "Start her up, but be careful passing by me. Anything looks funny, I shoot your wife. In the belly. Understood?"

Beau licked his lips. "I understand everything. You best believe that, sonny."

# 54

Beau slid behind the wheel. Consuelo followed closely behind him, turning and squeezing through the cabin door, trying to keep as much distance as possible from Miguel. As she passed, Miguel leaned into her and said, "This changes nothing. You don't escape from this, *puta*. When this thing with the fish is over, I still kill you and the other whore. And that old man at the wheel. The hombre in the chair, Mase, he can take me in sight of land. So don't get your hopes up. You're going to die. You and that thing that old man put inside you."

Consuelo said nothing, just slid past him with red cheeks and angry eyes. She sat down next to Beau. She squeezed his hand. "What are we going to do? He says as soon as the fish is caught, he'll kill all of us but Héctor. Him he'll force to drive the boat until he sees land. Then he says he'll kill Héctor, too."

"I'm sure he means to do all that," Beau said, busy and focused. "Man proposes. God, or his instrument, disposes."

"So what does that mean? What do we do, Beau?"

He smiled at Consuelo. "We fish." He started the engines. The marlin was currently dormant. Beau knew when the big fish felt the tug from the boat getting underway the marlin would be stirred to flight, to make another run and effort to throw the hook.

Beau called back to Hector, "Going to take her forward. Now listen closely to me damn it, Hector. Listen hard. Hector, you be *real* careful now. You don't want to have too much drag on that line. You know what happens with too much drag, yes?"

Hector smiled, his back to the others. "I can well imagine," he yelled back to his grandfather. "I know what the drag will do. I know what too much or too little will do. Especially if he's running in the direction opposite the one we're moving in."

"*Exactly*," Beau said. God bless my boy for being' a quick study, he thought.

Hector turned off the drag, letting the line run out slack between his fingers as Beau eased the boat forward.

Beau called out, "Important thing, if this goes badly, is knowing just when to let go."

"I understand," Hector said. "It's the way with everything."

Brinke said to Hector, "You two have any ideas for getting us out of this mess?"

"We're literally working on it as we speak," Hector said. "I need you to get behind me, casual like, darlin'. Get right behind this chair and you stay there. Pretend to massage my shoulders and neck again."

Beau yelled over the sound of the motors, "We should be seeing him now, don't you think?"

"You would think," Hector said.

"I'm going to open the engines up," Beau said. Whenever you think the time is right, you give the word, Hector. You understand me?"

Hector flexed his fingers. He freshened his grip on the pole and tightened the drag a bit to goad the marlin to action. As the slackened line was taken up by the boat's motion, Hector braced his feet on the stern's rail.

He jerked hard on the rod and felt a sharp pull back from the line. The fishing line started going out with a squeal and Hector put on a bit more drag, trying to reel back in some line and feeling the weight and strength of the leviathan on the other end of the line.

The marlin broke surface thirty yards off the stern, furious and frenzied. The fish sprayed Hector and Brinke with bloodied water droplets. There actually was some blood visible in the right gill slit, and now, behind the marlin, Hector could see a pair of fins, probably of tiger sharks, Hector figured.

Miguel said, "My God! Look at him!" The Cuban was clearly awed by the enormous blue marlin. Smiling, Miguel said, "Just look at him!"

Forgetting himself just a little, Miguel stepped a bit out onto deck, squinting and shading his eyes for a better look at the leaping fish. The marlin jumped again, thrashing its head side-to-side. "God, look at how beautiful!" Miguel quickly looked back over his shoulder to confirm Beau and Consuelo hadn't moved. When he saw they were still in their seats, he turned around again to watch the marlin.

Beau slowed the engine a bit, then said, "You're going to have to help us, Miguel, unless you let me back there."

Miguel said, "Then who would drive? You said it was important someone steer, old man."

"Consuelo could maybe handle it," Beau said. "Thing now is just to be ready to pull in the marlin. See, he's almost worn out," Beau lied. "There's a pole fastened there under Mase's feet. It's a gaff hook. You need to get it in the fish's mouth and pull him up alongside when Mase gets him in close. I'll stay on the engines if you'll help Mase. You can tuck your gun in the waistband of your pants. Not like Mase can do anything to you, not strapped as he is into that chair like that."

Miguel said to Beau, "You're *loco*."

"We have to hurry," Beau said. "Please! If it gets dark, and the fish ain't landed, if he has any struggle in him or time to recuperate...? I told you, we can't fight him in the dark."

Miguel gestured at Brinke with his gun. "And this one?"

"Marlin's past running at speed enough to need to cool the rig," Beau said. "Brinke can come in here with us."

The marlin leapt again. Miguel watched him, obviously excited and awed. "He doesn't look so tired, gringo," he said. "But, okay." He waved the gun at Brinke. "You, in with the others, *puta*."

Brinke said softly to Hector, "Do you want me to go, darling?"

"With all haste," Hector whispered. "Get in there where it's safer. Keep your head down. Bullets may yet fly."

Miguel made sure Brinke reached Consuelo and Beau. He then looked carefully at the rig securing Hector to the fighting chair. He was satisfied Hector couldn't easily free himself.

Hector shook his head and said, "Don't sweat it, fella. I'm no Harry Houdini. A straight-jacket couldn't tie me up any tighter than this rig does. Now pick up that hook and let's get to it. Figure that blue is about thirty-feet off the stern." Another lie: it was more like sixty yards, Hector estimated.

Beau called back, "You remember all I said, Mase?"

Hector yelled, "Sure. Short form, it's set drag. Then let go. Right?"

"Right-o," Beau hollered back. "And on your mark, I'll open up the engines. Get a little distance from those sharks when it's been done."

"Sounds jake," Hector yelled.

To Miguel, Hector said, "Put the gun in your pants and get that gaff. You'll need both hands. This thing we're going to try and catch is as heavy as a horse. Stand a little off to the left of the line. I'm going to hit the marlin one more time, to break him, then you step up close to that line as you can and be ready with that hook."

Hector notched up the drag again and called to Beau, "Just a tad more engine." He hit the marlin again and felt a sharp jerk as the blue began its hard run away from the back of the boat. Despite whatever the hook had done to its mouth, the fish was still strong and fresh. All its fight was undiminished. Hector opened up the drag to give the fish more line, to increase the speed of its flight.

"Now Miguel," Hector said, moving his feet to make room. "You step up here."

Miguel did that, leaning out with the hook. He warned Hector, "You get any ideas about trying to kick me over, I'll have time to grab the rail and put three in your chest. Then I'll rape your woman. That's what I'll do if you try anything."

"Thought of kicking at you never crossed my mind," Hector said.

As Miguel leaned out with the hook, Hector lifted the butt of the pole free from the brass chair socket between his thighs. He held the pole in his hands, careful to keep his fingers clear. Hector yelled to his grandfather, "Open her up now!"

When he felt the boat accelerate, Hector turned the pole a little to an angle and then set the drag full on.

Hector spread his fingers.

There was a loud *t-h-a-w-n-g* as the rod flew from his hands and struck Miguel and the gaff hook.

Miguel had half-turned at the sound of the pole's release. The rod struck Miguel just below the rib cage, then trailed up his torso. The handle of the reel snagged his priest's collar.

Hector winced as the Cuban and the pole were ripped from the boat and dragged quickly out into the Great Blue River by the massive marlin.

Beau kept the engines open a long time, putting distance between them and Miguel's body, just in case enough life remained in Miguel to take a shot back at them.

Hector ran to the cabin, grabbed a pair of binoculars and played with the focus pin, scanning the horizon.

He saw sharks' fins converging. Hector hoped the sharks severed the fishing line, freeing the marlin of the fishing rig and whatever the sharks left of Miguel, giving the blue marlin some possibility of recuperation, some chance for survival in reward for saving their lives.

Brinke was suddenly at his side. She shook her head and hugged Hector. "I almost felt sorry for him when the rod hit him. What a terrible way to die."

"At least it was quick," Hector said. "Maybe he was even dead before the sharks got him. A better, kinder death than the ones he was handing out. Surely better than Malú was dealt by him."

"You don't feel anything for Miguel?" Brinke's forehead wrinkled. "I don't believe that. You're not that callous, not on your meanest day."

Hector brushed her wind-blown hair back from her face and kissed Brinke hard. "You've never seen anything close to my meanest day," he said. "Old Miguel out there, he's just another fish story now, the one who got away."

"Not from the sharks he didn't," Brinke said. She buried her face in his neck. "I need to go see to Consuelo. I don't care how crazy Miguel was or what he just tried to do to us. She cared for that man once. Seeing that just now has to have hurt Consuelo, deep inside."

Hector handed her the binoculars to take back inside. He massaged his sore shoulders. "You do that then. Go see to Connie."

"You're sure you're okay, Hector?"

"I'm fine," Hector said. "That son of a bitch is not a bit close to my conscience."

"Then what are you going to do, Hector?"

"See to Pap, I reckon. Man lived seventy years without taking a life. Now he's done it twice. And, hell, we're hardly halfway through twenty-five. What a bloody year this is shaping up to be."

# LABOR DAY, 1925

*"The soul is healed*
*by being with children."*
—English Proverb

# 55

Hector said, "Seas are calm enough, we could take the boat out. Get a little time in before the storm season really settles in deep." He stroked Brinke's damp forehead. "If you're up to it, I mean."

Brinke was sitting beside him on the sofa, fanning herself. She was wearing shorts and a loose-fitting T-shirt of Hector's.

Brinke had grown her hair out even longer over the summer and it reached below her shoulders, longer now than Hector had ever seen it. Brinke's hair seemed to Hector to also be thicker and glossier of late. Her breasts were fuller and the texture of her skin had changed, he thought. Pregnancy seemed to agree with her.

But Hector had also caught Brinke a few times looking in the mirror, searching her part for gray hairs. He'd tried to kid her about it, but Brinke wasn't having any of it. "Five years between our ages, Hector, half-a-decade. Hell, in some ways, you're still just a kid."

Hector had shaken his head. Smiling, he had said, "Actuarial tables indicate most men predecease their wives by just about that many years. Least this way we can maybe check out of this world together, or close to it." He smiled and kissed her. "You won't have to shoulder the trauma of mourning me, darlin'."

Brinke had shaken her head with a forced smile. Hector had to confess he hadn't found it so funny himself, not after the bloody winter-into-summer of 1925. Hell, 1924 had been a bloodbath, too.

He was hoping for a quieter, happier autumn. Maybe 1926 would be their banner year.

But so far, Hector had found himself walking on eggshells. Brinke was obsessive about her diet and health. Since the doctor had told her she was pregnant, she eschewed liquor and cigarettes and shamed Hector into doing the same. He had to admit, he felt better, felt more clear-headed, for living the clean life.

But all the colors of the world seemed somehow drabber.

Brinke lifted her hair from the back of her damp neck. "Key West is just no place to be pregnant," she said. "I'm actually homesick for Paris, for Paris in the winter. And for our friends still there. I wish I could go back there with you. See them. Let them know I'm still around. Hash and Hem, especially."

Hector stroked her cheek. "We could head north around these parts for the winter. New England, Michigan. Really feel the seasons."

"Maybe Key West is no place to raise a child," Brinke said. "I know we just got here, but maybe we need to look somewhere else. Maybe out west, where we can have all those seasons. Idaho. Maybe Montana. Big Sky country. We could get a little ranch, and we could have a horse. When I was a little girl, I always wanted a horse. Wouldn't you like one, Hector? You were cavalry, right? A horse for our daughter or son to ride? A big strawberry roan we could ride high up into the mountains. Wouldn't that be wonderful?"

"If we're going to sell this place, now might be the time," Hector said. "Move before the Florida land boom goes bust, which I read in the paper some think is a real threat."

"I was just saying," Brinke said. "A ranch some day, a horse, would be nice." Brinke half-smiled. "But let's do get out on the boat now. Out from shore, with the sea breeze, it will be cooler, at least."

"You're up to it?"

She nodded. "I'll be fine. Really. I'm just fine."

They were two days at sea and headed back into port ahead of a storm front.

Hector thought the tropical storm season was finally taking hold in the Gulf; hurricane season had arrived. The waters were choppy and the sky an ugly shade of gray. Hector could just see the top of the lighthouse on Whitehead Street poking up over the horizon.

Because of the holiday, the waters were getting more crowded as they neared the Key and Brinke decided it was time to dress. She stepped back into her white swimsuit, pulling it up over her hips and breasts and then tugging its straps over her bronzed and now-freckled shoulders. She wrapped her arms around Hector's waist. "How long?"

"Ten, maybe fifteen minutes."

"It was wonderful to get away. I so love this boat."

"Me too." Hector wrapped an arm around her waist, steering the boat with one hand. He frowned at the heat he felt coming through her swimsuit. He raised his hand to her forehead. "It's hot all right, but you don't feel hot in that way. That's a fever you've got, I think." He thought that even with the sea breeze, he could smell the fever radiating from her now.

"Really don't feel so well all of a sudden," Brinke said. "Haven't felt great all morning. But standing up now, I feel woozier." Brinke suddenly leaned into Hector, clutching at her belly. "My stomach hurts." She groaned and went down to her knees. "Oh, God! It hurts so much!"

Hector saw it then, this spreading crimson stain between her legs. Her swimsuit there was red with the growing stain of blood. Brinke's gaze followed his. Brinke put a hand between her legs and it came away red. She held up her hand, slick with her own blood, and said, "Oh my God, Hector! What's happening to me?"

"Lay back, sweetheart," Hector said, his voice urgent. He pulled down a life preserver and tucked it up under her legs, elevating them. "Just lay back, darling." He opened up the throttle. "I'll have you to a doctor in five minutes."

Brinke was groggy now, her eyes half-closed. She had curled into a fetal position, groaning and clutching harder at her belly and between her legs. Hector could feel her blood, warm and slick under his bare feet as it spread across the deck. It was a massive internal hemorrhage. He'd seen soldiers bleed out from belly wounds in a matter of minutes.

Hector didn't trust the civilian hospitals to cope with the kind of internal bleeding Brinke was enduring and those hospitals were all inland, anyway—they would take far longer to reach. Hector steered toward the naval base and the hospital there. Hector was counting on his veteran's status and Brinke's obviously life-threatening internal bleeding to secure her treatment there.

Hector stole another glance down at her. Brinke was unconscious. Only the flutter of her pulse under her chin gave Hector indication she was still alive. Frantic, he got on the radio to the base.

Hector contemplated the mounting pile of cigarette stubs at his feet. With shaking hands, he shook out another Pall Mall. His shirt tales and shorts were stained with Brinke's blood from where he had carried her from their boat to the hospital. He'd run with her, screaming all the way for help. Now Hector struck a match on the stucco wall of the hospital and lit his cigarette. It was starting to rain and he ducked under the eaves to get out of the cold shower.

"Mr. Lassiter?"

The doctor was fiftyish, tall and slender.

Hector said, "Did I make a mistake, coming here?" His voice sounded strange to himself, hoarse and fragile. He said, "I mean, you probably don't treat many pregnant women around here, do you, Doc?"

The doctor patted Hector's back. "Bum a cigarette?"

Hector passed the doctor a Pall Mall and lit it off his own butt. The doctor said, "You did the right thing, Mr. Lassiter. The extra fifteen or twenty minutes spent getting to those other hospitals would have cost you your wife. You'd have lost her for certain. You saved her, coming here."

"She going to pull through, you're saying?"

The doctor hesitated. "The problem is plasma. I need more AB-negative and the place here is a bit short of potential donors. Everyone's off base."

Hector tossed his cigarette to the ground and twisted the toe of a sandal over it. "That's my blood type. Let's go, right now. You can drain me dry if it'll help Brinke pull through."

The doctor cast down his own cigarette and opened the door. "You're sure of your type?"

Hector nodded. "I've shed enough of it over the years to know. I was a medic, and so constantly getting tapped during my service in Europe."

The doctor took Hector's arm, walking him briskly down the hall. "That's very good luck for us, then. It should make the difference."

"What's happened to her?"

"She's sustained at least a partial ectopic pregnancy," the doctor said, urging Hector around a corner. Hector was already rolling up his shirtsleeves. "The fetus developed outside the womb," the doctor continued. "It developed in the fallopian tube. I'm sorry, Mr. Lassiter, but she lost the baby. I've had to take the fetus, the placenta and both of her tubes. She also is likely to lose her right ovary. She shouldn't ever risk another pregnancy, and frankly, after what's already been taken from her, it's unlikely to be an issue of choice."

"Just keep Brinke alive," Hector said. "That's all that matters anymore. You can pull her through, can't you?"

"With your blood, yes, I believe I can."

"Then like I said, you suck me dry if it will save Brinke."

# 56

For the next several days, Brinke's condition was judged "guarded" by her Naval doctor. Returning bellbottoms were screened and tapped for more blood.

For the first day, Hector had been the sole source of blood for Brinke's needed transfusions and for two days following her admission, Hector was woozy and weak from his own blood loss, living on sugar cookies and orange juice.

He was sleeping on a couch in the waiting room. An orderly shook him awake. From the orange glow through the seaside windows, Hector guessed it was sunset. "She's awake now, and she's asking for you," the orderly said.

Hector struggled up into a sitting position and ran his hands back through his hair. He was still wearing the clothes he'd had on when he carried her into the hospital. Brinke's blood had dried and darkened to the color of mud. He felt his jaw; six days since his last shave.

Brinke winced when she saw him. "My God, Hector," she said, her voice weak and hoarse. "Were you injured?"

"That's not my blood," Hector said, absent-mindedly fingering his blood-crusted shirt.

"The baby?"

"Hush," Hector said. "Rest. Sleep."

"I just woke up and don't need more sleep," Brinke said. "I lost our baby, didn't I?"

Hector stroked her forehead. "Thing that matters is that you're here and you're going to pull through." He tried to make a joke. "You're going to be fine now. You're full of that crazy and intrepid Lassiter blood now. Seems we're the same blood type, and a good thing it is that we are."

"It's Stryder blood that buys a woman miles," Brinke said trying to joke. "Or so I hear."

A tear slid down her cheek. Hector wiped it away with his thumb. "What have the doctors told you, Hector? What has happened to me? How bad is it? And no kind lies, Hector. I need the whole truth, straight up. And I need to know, can we try again? Can I have another baby?"

Hector stroked her cheek. "No. And even if it was a remote possibility, you shouldn't try. I wouldn't let you try. I can't risk you again. I can't go through another week like this one."

Brinke scowled. "A week? I've been here a week?"

"You were in shock before I got you off the boat. You nearly bled to death. You were in something like a coma for several days. We can't try again."

"What did this cost me?"

"I think the doctor should talk to you about that. I don't know that much about female anatomy, I mean not the inner workings." Another lame joke.

Brinke nodded. "But he's sure I can't conceive another?"

"Yes. That's a certainty."

She bit her lip and her chin trembled. She said, "You can have a divorce, Hector. You should have a family. Babies of your own. That can't happen with me now."

"Jesus! Stop!" Hector squeezed her hand. "Stop it! I don't want a divorce. Hell, I don't need family more than just the two of us, darling."

"Don't need isn't the same as don't want, Hector."

"I don't want more than you," Hector said. "You're all I want and all I need. And that's the gospel truth."

Brinke hugged him to her. "Later you might feel different. You can go then, if you need to. I just want you to know that. I can't lay claim to you now. Not when I'm not a true woman anymore. I'm sorry, Hector. I'm so, so sorry I failed you. Failed our baby."

"You have nothing to be sorry for and I don't ever want to hear you talk about yourself like that again, as damaged or incomplete. You just need to focus now on getting better. Get stronger so we can back to our sweet quiet life. Turn your mind off about all the rest."

"I don't think I can do that, Hec."

"You have to, darling. Get well. Then we'll get back on the boat, and we'll go someplace neither of us has ever been. Just you and I and our writing tools. We'll go wherever you want, New Orleans, Bimini. Maybe the Bahamas."

"Cuba," Brinke said. "Havana. I need to finish revisions on *Havana Bounce*. Would be good to do that in situ."

"Okay then," Hector said. "Havana it is." Her talking about her writing gave him some heart and hope that fight remained in her. Brinke still saw a future for herself, he thought.

She said, "I need you to do something else for me, my love."

Hector said, "Name it." He figured she might ask him again if she was the one. If so, he was prepared to tell her so again, this time without hedging or reservations.

"Go home now," Brinke said. "Go home and wash up and get some sleep in our bed. Come back tomorrow shaved and showered and rested and having had a big, good breakfast. Do that for me, yes?"

Hector squeezed her hand.

"Promise me."

"I promise," he said.

"And bring my manuscript, would you? I need to put my mind to something. I need to work." A strange and sad smile. "I need to create. Need to finish something."

A week later, Brinke was released from the hospital. She seemed fairly miserable. "I'm pretty mutilated," she said on the ride back to their cottage.

Jack Dixon, new sheriff-elect, had loaned Hector an official car to transport Brinke home. Brinke rolled down the window and leaned her head out, letting the wind whip her long black hair. "You've seen me naked for the last time, Hec. I look like Frankenstein's monster down there now."

"The doctor said there will hardly be a scar in three months," Hector said. "In a year, you won't even notice it."

"I want to swim, but the damned stitches preclude that."

"Just for a short while longer," Hector said.

"I've been thinking again about us adopting."

"That's fine, and we surely can think about all that," Hector said. "But later. For a few months, let's just be you and I, please? Our time in Paris was frenzied and strange. Our time together in Key West so far hasn't been much different in that sense. I want to just loaf and love you. Okay?"

Brinke rested her elbow on the car window and propped her head on her hand. The wind through the car window fingered her black hair. "You're sure you're not still with me because of guilt?"

Hector sighed. "I'm sure, and that's the last time I want to have this conversation. I mean that. Do we understand each other on that point?"

"I understand what you're saying." Brinke scooted over and rested her head on his shoulder. "The doctor told me what you did for me, all of it," she said. "Racing into port, carrying me across the base. Then giving so much blood they were afraid you'd be at risk yourself. He said you told them they could have it all and he believed you meant it. I have never had anyone make even minor sacrifices for me. He said you drew your Colt on him to make him take another pint from you when he knew he shouldn't. What you did, what you're doing…?"

"You act as if there's a choice to be made."

"Of course there was. There are always choices, Hector."

Hector wrapped his arm around her shoulders and hugged her. "Like I told you before, there's no choice. Not where you're concerned. Not loving you as I do."

# 57

The first several days with Brinke back home were fiercely tumultuous. Her moods swung wildly between a kind of exhilaration or mania and terrible valleys of black despair that terrified Hector. Her depressions were so dark and fearsome Hector toyed with taking Brinke's gun and his own out of the house. He thought of hiding the Colts somewhere on their boat.

Brinke's appetite, always prodigious, was all but gone. She picked at her food and he could see the weight-loss in her face and now-smaller breasts. Sullen, she'd sit at her writing desk, doggedly working and reworking the opening pages of her manuscript, or simply staring out the window as the neighbor boy, a fatherless child, played catch by himself.

The boy quickly became an issue between them.

Brinke urged Hector to go out one morning, to have a catch with the lonely young boy. Reluctant, Hector nevertheless went out and offered to toss a few balls to the delighted boy in order to placate Brinke. Hector had no glove and so had to catch the ball barehanded, which stung. Brinke watched them through the window above her typewriter.

At some point, Hector looked up and saw Brinke leave her desk, doubled over. He excused himself to the boy. Hector found Brinke in their bedroom, curled up on the bed, sobbing. "You should be across the street," Brinke said, barely intelligible between ragged sobs. "His mother is pretty and lonely. You should be loving her and raising that boy. Having a real family. Something to leave behind beyond just damned books."

"That's crazy talk," he told her.

The following morning, Brinke again raised the prospect of Hector divorcing her. "Not in this lifetime," he said. "Closed subject."

After three weeks, Brinke's stitches were removed and they returned to their old swimming place. They were both careful their first day back as their tans had dimmed in the intervening days loafing around the house, mostly writing. "You'll be fine in the sun of course, with that skin of yours," Brinke had said. "But I'll burn. And please, Hector. No looking at my body."

But she looked very fine to Hector. When he tried to make love to her she pushed him away. Scowling, she said, "What's the goddamn point now? Nothing can come of it."

"Was a time," Hector said, searching her eyes, "when we made a point of seeing nothing would come of it. It was about making each other feel wonderful and to no other end. I want those times again. I need you that way again, darling."

He pressed the issue until she surrendered. They made love on the beach, slow and sad at first. At some point, Brinke began to move with more intent under Hector. Her mouth gave way to a passionate snarl and she nicked his gums with her teeth as if she was intent upon actually devouring him. Her kisses grew hungry and deep.

They peaked together, bodies cooled by a soft summer rain. "Maybe we can be all right together," she said after a time, slowly unclamping her fingers that were knotted in his hair. She traced his jaw with her other hand. "Maybe it will all be fine in the end."

They ate dinner at the place that Brinke had taken them Hector's first night in Key West. Her appetite was more like the old Brinke. She put away a couple of appetizers, her own entrée and most of Hector's. They split a piece of Key Lime pie. Patting her mouth with her napkin, Brinke said, "Tomorrow, let's leave for Havana. We can do that, can't we?"

Hector smiled, feeling like some corner had been turned. "Sure, we can do that. We'll leave just after noon." Hector first needed the early morning to get the boat in shape, to swab up the dried blood from Brinke's miscarriage.

He thought about how he'd seen far too much blood shed from the women he had vowed to spend his life with. He told himself he would build a wall a mile high around her to keep her safe. He made a private pledge never to see Brinke at risk again. He swore to himself to protect her forever.

# 58

Mike Rogers sat along the docks, watching the rich men's yachts coming in. He'd shed a few pounds over the last several months and lost more hair. Tight as money was, the former newspaperman treated himself to a drink once a week at the docks, spending a little of the stingy wages paid him as a freelance correspondent for the wire services.

For some time, Rogers had been contemplating a return to the States, but he hadn't yet accumulated sufficient money to make a go of it.

And where would he go if he could afford it? That question still perplexed him.

He wouldn't go back to Key West, not to live.

Oh, he knew now what had happened to him. He knew how they'd contrived to take everything from him.

Rogers knew now that that stranger in the bar had snookered him, tricked Rogers into believing he was a whore killer.

A passing acquaintance from Bone Key had come over in June and stumbled across Rogers on the dockside of Old Havana. The man had been surprised to find Rogers living in Cuba. The two of them got to talking over beers and the Key Wester, a man of low morals and loose-tongued in his cups, well, he'd gotten to jawing about one particular young Key West whore with whom he'd grown enamored.

Six minutes into the man's obscene rant about the whore's "virtues" Rogers had realized the prostitute whom the man was rhapsodizing about was the very one Rogers was supposed to have murdered in a drunken fit several months before.

Rogers put several questions to the Key Wester and found himself convinced that the man had spent the night in Rogers' so-called victim's bed just hours before crossing paths with Rogers in that Havana dockside saloon.

So Rogers wrote some letters home. He made some further inquiries back in Key West. The journalist confirmed the working girl he had "killed," a taffy blond named Janice Henry, was still alive and well and turning tricks with her customary zeal to please.

He was told his landlord had seized his press and other pieces of printing equipment in lieu of owed back rent on the newspaper office. His chief competitor, he learned, had bought Rogers' subscriber list from his landlord and then used it to raid his client base—drained away all of Rogers' potential circulation for his paper.

In terms of reclaiming his business, there was no longer anything to take back, no hope of that at all, it was clear.

And his swanky new convertible?

His new car was now reported to be being driven around Bone Key by the fat madam who ran the sporting house in which Rogers had been bamboozled by that man who got Rogers drunk and talked him into visiting the brothel in the first place.

Everything. Every last thing had been taken from Rogers.

But according to his Key West correspondents, more had happened back on Bone Key than just the destruction of his own life. Rogers was told Sheriff Hoyt had gone missing and was presumed dead by many living around the Key.

The mayor and three council members had been indicted for stealing city funds and were expected to actually draw significant stretches of hard prison time. The realtor, Denton Stokes, had lost his real estate license and was also facing charges of fraud and conspiracy.

In that sense, Rogers figured he maybe was lucky to have been chased off the Key before he could fall prey to the same fate as his associates.

But those other men hadn't endured months of cold sweats in the dark hours of the sultry night, thinking themselves a whore killer.

Rogers couldn't really afford it, but he'd nevertheless bought himself a cheap gun and two boxes of bullets. His notion was that he'd return to the States via Key West. It only made sense to return via Bone Key. Staying incognito, Rogers figured he'd track down that bastard who took him to that whorehouse and he'd empty his gun in the son of bitch's too-handsome face.

A yacht was pulling in. A pretty, dark-haired woman was on the deck, tossing mooring lines to the boys who worked the dockside to make fast. The woman looked vaguely familiar to Rogers but he couldn't put her in context. The name of the boat was "Devil May Care."

Rogers took another sip of his Cuba Libre. He wondered what kind of man it took to win the companionship of a woman like the one moving around the boat. A shadow crossed his face: his waiter was hovering, getting in the way and blocking Rogers' view of the pretty, black-haired woman. The waiter asked if Rogers wanted another drink. Rogers knew he shouldn't spend the money, but the improved view decided it for him. "*Sí, por favor.*" The waiter slunk off to fetch Rogers another rum and cola.

The yacht's owner was on deck now, helping tie the boat fast. The man was tall and well-built and very bronzed. The man's back was to Rogers. When the big man turned and leapt over the side of the boat, Rogers had a jolt of recognition.

The stranger turned his back to Rogers again, extending a hand to the woman still on deck to help her down. The man put two big hands around the black-haired twist's wasp waist and sat her down on the dock. The man hefted a suitcase from the deck and the couple wrapped arms around one another's waists, making their way up the inclined ramp to the dockside and passing right by Rogers.

The journalist ground his teeth, watching them approach and then pass. It was him, no doubt of that. It was the son of a bitch who had cost Rogers his sweet life back on Bone Key.

And the woman with that son of a bitch?

It was that bitch who had run out of him in the bar just a couple of days prior to the so-called murder. It was "Tessa Templeton."

So, "Tessa" had obviously been playing Rogers all along. She was in cahoots with the bastard who had made Rogers think he'd nearly twisted off some whore's head.

They were just a couple of slick grifters who had conspired to burn down Rogers' sweet life back in Key West.

The journalist slammed back his drink and followed the couple to a hotel across the street from the big, baroque Grand Theater of Havana.

Rogers slid into the lobby and stood off in a corner to confirm the couple was indeed checking in. When the pair went upstairs with their suitcase, Rogers ran to the front desk. He held up his own eyeglasses and said to the clerk, "Excuse me, but that man who just registered, he left his glasses in my watch repair store. I ran three blocks to try and catch him, but just missed him at the elevator there."

The desk clerk said, "You mean Mr. Lassiter?"

"Lassiter?"

"Héctor Lassiter, *sí*."

"Could you give me his room number, *por favor*?"

"Three-twelve."

"*Gracias*," Rogers said, smiling.

Rogers set off under the pretense of climbing into the elevator to return the glasses. When he saw the clerk was busy with another guest, Rogers doubled back and crossed the lobby fast, intent upon fetching his gun.

"Some help, please?" Brinke held her hair up off her back. She wore a strapless white dress. "Zip me, please?"

Hector did that and kissed the back of her neck, brushing his nose against the soft, short down there. "You feel okay, darlin'?"

"Wonderful," Brinke said. She picked up a brush and began running it through her hair. Hector slung on his shoulder holster and slipped in his Colt. Brinke sighed. "Oh, Hector, a gun tonight? Must you?"

"It's Havana on a Saturday night and the whole crazy country could lurch into revolution before we're served our appetizers." Hector shrugged on his white cotton sports coat to cover the big old six-shooter. He wet a comb and ran it back through his dark hair.

"I could eat a horse," Brinke said.

Hector smiled. "Given the look of some of the joints in this town, you might find yourself doing just that."

The waiter had taken their order and brought them their drinks.

They tapped wine goblets. "To what do we toast?"

Brinke thought about it a time, then said, "I'll get back to you on that, okay?"

"Night is young."

"It is." Brinke took his right hand and smiled. "My God, you're handsome tonight. Do you know how much I love you, Hector Lassiter?"

"How much, darling?"

"Without reservation," Brinke said. "Outside time. I'll love you forever."

Time went haywire then.

Before he could respond, Brinke said, "Why do I feel like I know that guy there?"

Hector glanced at the man approaching their table, then turned away. Something clicked in his mind just as he heard a woman say in Spanish, "My God, he's got a gun!"

Hector tried to free his right hand, his gun hand, from Brinke's grasp. He pulled the lapel of his jacket away with his left hand to quicken his draw.

As his Colt cleared his coat, Hector locked eyes with the ex-reporter and snarled, "Rogers, don't you make me kill you!"

Wyatt Earp had a winning strategy for gunfights that had always hung with Hector. Earp said, "You must learn to be slow in a hurry."

Everything was slow, yet hyper-focused for Hector.

The two shots came almost simultaneously.

Women at adjacent tables screamed. A few men screamed, too.

Rogers tumbled backwards, his face a red smear. Hector said, "Goddamn you for making me do that to you, you sorry son of a bitch!"

Hector holstered the old Peacemaker. He said to Brinke, "Thank God there are plenty of witnesses in this joint to testify he drew and fired first."

He turned around to check on Brinke and Hector's eyes widened. His legs began to quake.

Brinke's head rested on the table. Her longer black hair was spread out on the white tablecloth. Streaks of scarlet were spreading around the long black strands of her hair.

Hector put a shaking hand to the back of her neck and said, "Brinke? Darling?"

Hector couldn't bear to see her face. He felt under her chin with trembling fingers and found no pulse.

He took a deep breath, empty suddenly, weak in the shaking knees.

With a bloody, trembling hand, Hector turned around his chair and collapsed into it. Hector rested his head on Brinke's bare and still warm back and he began to sob.

# *59*

They were anchored just off Old Fort Jefferson.

Sheriff Jack Dixon and Beau Stryder stood either side of Hector, the wind at their backs, the blast-furnace breeze whipping their white shirts and their hair.

Hector took the lid off the urn and handed it to his grandfather to hold. Hector scooped up a handful of ashes. He let the wind work the ashes from his hand.

Beau squeezed Hector's neck.

His chin trembling, Hector watched the dust sift from between his fingers.

# *60*

It was two days since he'd scattered Brinke's ashes at sea. Beau had returned to his pregnant young Cuban wife, urging Hector to come to Texas, to put some distance between Key West and his memories.

Hector couldn't tell Beau how much he resented Consuelo and the life growing inside her. He couldn't confess to the pain it gave him thinking of Connie, of the prospect of seeing her and seeing the baby that would come with the New Year.

Hector sat alone on his front porch with a bottle of beer and lit another cigarette, trying to think of something he might write. Groping for something to do that wouldn't result in him getting drunk, getting in a fight, or doing something equally stupid to punish himself or some luckless other.

"Hey mister!"

Hector squinted, holding up a hand to shield his face from the sun. It was the neighbor kid, Billy. The boy held up a brand new glove. "My mom bought me an extra glove, a big one," the boy said. "It should fit even your hand. Wanna have a catch?"

Hector thought about it. He smiled and shook his head. He cast down his Pall Mall and ground it out with the sole of his sandal. "Sure, why not," Hector said.

They stood in the middle of the street, under the shade of the tall old palms, tossing the ball back and forth.

Between lobs, Hector sometimes stole glances at the empty picture window of his house, remembering Brinke watching him, remembering the look in her eyes. She was lost to him forever now.

The ball snapped into his glove again.

Forever. What was that Brinke had said to him?

"Forever is just pretend?"

Hector flung the baseball back at the boy, long and high.

That night, Hector had a dream about a dark-haired woman at the top of some hill somewhere in the borderlands.

The woman with the black hair was astride a strawberry roan, silhouetted against some bloody sunset, waving to him. A little girl held Hector's hand, walking him up the side of the hill.

Hector awakened from the dream shaken and cotton-mouthed; sweat-soaked and frightened.

He found his Peacemaker, emptied the bullets into his hand, one at a time, then opened the back door. He slung the bullets far out into the night where it would be harder to find them.

Hands shaking, he turned on the lights, brewed some black coffee. No goddamn way he wanted to try and drift back into sleep just now.

He couldn't fathom laying there at the mercy of his dreams.

No, strike that, stretched out there, hostage to his *nightmares.*

Hector scrolled a virgin sheet of paper into his typewriter, intent upon pouring all that poison onto the page, desperate to use his hurt. He was determined to find one true sentence. On a hunch, Hector typed, "Forever's just pretend."

## THE END

# READER DISCUSSION QUESTIONS

1. *Forever's Just Pretend* is the only novel in the Hector Lassiter series to incorporate no significant cameos or supporting roles by historical figures. Did their lack in any way change your regard for Hector Lassiter? Did the story seem less "real" to you as a result of their absence?

2. Key West has evolved into a kind debauched tourists' Mecca over the past several decades. Did its Prohibition-era portrayal surprise you in any way?

3. If you've read *Toros & Torsos*, did you find yourself comparing circa-1925 Key West to circa-1935 Bone Key? What most struck you as a result of a decade's passage?

4. A certain surviving grand house in the otherwise burned out section of Key West—a nod to an all-too-real Key West fire—makes a cameo appearance that pays off in the aforementioned *Toros & Torsos*. Did you catch the allusion to the house and the foreshadowing of its eventual famous author-owner?

5. Ernest Hemingway is a significant character in the Hector Lassiter series and noted former Key West resident: Aside from the obvious moments where he was mentioned by name, how many allusions or nods to Hemingway did you catch in the course of *Forever's Just Pretend*?

6. The Hector Lassiter series frequently toes the blurry line of meta-fiction. Beau Stryder makes a couple of asides that reference a certain pop-culture confidence man and gambler of some note. Did you catch that allusion? If so, what popular 1950s TV Western series or character is it hinted Beau played a pivotal role in inspiring?

7. Now that you know the arc of Brinke Devlin's character, apart from driving Hector to write crime fiction, in what other ways do you now see her as having affected the course of Hector's life and/or art?

8. Beau Devlin is the man who raised Hector from childhood. Are there any ways in which Beau's unusual avocation shaped Hector's eventual career that you can identify?

9. As noted earlier, no historic figures are featured in *Forever's Just Pretend*, but the Florida land boom of the 1920s is a prominent plot point. The Key West Clubber is also based on a historic cycle of actual crimes, though they have been moved by several hundred miles. Do you know what historic murders inspired the Clubber?

10. As the Lassiter novels are now being presented in chronological order—and presuming you've already read *Toros & Torsos*—how do you see Brinke's newly revealed Key West adventure informing *T&T* and its Key West-set events and rather unusual love story?

# ABOUT THE AUTHOR

Craig McDonald is an award-winning author and journalist. The Hector Lassiter series has been published to international acclaim in numerous languages. McDonald's debut novel was nominated for Edgar, Anthony and Gumshoe awards in the U.S. and the 2011 Sélection du prix polar Saint-Maur en Poche in France.

The Lassiter series has been enthusiastically endorsed by a who's who of crime fiction authors including: Michael Connelly, Laura Lippmann, Daniel Woodrell, James Crumley, James Sallis, Diana Gabaldon, and Ken Bruen, among many others.

Hector Lassiter also centers short stories that appear in three crime fiction anthologies, *The Deadly Bride & 19 of the Year's Finest Crime and Mystery Stories*, (Carroll & Graf) and *Danger City II* (Contemporary Press).

Craig McDonald is also the author of two highly praised non-fiction volumes on the subject of mystery and crime fiction writing, *Art in the Blood* and *Rogue Males*, nominated for the Macavity Award.

To learn more about Craig, visit *www.craigmcdonaldbooks. com* and *www.betimesbooks.com*

Follow Craig McDonald on Twitter *@HECTORLASSITER* and on FaceBook: *www.facebook.com/craigmcdonaldnovelist*

*Forever's Just Pretend*

Made in the USA
Lexington, KY
20 May 2018